Tonight, it's My Turn

To Friendship.

In Memory of

Barclay William John Nesbitt
&
Jeanie Scott Carmichael Nesbitt

"The greatest Oaks have been little Acorns."
Thomas Fuller's Gnomologia, 1732

"Very few things happen at the right time and the rest do not happen at all. The conscientious historian will correct these defects."
Herodotus

Author's Note

A friendship can be a difficult as well as a wonderful thing. It begins tentatively and flourishes only with care. Even when it has been nurtured and is in full bloom, the world and the day-to-day events of our lives can wedge themselves between us and the people we love. This is the story of the beginning of a friendship: its end is held dear in my memory. The reality of the friendship, too, was very different from the one in the book you are about to read, for this is a story suggested by a friendship, not the biography of one.

In the early summer of the year 2000, I got it into my head that my church should hold a collegial (and, yes, possibly even a money-making) event when we came together after Labour Day. Out of so small an acorn, what was really a very innocent and totally naive thought, came a theatrical adventure, the friendship I have mentioned, and, now, in 'Tonight, It's My Turn,' a novel. The theatrical adventure, The Deer Park Very Little Theatre, lasted some five years. We produced plays, organized concerts, mixed professional and amateur actors and, as a high point, even took a surprisingly successful shot at a three-act, five-night musical. And contrary to the prophets of doom, we always made a profit.

It would all have been impossible without Mr. Barclay William John Nesbitt, although I hardly knew him when we started out. Barry — who knew him as anything else? — was an actor, singer, emcee, Toronto radio personality and raconteur. Without him the idea would have died on the vine before it even got started. He was an enthusiast. He took my original thought and ran with it. I spent much of my time trying to keep up. 'SeptemberFest,' as that first event came to be called, was also the beginning of a friendship which both of us were to cherish.

It is not easy to make new friends in one's old age and we were both circling the drain of that phenomenon rather quickly, Barry even more so than I. The friendship also came to include Barry's wife, Jeanie, and my wife, Sonia, and, if four less similar persons ever banded together, I challenge you to find them.

The theatre ran out of steam when Barry became ill. He recovered slowly and although there was the occasional event later on — a radio version of 'A Christmas Carol' and a first class concert put on by professional artists — it was our friendship that endured. The four of us dined out before going to the theatre, he baked his scones, and he and I went for dapper afternoon strolls along St. Clair. Barry read, and critiqued, everything I wrote. He and I could hardly have been more different, but we enjoyed each other tremendously. He was the gentleman, always on the go. I came to admire his determination and his very principled kindness. I, for my part, could always make him laugh. Only in politics were we alike, but whereas Barry rarely had a bad word about almost anyone, I, I admit, rarely had a good one about most.

Then Jean died. Barry was devastated. Months later, I persuaded him to buy a computer and encouraged him to write his memoirs. They were published as 'What's On The Air Tonight.' After that, I think, he had had enough of this world. He went to live in Vancouver to be near his family, and we stayed in touch weekly. Sonia and I spoke to him just three days before his death and, although he was very ill indeed, he was the same Barry we had always known — warm, caring, upbeat, intelligent. As usual, he inquired about Clio, our cat.

'Tonight, It's My Turn' is dedicated to both Barry and Jean, but although it is the story both of a neophyte theatrical event and a burgeoning friendship, it is a work of fiction. Let me repeat that in capitals: THIS IS A WORK OF FICTION. Oh yes, you may see bits and tiny pieces of Barry and me along the way — we always knew how to make fun of each other — but you won't see either one of us in full. Nor will you see our wives. As anyone who ever met them would agree, my wife is no shy, retiring violet and Jean, well, Jean was definitely a Scot's lady to the very twinkle in her eye. Also not in the book is any of the people who participated in that first evening of entertainment.

If anyone suspects that he has found himself somewhere among these pages, it is time to schedule cataract, if not brain, surgery.

Enjoy the tale of the Fall Follies in 'Tonight, It's My Turn.' I will always be grateful for my original thought, that very small acorn which became 'SeptemberFest,' and for everything that came after, hard work though it often was. That acorn also provided the germ of the idea for this book and I am grateful for that, too. Most of all, I am grateful that the acorn introduced me to two very special persons, Barry and Jeanie Nesbitt. They would have enjoyed the joke.

The Playbill In Chapters

1. The Smallest Of Acorns 1
2. The Business Of Pleasure 12
3. Lampposts and Other Flights of Fancy 20
4. Meeting La Belle Mabel 27
5. Cappuccinos… 36
6. …And Cucumber Sandwiches 46
7. Soft Shoes In The Sanctuary 52
8. Casting A Net And A Play 60
9. Life Is A What Again, Old Chum? 68
10. The Summer of Stanley's Discontent 75
11. Hector Hums Along 83
12. An Amity Of Opposites 88
13. Marriage and Maternity 91
14. Oh God, Not Atheism! 97
15. Laddie's Lament 104
16. The Blithe And Bonny Noni 110
17. Scripts And Superstitions 117
18. Of Pregnancies And Prompters 121
19. A Diva Disinterred 127
20. Mirror, Mirror On The Wall 131
21. A Weighty Dress Rehearsal 135
22. Rude Awakenings 141
23. The Day Goes Slowly By 145
24. A How-To Guide To Popping Pills 153
25. Clarence, A Corpse Becomes You! 158
26. The Play's The Thing, Of Course 164
27. Little Eaten In The Entr'acte 174
28. A Great Reckoning In A Little Room 182
29. It'll All Be All Right On The Night 188
30. Stanley And The Hatstand 193
31. Pigalle Would Have Been Proud 196
32. Hector's Turn 207
33. Exeunt All 210
34. Whither They Went Afterwards 219

Cast Of Characters

Hector Hammond: Entertainer, Impresario, Devoted Spouse

Fanny Hammond: Wife, Exotic Flower, Accomplished Flirt

Stanley Parkinson: Banker, Idea Man, Embryonic Talent

Faun Parkinson: Helpmeet, Budding Bernhardt, Avenging Angel

Gilbert Gilchrist: Vicar, Overbite Enthusiast, Blimp

Lilith Payne: Graduate Student, Jungian, Godawful Girlfriend

Mabel Green: Church Lady, Dog Lover, Fuhrer without an Umlaut

Vera Tilsley: Secretary, Mother To Be, Woman Scorned

Laddie Harland: Accompanist, Despoiler, Inebriate

Noni Figueroa: Chanteuse, Collagen Cutie, Tweetie Bird

Roger St. J. Mountjoy: Actor, Apprentice Automaton, Dipstick

Clarence Moran: Janitor, Corpse, Monosyllabic Man

Elmer Simms: Parishioner, Curmudgeon, Commentator

& Several Other Rather More Anonymous Persons

The Smallest Of Acorns

Who would have thought that anything like this could have come to pass? I mean, the whole thing just grew, spiralled out of control, you might say, at least at the end. No one had any idea. It began with the merest suggestion and took off from there: no one's fault really, if you are looking to assign blame, which I am not. There is an old saying, 'Tall oaks from little acorns grow.' It almost fits, although I am not sure that they ever quite got to the tall oaks part. Except possibly in Hector's mind. Hector Hammond's mind was complicated enough to begin with. It had plenty of space for pithy metaphors and still more for grandiose ideas that took off faster than he could get the words out. But Hector didn't begin it, although he might have implied sometimes that he did when he got carried away. It was the other one, the passive aggressive one, who started it all.

The other one, Stanley Parkinson, was very different from Hector Hammond. Chalk and cheese, night and day, hot and cold, don't begin to cover it — although perhaps there might be a degree of truth in the last of the three. Stanley reminded me of those everlasting flowers that people used to hang, upside down, in the basement for six months before taking them down to use in an arrangement. There was no fragrance to Stanley. Composed and rather brittle, you could say, thin and dried up, with a skin like a fine parchment that seemed to shed a kind of epidermal dandruff even on the most humid days of summer. And summer, of course, was when our story began.

He had a good heart, Stanley did, no doubt about that, but he didn't wear it on his sleeve or anywhere else that might have soiled his three-piece suited look of affluent caution. Nevertheless, it was Stanley's idea. With his usual throat-clearing carefulness, it was he who approached the Vicar after the Sunday service, making sure that that personage was not, at that precise moment in time, too busy to listen and that they would not, in fact, be interrupted, although he, Stanley, would have been fully willing to cede the limelight to the leviathan bulk of his liturgical leader had that was been required of him.

"I have been thinking," said Stanley, the usual aspirated sound of his voice half an octave higher at having to broach a subject, any subject, before his spiritual leader. "I have been thinking," he said again, just as the Vicar expected he would, "that it might be a good thing to organize a social event, an evening event, at the beginning of September." At this point Stanley gulped before speeding onwards, "To bring the congregation together and to," here for reasons, known only to himself, Stanley shrugged his unfortunately ovoid shoulders, "to engender a greater sense of camaraderie."

It was, for Stanley, quite a speech and the Vicar took a step backwards, unused to such loquaciousness in his parishioner. He knew, of course, that Stanley had the power of speech — Stanley was the Church Treasurer — and he had been known to run on at length — considerable, even interminable, length — when discussing congregational finances; but, in general conversation, Stanley usually stood or sat, depending on the situation, mute.

The Vicar cleared his throat.

"What I mean is..." Evidently, Stanley had merely paused to take in air, "if we had a little supper and perhaps some small in-house entertainment, we might feel its benefit in bringing us all together and..." Here he seemed to run out of thought processes, or words, or, possibly, steam. He spoke next as in extremis, "What do you think?"

The Vicar, all four hundred and fifty-seven pounds of him, did not know what to think. He knew his weight because his doctor had put him on a diet and told him that if he did not shed a hundred or so of these pounds, someone would have the difficult task of closing the lid on his coffin. The Vicar had understood what the doctor was saying, and was attempting, in his spare time, to act accordingly, but Stanley's less threatening words proved far more difficult to take in. Stanley and "social" and "entertainment" and even "supper" did not really compute. He had been invited to dine at the Parkinsons' several times and they were not evenings that he would ever include on a list of ten — or even twenty — bests. If there was one person on God's good green earth generally filled with less vivacity and/or outgoing conviviality of any sort than Stanley himself, it was his wife, Faun. The thought of Stanley and Faun organizing an evening of light entertainment, of gaiety, with food no less, was not something the Vicar cared to contemplate, and not one, when he finally came to himself and swallowed the half litre of saliva that had welled unbidden at the back of his throat, to which he might be persuaded to look forward.

You did not get to be an urban Vicar without brains, however, even in an Anglican parish, and he wracked his. Never doubting the efficacy of prayer, he also prayed. "Jesus Christ!" he said, under his breath. "What am I to say? What do I say to this good, kind," he searched his repertoire of suitable adjectives to locate something apposite to describe Stanley, "this worthy soul?"

And, of course, his prayer was answered.

"Hector Hammond!" he said. "Hector Hammond can help."

The Vicar was well aware that while alliteration can be immensely useful when making a point in a sermon, its use in normal conversation can ring less than true, but other than registering this fact, he remained more concerned with having found a solution, a solution that would obviate his congregation having to sit down to any putatively pleasurable function organized by Stanley Parkinson, abetted by his adoring spouse, the fragrant Faun.

"You know Hector," said the Vicar, the jaunt of his voice restored, "He used to act. He'll help. He'll want to help."

The Vicar noticed that Stanley was regarding him with a look of bemusement.

"Who is he?" Stanley asked, the "who" uttering from rounded lips like a baby barn owl trying out sounds. He inhaled. "Is he new?"

"No, no, no! Hector? He's been coming for years! He's an adherent! He's over there!"

The Vicar was tempted to try a little dance to go along with his exclamation points, so pleased with himself was he for coming up with the name of the one person in his whole congregation who might be able to enliven Stanley's evening of fun and give it some slight chance of success. He did not, however, give in to temptation, adding instead, "He's married to Fanny!"

Stanley's continued look of blankness was disconcerting. It was true that he blinked twice and jerked slightly when the Vicar said the name of the spouse by whom he was trying to identify Hector, but a kind of polite passivity then returned. Like many of their fellows, the Parkinsons tended to regard adherents as lesser mortals. Stanley himself, in his role of Treasurer, tended not to take much note of them on the grounds that they did not put their money where their mouths were: they talked at meetings, yes, but, generally speaking, they did not give. Giving, Stanley considered, was what made a member of the congregation. The long and the short of it was that he, honestly, did not know who Hector Hammond was. As for the wife, even one with such an indelicate name, he could not recall her.

The Vicar was becoming exasperated and his chins began to quiver.

"You know," he said in a whisper, bracingly. He looked cautiously around. "The black woman! Over there! Fanny!" The diminutive of Mrs. Hammond's good given name was hissed. With exclamation points!

The penny dropped. Stanley understood. Of course, he knew the divine Fanny. Everybody in the congregation knew Fanny. How could they not? Not by name, though. What had given it away was the adjective used to describe the name. Fanny Hammond was the only person of colour in the entire congregation. (The relief janitor was an Afghani Muslim, but, as an employee, he hardly counted.) Fanny, née Constance, Hammond was — and she would have been the first to confirm it — black. Spectacularly so. Her skin gave off a purple mahogany shine which on her initial appearance at the church three or four years ago, had brought its anglo and saxon denizens up short. Fanny relished this. She was vivacious and gregarious; she had a loud personality; and she had a habit of throwing her head back in laughter at every opportunity. Fanny Hammond's laughter regularly stunned the older males of the congregation. There were, of course, no younger male members in the congregation. It had certainly stunned Stanley, and it was this that explained how he had never become acquainted with her spouse. He had shied away from both of them.

If Fanny's hue and her outgoing personalty were not enough, there was one other feature that tended to mesmerize all those of the male persuasion who met the lady — her superstructure. Fanny's breasts were super-sized and because of a somewhat flamboyant style of dressing, they were, on occasion, rather more visible than perhaps was typical in the sanctuary of an indubitably conservative congregation. Stanley spied her now across the room, while he tried to gather his thoughts. She was talking animatedly to the Choir Master, breasts jouncing independently, seemingly suspended above a short, tight skirt into the bottom of which a pair of shapely slim legs had inserted themselves. Fanny loved her legs. She called them her lucky legs: they had taken her all over the world and they had brought her back again. At the nether end of these legs were a pair of red, patent leather, four inch high-heels.

Stanley, instinctively, wanted to balk. A vague sense of unease began to lap at his consciousness and he was beginning to regret his conversation last evening with his spouse and helpmeet, Faun.

"You know," he had said, as they sat on the back verandah wallowing in the warmth of a Canadian June, "what we lack is not money and not even numbers, though, of course, we could do with more of both of those."

Faun hung on his every word. When her Stanley spoke, it behooved the world to listen.

Having described Fanny in such detail, you might expect that I would describe Faun similarly. She is, after all, to be a major character in our story. In truth, however, Faun has already been described. Her parents, in one of their few flights of fancy, had named her, in error, after a type of pastoral goat, but "Faun" spelt another way provided the most accurate of all possible descriptions. Her parents might just as well have named her "Beige."

"What we need, my dear," said Stanley, coming alive, "is spirit!" He thumped the arm of his chair in emphasis, nearly dislodging his glass of Vernor's ginger ale as he did so.

"Oh, careful, my love," Faun cooed in fright, "you'll wet your pants if you don't watch out."

It was an infelicitous turn of phrase and Faun did not dwell on it. "What do you think we should do to find it, Stanley?" She spoke as though "spirit" was something to be ordered from the Bay, that could be delivered first thing Monday morning. Certainly, if what the church required was "spirit," her Stanley would be the one to obtain it. Faun, you see, loved Stanley Parkinson and had done so since the first time she had clapped eyes on him thirty plus years past, she a new teller, he already a junior accountant at the bank. In those days Stanley had not been as thin and desiccated as he came to be. Neither had he yet tamped down the more joyous edges of his personality, the better to be able to get ahead of his peers in the world of middling to high finance.

Faun even thought him fun. In those days, his mother still kept him fed and watered, and old Mrs. Parkinson had been a better cook than Faun would ever be.

Stanley jutted out his chin and closed his eyes.

"Spirit!" He was ruminating. His spouse forbore to interrupt him. Still conducting an internal gloss on the subject, Stanley opened his mouth and allowed his tongue to emerge. Unconsciously, he licked the tip of his nose with the end of it. It was an unusual feat and an unfortunate habit and not one that had done his career a great deal of good in the halls of head office commerce. It had taken him years to train himself out of it, but, occasionally, the tongue would still appear all unbidden in the sanctity of the Parkinson domain. Faun, glancing at Stanley in the fading light, swallowed, made slightly feverish by its appearance.

"What about a social?" he said, and neither waiting for, nor expecting a response, continued, "That's it! We should have a social. Some activity. Perhaps a soloist or two from the choir. Then a little light refreshment. And a sing-song to finish."

"Dancing?" Faun breathed the word with anticipation. "Do you think?"

Stanley's eyes snapped open and he observed her balefully. "Oh, I shouldn't think so, should we, my love?"

"It was just a thought, Stanley," replied his spouse, secretly rather disappointed that it had been turned down. "Just a thought."

"But just the kind of thought we need, Faun. The kind of thought that will help get us into the swing of the thing." Stanley thumped the arm of the chair again and this time the ginger ale went crashing onto the flagstones.

Faun's little shriek put an end to the conversation, except that as they lay, side by side, lights out, all tucked up tightly in their double bed, Stanley uttered an addendum on the subject, "I'll have a word with the Vicar after the service tomorrow morning."

And so, of course, he did.

The Vicar interrupted Stanley's train of thought. "You don't know Hector then?!" It was a question as well as an exclamation. "Would you like me to introduce you? You would work well together." The Vicar did not believe this for an instant. He had often thought that

Stanley's crib must have come with a sign that said, "Does Not Play Well With Others," and he could not credit that Stanley alone, for all his undoubted fiduciary expertise, would be able to organize and get off the ground anything that even in the loosest of terms could be labelled 'a social.'

"Come," he said, "permit me to introduce you."

The Vicar took hold of Stanley's boney elbow and together they moved slowly across the room, the one a vast supertanker of a man, the other a diminutive row boat bobbing alongside. People eddied out of the way of the Vicar's bulk to let the two of them hove on by and, as they moved forward, Stanley tried to examine the man who, it appeared, was to be their destination. He did recognize him — not so much for himself as for the beauteous Fanny with whom the man usually stood during coffee hour. Stanley himself was not much for chitchat — an understatement as even he would have admitted — and he was reasonably sure he had never had words with Mr. Hammond. Examining him as they came alongside, he was not entirely sure that it was a good idea that he did now. The man, Stanley determined, was a little flashy.

Hector Hammond was, indeed, just a tad flashy. It would have been strange if the man married to Fanny were not, for otherwise he might have been invisible. What Stanley found just that little unsettling, however, was not the fact that Hector was wearing a blazer rather than the requisite Sunday suit, but that around his neck was a paisley cravat with a stickpin running through it. The man, thought Stanley, had an unfortunate air of frivolity about him. He was also standing rather peculiarly; one leg out slightly in front of the other, knee bent, shoulders thrust back and chin raised. Stanley suspected that it was a pose.

In reality, there was something of the poseur in Hector. He was a retired actor, or rather, more accurately, since actors never retire, an unemployed one, and at this time in his life, at the beginning of his golden years, he was his own production. A twinkle in his eye informed those who guessed correctly that he knew he was posing. He was known to say among his intimates that if he did not affect there would be no effect, and like most of his profession, he enjoyed that effect. Had it not been for the fact they were inside, he might have added a holdered cigarette, à la Noel Coward, to his outfit and, if it were a special occasion, a boutonniere.

Noticing the imminent arrival of the Vicar and his acolyte to port, Hector drew on another of his arsenal of theatrical shenanigans and boomed in a voice that erupted from deep within the recesses of his abdomen and made its way up and out as though a trombone was wedged somewhere beneath his esophagus, "Vicar!"

Stanley winced.

"Hector," said the Vicar, "I want you to meet Stanley Parkinson. He has an idea that you might interested you. The two of you could work together on it. I'm sure you will do well together." The Vicar was not a deluded man, but he could be wilfully optimistic on occasion. This was one such occasion. "Stanley wants to put on a social." He searched for another word, one not so tired or so churchy. Inspiration pounced. "To put on," he wheezed, "a show."

There was possibly no other word in the English language that could have had a greater effect on Hector Hammond. It was pure catnip to a thespian whose very life had been theatre and whose nickname in the trade was Hammie. Hammie Hammond. His directors, his co-stars, even his wife, called him this, but, it must be stressed, with great affection and only behind his back.

"A Show!" Hector hallooed the word, and capitalized it, lengthening it so that it seemed multi-syllabic and even orgasmic. "A Show!" he repeated it even more loudly and with considerable reverence. His baritone filled the room. People turned to stare. "Tell me more!" he commanded. "Tell me more, my friend. Do tell!"

To Stanley Parkinson's total consternation, Hector Hammond flung a blazered arm around his knobbly shoulder and hung on tight.

Stanley felt himself at sea. A modern Jonah, he was being chomped on and spat out, and even though the spitting was purely metaphorical, the physical effect was real. A vein in Stanley's forehead began to palpitate and he blanched. Faun, serving tea on the far side of the room, noticed both phenomena quite clearly and her bosom heaved with concern. This heaving, however, went quite unnoticed by the fellowship: nature, in that particular area, had not been munificent. In this respect, as in many others, Faun, as you might guess, was the polar opposite of Fanny.

"A Show!" Hector had repeated the word a third time. Each time it seemed to have a different emphasis, a different implication. Focusing his complete attention on Stanley, he asked, "My dear fellow, what did you have in mind?" Since his arm was still around Stanley's shoulder, their proximity was extreme. Faun had borne Stanley two children and he could not remember ever having been this close to her. He became enveloped in Old Spice, an aroma to which Hector Hammond was more dedicated than the Pope is to incense. Stanley felt his uvula closing down in protest. Only vaguely aware that he had been asked a question, he was, nevertheless, about to learn a salient fact concerning Hector Hammond: Hector might ask questions but he did not necessarily expect answers.

"How about making it an all day affair? A proper event? One culminating in a full evening's entertainment? Perhaps even a cabaret?"

"Well, gentlemen," said the Vicar, when he could get a word in edgewise, "I'll leave you to get acquainted."

The departure of their spiritual councillor left Stanley feeling bereft. He was still fastened to Hector, he was still being breathed on and it was quickly becoming apparent that his idea of a nice little social event was about to be hijacked.

"I've got an idea," said Hector. Stanley hadn't liked the last several of Hector's ideas, but he had no choice but to listen. "Come over for tea on Tuesday, and we'll get organized. Fan will be there and we can flush out the basics."

Stanley felt as if he had already been flushed, but, suddenly, he felt himself dragged as well. Without releasing him, Hector began to waft him across the room to where two seniors stood, eyes locked on Fanny's frontage. She was retailing for them, at their particular request, the finer points of cricket with its silly mid-offs and maiden overs. "Fan," he said, interrupting her in mid-sentence, "Stanley is coming over on Tuesday for tea. We're going to plan an entertainment! You know Stanley, don't you? He's going to be in charge."

Stanley heard these last words and even as they passed through his consciousness he knew them to be nonsense. He knew this as surely as he knew that his idea of a pleasant social evening at the church would never be heard of again. Oh, lip service might occasionally be given to it, but its essence, the politeness of a sit-and-sip anglo-catholic tea-party, was gone forever. Before this thought had even properly registered, however, Stanley replaced it with another: to wit, Fanny Hammond's breasts were stupendous. Unbelievably stupendous. And they were now approximately eighteen inches in front of him. He did not know from whence the thought came — it certainly was not typical — but there was no doubt about its currency. Unexpected it might be, and, yes, totally atypical, but, oh my, it was there.

"Hello then, Stanley!" declared the owner of the bosom. She held out her hand to be shaken. "Do you like pineapple upside-down cake? Hector doesn't like pineapple upside-down cake, but I will make one for you. Will you bring your wife? She would make four." Stanley was barely able to keep up. He seemed to be embroiled in a conversation adorned with insidious sexual innuendo, and he knew neither what to say nor do. Did he have a wife? He really couldn't remember. Why did the woman's breasts rise and fall like that? How? He was reaching out to shake one of them — the left one seemed to be particularly friendly and it was apparently coming forward to meet him — before he recalled that it was her hand he was supposed to take hold of. At the last minute he diverted his eager fingers and avoided what would have been a blunder of story-ending proportions before we even get started.

"Yes, of course, do bring your good lady!" said Hector, still declaiming his sentences. Like the Vicar, Hector had a tendency to speak in exclamation points. "What a team we will make! Which one, er, of these lovely ladies is your good wife?" He looked around at the bevy of possible prospects, few of whom would, in the normal course of events, have expected to be called lovely.

"Hector Hammond!" laughed Fanny, "How come you don't know Stanley's Faun? Everybody knows Faun." Weighed objectively, her statement was probably accurate. Everybody did know Faun. They might not have known her name but most of them had come to realize that although she might not say much, she was actually Stanley Parkinson's missis, and everyone knew Stanley Parkinson. Faun was on the tea committee with her, and Fanny made it her business to know people's names. She was like that. Names were important. She pointed towards the tea trolley. "That's Faun, with the tea pot," she said.

"Aaah," said Hector. Releasing his captive, he moved once again across the room, this time his arms outstretched, navigating round the trolley when he came to it until he was able to envelope Stanley's considerably confused spouse within the safe harbour of his arms. Unfortunately, since Faun only came up to Hector's armpit, she was in immediate danger of suffocation. Whereas, however, Hector's toiletry excess appalled Stanley, who did not believe that men should apply anything more noxious than Irish Spring to their dermis, Faun went entirely in the other direction. Had the makers of his aftershave been aware of the effect their product was about to have on Faun, they might have considered adding a warning label, or at least a disclaimer, to the container, but it was too late. Faun had already inhaled.

The Business Of Pleasure

The four persons who gathered in the Hammond apartment for afternoon tea the following Tuesday came with very different agendas. Fanny, who knew she had caught Stanley's eye and having done so, was more than willing to throw him back into the vast pond of tiddlers from whence he came, was bopping reggae in the kitchen when the doorbell rang. Her pineapple upside-down cake had not come out well and she was too busy reassembling broken pineapple rings to attend to it. She wanted the tea to be a success, just as she wanted everything that involved Hector to be a success. He hadn't been well lately and she thought that organizing a show, even a church show which didn't sound much of a challenge, would give him a boost. She frowned and licked her fingers.

"Hector, get the door will you," she said, "they're here."

It wasn't that Hector hadn't heard the bell but when Fanny called out he was sitting rather abstractedly shuffling papers on the couch. He had sat there all morning roughing out, he said, a plan for the day's entertainment. He was not yet satisfied with the whole thing, but he felt that he did have something to present to Stanley and, as he said to Fanny over a quick lunch, at least they had some talking points. Fanny, who knew her husband inside and out, merely nodded and said she was sure it would be great. In her opinion, the Panama Canal had probably been built with less detailed plans than those strewn across her carpet.

"Okay," said Hector. He pushed himself up from an over-upholstered couch, and passed in front of a mirror, just happening to steal a glance to see that his bow-tie was straight. He walked slowly towards the vestibule with a slight swagger, a silent whistle on his lips and the usual twinkle in his eye. "I say, old thing," he said, calling out to Fanny in the kitchen behind him, affecting a mock accent, "Will that be one lump or two? Pip, pip and all that!"

Fanny laughed. "Now you behave, Hector, or you'll find out."

Opening the door to welcome his guests, Hector had no time to ask what he would find out. What he saw standing in front of him was not quite what he expected. Stanley, formally attired in a three piece suit that rather looked as though he had borrowed it from Humphrey's Funeral emporium, had left work early to be there and was wilting in the summer heat. Hector, if he considered the matter at all, had assumed that Stanley was retired like everyone else. Slightly behind her husband, and peeping out from under the brim of a large straw hat, Faun seemed embarrassed to be there, but essayed a slight hello.

Knocking on the door before it opened, Stanley had had two objectives. The first was to keep his mind — and his eyes — off his hostess's frontage. This, he had decided on the journey over, should be easy enough since he and Mr. Hammond would have a lot to discuss. The second objective, the more important one, of course, was to disabuse Hector of the idea that the event they were going to plan would last any longer than a couple of hours or involve more than cups of church tea and a concomitant selection of dessert. Faun, who had been in a daze since leaving the church on Sunday morning, hardly had an agenda at all. She just wanted to take everything in: the apartment, the ambiance, and, perhaps most of all, if she had admitted it to herself, Hector Hammond.

Hector reached out to shake Stanley's hand, drawing him forward into the apartment. Shaking the hand heartily, he threw his left arm over Stanley's shoulder and held on to him. Hector, as everybody who met him found out, was a toucher. Stanley was not. "Come on in, old bean," said Hector, "welcome to our happy home." And calling out, when he spied her, he added, "You too, my divine Faun."

"They're here," hallooed Hector, stating the obvious, as Fanny emerged from the kitchen smoothing her hands down the front of her frock. The smoothing had the effect of causing her superstructure to dip a little before it bounced back when she ceased the downward motion. It also had a decided effect on Stanley, who found himself staring at the one place he had determined not to. "Stanley's looking very hot and bothered, Fan. Perhaps our guests would like a cool drink. It's a scorcher out there."

Fanny spied Faun, still half hidden behind the menfolk and reached out to her. "Hey there, m'dear," she said, "come in. Don' mind this man! He has no more manners than a delinquent youth. Hector, mind your manners, man. Come sit down, m'dear." She led Faun over to the couch and tipped her gently down into it. Faun half disappeared into the cushioned excess and had to fight her way back to sit on its edge. She resembled a sparrow perched on a wire.

"Yes, indeed," said Hector. "You must forgive me, my dear. What was I thinking?" He gave Stanley a hug and let him go, prodding him with his elbow as he did so. "Just wanting to get down to business, I guess, eh what!" Rubbing his hands together, he looked at each of his guests in turn, "What can I get you to drink then? Gin? Scotch?"

The Parkinsons had been invited for tea and being literal-minded people had assumed that tea meant tea. In any case, neither one of them drank much, and certainly not at four o'clock in the afternoon. The Hammonds, more cosmopolitan and always thirsty, assumed that everyone drank and never had a thought otherwise.

"Oh, no, I don't think so," said Stanley shaking his head, "nothing for me."

"Oh, come now," replied Hector, "we can't have the Hammonds drinking solo, can we? What about you, my dear Faun? A little sherry, I'm sure."

Hector's question took Faun off guard. So did his gaze. He was standing in front and above her, leaning slightly forward, a blinding smile giving all his attention to her.

She hardly knew what she was saying.

"Well, yes. A little one wouldn't go awry," she said with a giggle. "I don't usually, but, umm, perhaps I will."

Faun didn't dare to look directly at Hector. She didn't know what she would do if she did. She didn't dare look at Stanley either. She could feel him frowning in her direction and she heard him take a breath. "Are you sure, Faun? It's not like you."

Faun raised her chin. "Well, yes," she said before adding coyly, "just a teeny teeny teeny one though."

The sherry that arrived was far from small although compared to the martinis that Hector made for Fanny and himself it might have seemed so. Stanley had been persuaded to have a glass of ginger ale and they all sat down.

"Let's get to work, then," said Hector, rubbing his hands together, "I've put together a couple of thoughts."

Stanley looked at the sheets of paper that Hector was waving in his direction. "I hope you haven't been put to too much trouble with this," he said, not quite sure what the papers meant but wanting to take control of the situation. "It's nothing big or complicated. Just an evening of fun and frolic."

"Absolutely!" agreed Hector. "An evening of fun!" He beamed. "And we're Bialystok and Bloom. The producers!"

Stanley hadn't the foggiest idea who or what Bialystok and Bloom were, but he had become aware that Fanny, seated to his left, had her martini cradled in her cleavage. The amber liquid in the glass illuminated her bosom, and it, it seemed, was beckoning to him. Fanny was smiling at him as well and, as she did so, she rotated the glass slightly from side to side. Stanley not only lost his train of thought, he became derailed.

"Umm," he said, gathering his wits as best he could, "I, er, thought, a couple of solos and perhaps a recitation or two before refreshments and then a sing-song to finish. Not too late a night, you know, so the older folks can get home early, but an enjoyable occasion for everyone."

Hector glared at Stanley as though doubting he had heard correctly. He shook his head, although more to clear it than in actual disagreement. He stood up and threw out his arms, spilling half of what was left of his martini on the carpet.

"Oh," he said, "I think we can do a little better than that, my friend. Let me show you."

To Faun's consternation but also to her illicit joy, and to Stanley's greatly embarrassed annoyance, their host sat himself down on the couch between the two of them, opened a double spaced concertina of paper on his knees and threw his arms around both of them.

"What I was thinking is this!"

What Stanley and Faun were being directed to look at appeared to be a timetable, divided into hours, for Saturday the seventh of September. The hours between eleven in the morning and ten at night were shaded and capital letters occupied each block of time. That much was certain. What the capital letters signified was less clear. Hector suffered from arthritis in his thumbs and his writing was virtually illegible. As they were about to find out, even he had difficulty deciphering it. Using his left hand, the arm of which was still round Stanley's neck, he pointed at the shaded eleven o'clock space, nearly strangling his fellow producer in the process.

"The morning should be for the kiddies. We'll begin with a scavenger hunt in the church and then I thought I would get a police car so they could see what it is like inside one." Hector paused and squeezed the necks of both his captives. "In case they ever get arrested!"

Stanley congealed. There were so many things wrong with what Hector had just said that it was difficult for him to decide which to address first.

"We can't have a scavenger hunt in the church. The executive would never permit it." Neither, if it came to that, would Stanley. "The Vicar would be most upset."

Hector turned to face Faun and winked. "Don't worry about that. We'll have Faun work on him."

Faun did something she had never done in her life before. She simpered.

"And, and, and," said Stanley rushing on, still marshalling his thoughts. "We don't have children in the congregation." This was true. The congregation lacked anything that could remotely be labeled a kiddie.

Hector bounced on his seat.

"Leaflets! We'll do a postal walk and paper the district. That'll bring them in, eh, ma belle?" Hector looked to his wife for support.

She nodded back at him, grinning. "It will have to be done the Saturday before so that people get enough notice."

"A splendid idea. Absolutely splendid." Hector beamed at Fanny and hugged the necks of his guests.

Stanley was staring down at the eleven o'clock section of the schedule. He had deciphered the word "Police" and he was not happy with it. "What is this about a police car? We cannot afford a police car. Why would we buy a police car? What would we do with it afterwards?" Even as he spoke, Stanley realized that, if Hector was not making sense, he was hardly doing any better, and he did not appreciate the fact that both Hector and Fanny had burst out laughing.

"Public Relations, my friend. That'll get us a police car. Free. I know the commissioner. And a couple of off-duty coppers. We'll need them anyway for crowd control."

Nowhere in Stanley's ruminating about the social event had the words 'crowd' or 'control' entered the picture. He was not a man to pour water on enthusiasm but, clearly, Hector had gone too far. Stanley cleared his throat.

"I really don't think there will be any need for that. Our ushers would be all that we need," he said. Even as he said it, he knew that Hector was not listening.

"Then, at one o'clock, lunch!"

"Hot dogs and hamburgers." Fanny clapped her hands and Stanley looked over at her, startled.

Hector rolled on. "Barbecue! Faun, I thought you and Fan here could be in charge of that. What do you think? Any thoughts?" Faun's neck was beginning to ache but the enticement of Old Spice had long ago made her head swim. She had also just drained the largest glass of sherry she had ever put her lips on. She was vaguely aware that Stanley was sitting rigid on Hector's other side, but what else was she to do but accede to Hector's instructions?

"Oh, yes, I'll do the hamburgers."

"Mmm," said Fanny, with a wink at Stanley, "and I'll be in charge of the hot dogs. Foot longs, wouldn't you say?"

Stanley, to do him justice, did not have a salacious bone in his body. Nevertheless, he caught the innuendo and he clasped it close to his chest for several glorious moments before his fiduciary soul managed to wrest it from him. Only then was he able to frown and shake his head. Stanley had the responsibility of keeping the church afloat financially after all. "Oh," he said, "we couldn't possibility afford to have a lunch and a supper as well." Even as he said this, he was aware that he was giving ground, and that Hector might think his grandiose scheme for the morning was somehow approved. He added hastily, "Not that we could afford the police either. They'd have to be paid, after all."

He felt Hector shrug next to him, and heard him say in a mock Jamaican accent, "No problem, mon, we'll go to the local merchants for a donation. The banks, the supermarkets, and there's the pub on the corner." Turning towards Stanley so suddenly that he almost flinched, Hector added, "You're a banker! You can be in charge of that."

"Me?!"

Disbelief was the major emotion that Hector might have detected, had he been listening. He wasn't.

"The hotdogs and hamburgers we'll get as a contribution from Loblaws. And give an acknowledgement in the programme, of course. Are you an IT fellow, Stan, old boy? We'll need an IT chap to handle the programme."

"And the posters," added Fanny across the room, again clapping her hands. "Could you do that, Stanley?"

Stanley's computer skills were minimal, but he was hesitant to admit it. He was not sure why. "Well, I suppose I could. At a pinch." His secretary could be put to the task. Again, however, Stanley recognized that somehow, in some way, he had given ground and he struggled to reclaim in. "But, again, Mr. Hammond, Hector, who's going to pay for it?" He appealed to Fanny. "Fanny," he said, the word seeming to struggle off a swollen tongue. British background on not, he had never said the word in his life before. So he said it again. "Fanny! Surely you see what I mean."

Fanny shook her head and laughed. "Once Hector gets the bit between his teeth there's no stopping him. And it'll be fun. We'll have fun." She gestured to the group and stood up. "We'll all have fun!" To illustrate her point, Fanny began to move from foot to foot, gyrating her hips infinitesimally and flicking her fingers to an internal beat.

Hector paid no attention to her. "I think the afternoon should be for everyone," he announced.

"The afternoon?" stuttered Stanley, his attention focused rather too completely on Fanny's mid-section.

"Games for the whole family, I was thinking. Crafts in the Latimer Room, skittles and musical chairs in the auditorium as long as they finish early enough so that we can arrange the chairs for the cabaret, bridge for the older heads upstairs in the nursery. Things like that. What do you think, Stan?"

Stanley didn't know what to think. Every time Hector opened his mouth, Stanley seemed less able to think. He was, for instance, wondering why Hector kept using a stage Englishman accent and whether this was somehow a dig at him, Stanley, just because he did still have a little of his original English accent left. He was wondering too how his little social event for a Saturday evening had suddenly become a cabaret, of all things. And he was wondering what his boss at the bank would have to say if he were to appear, cap in hand, asking for a donation to fund a church function of any kind, even with attribution in some kind of programme, one presumably printed on bank stationary and designed on company time!

He held up his hand. "I really think," he said, "we have to think." This was not the most coherent of sentences, but it had to be said. "My idea," he paused at the word, searching for one that would be more in the spirit of the endeavour, "My vision is for an elegant evening of fellowship." The word elegant had fluttered into his brain unbidden and he wasn't sure it was appropriate. It was, however, he thought, the kind of word Hector might use and which he should be able to understand. At least it would take them away from hotdogs and police cars and Fanny's burlesque. He had considered 'intimate' but a glance at her dancing had convinced him that it would be unwise.

"Oh," said Hector, beaming, "We'll have elegance, won't we Fan?" And, so saying, he stood, reached out a hand to her, and twirled her under his arm. They began to perform a sedate version of the frug in front of their astonished visitors.

Stanley felt as though he were on the Titanic. Faun was still seated on the sofa, leaning forward, chin resting on her hands, with a look on her face that Stanley could not fathom. It was part smile but, had he but known it, also part swoon. And, indubitably, envy. Whatever it was, it was of no help to him. He had to get the situation under control, have his say about all this or everything would be lost.

"Well," he began, with as much joviality as he could muster, "I don't know what the Vicar would think, but I'm afraid that he would say it was all far too ambitious. And who would do the work? Who would clean up and get everything ready for church on the Sunday morning? And, well, we've not done anything like this before, so…"

Leaving Fanny twirling round by herself, Hector bopped towards Stanley, apparently intent on sweeping him into his arms. Stanley flinched. Hector laid both hands on Stanley's thin shoulders. "My dear boy," he said, "I ran everything by the Vicar on the phone before you came, and he said everything was up to us. Just, he said, and I believe his words were, 'Don't wreck the joint or the Ladies of the Church will have my head.'"

Lampposts and Other Flights of Fancy

"Now, let's get on with the show!" said Hector, and changing his mental music, he began clapping his hands, affecting the pose of a rather geriatric flamenco dancer.

"Ole!" trilled Fanny, throwing her head back and stamping a foot.

To say that the Parkinsons were in shock understates the case. Faun was almost in a fugue state. Stanley, though made of sterner stuff, was, nevertheless, having trouble controlling his bladder. In the past five minutes, Hector had put forward the idea of a jazz ensemble to play quietly during tea, and a car service to provide transportation for the lame and the halt who might otherwise be unable to attend the day's festivities. Stanley had almost been struck dumb during his host's monologue on the feasibility of playing board games in the vestry. He became entirely so when Hector began to rhapsodize on the possibility of finishing the evening off with a theatrical event of some sort. The very idea seemed likely to finish Stanley off.

Hector continued apace.

"Do you sing, Stanley? Should we put you down for a number?" he asked.

Stanley's verbal response to these questions was a hollow and strangled, "Me?" and a half-depreciatory guffaw. This was what appeared on the surface. Beneath that surface, however, Stanley's emotions began to roil, and, although his bladder might have remained in control, much of the rest of him did not. His whole life, Stanley had had a horror of performing in public. Oh yes, he could explain a balance sheet using a flip chart and pointer. He could speak to, or more likely against, a motion with the best of them, but to get up on a stage and entertain was beyond him and he knew it. He knew it in his soul and he knew it because, against all caution and self-knowledge, he had once tried it. He had, long ago in college, played the counsel for the defence in 'Trial By Jury.' How he got through it, he could not remember.

The why of it involved being told that he had an excellent voice — which was stretching it just a little — when an acquaintance at his residence heard him singing in the shower and cajoled him into an audition. It did not go well but he got the part anyway: his voice suited the role. The audition, however, was streets ahead of the actual performance, a performance that was, unfortunately, repeated each night for a week with a Saturday matinee unexpectedly attended by supporters of a visiting football team whose game had been cancelled due to weather so inclement that whales would have drowned in it. And the catcalls they hurled in his direction were nothing compared to the reviews. These were etched upon his brain. 'Unfortunately uninspired' had seemed almost complimentary when put alongside an entirely accurate 'rigidly stuff' but, almost forty years on, both still hurt.

And yet, truth be told, there lay hidden within the dry and untilled heart of Stanley Parkinson, a desire to try again.

"Me?" he said again, vehemently shaking his head in the negative. "Oh, no, not me!"

Hector, however, had seen it. He had seen that glint of desire in Stanley's eye, that slight swelling of a performer's bosom without which the boards cannot be trod. Hector knew what it meant to be told that on a certain date the house lights would dim, the curtains would rise and a single spotlight would seek him out centre stage, and that he would then begin to entertain, to enchant, to perform! And, somehow, in some way, as a prospector might sift through the dirt panning for specks of the purest gold, he saw this in Stanley.

"So you sing!" In a lusty baritone, Hector almost sang himself. "Or perhaps, my friend, you would like to act! A one act play! That's what we could do. Even a play with music! Forty-five minutes of words and music! Noel Coward! Ivor Novello!" Hector's use of exclamation points was excessive even for him, and he was not yet finished. "Or a solo! In an evening suit!" He raised his hands and looked between them like a photographer arranging his subject. "I can see you on the stage! Singing! Yes! Wonderful!"

Despite every iota of the common sense that had helped Stanley navigate some fifty-nine years of life, something inside of him stirred. His chest heaved if only slightly. He gulped. The flesh of his normally pale slightly yellowing skin began to achieve a pinkish tinge not normally seen in nature, well, not in Stanley's nature anyway. His eye, that eye which so often looked jadedly upon an unhopeful world, glistened.

And Hector saw it. He knew.

Stanley took a breath. It was not a deep breath, and it made no sound. The intake of air was scarcely enough to allow him to utter the one word he was finally able to enunciate. "Formby," he said, and, taking multiple gulps of oxygen like a fish gasping for air in the back of a boat, he continued. "George. Formby. I've always wanted. You know. To sing. 'I'm Leaning On A Lamppost.'"

Then, perhaps fearing he was speaking a language foreign to his companions, he tried to explain. "It's about a man standing at a lamppost. He's waiting for a woman."

Hector, who knew teasing, couldn't resist. "It doesn't sound like the kind of song for a church social," he said, trying to appear scandalized, just a little.

"Oh, no," replied Stanley, hastily, beginning to blush. "Not that kind of woman."

Hector laughed. "Well, you never know with Formby. His song about having his little ukulele in his hand was almost banned."

Stanley did not know what Hector was talking about and stuck to his guns.

"I've always loved George Formby," he said, mulishly.

It was news to Faun.

Faun was seated at the other end of the settee unable to believe just about anything she had heard for the last hour or so, and, unable to believe it, she was having a similar difficulty in knowing how to comport herself. The muscles of her face had taken on a life of their own and they seemed to change patterns as do the eddies of the tide in the sand. The muscles in her lower back had given way a while ago and she sat scrunched into a question mark, one knee vibrating against the other, a quivering which, in itself, matched the twitch that had appeared in her left eyelid. Part of her wanted to giggle. Another part wanted to cry. She understood neither part. A thought, a random thought it had to be since she was currently incapable of rational thinking, lurched into her mind and centred itself there. She heard herself speak.

"I like to dance," she said. "Perhaps there will be dancing."

Whence the thought came, Faun did not know. Stanley and she did not dance. They never had. Oh yes, there had been that dance at their wedding, the first dance they called it, but in their case it had just about been the last one as well. Whatever else he was, Stanley was not a dancer. He had ripped her hem and practically ravaged her mother when it came to her turn. Faun herself, heaven knew, was not the most rhythmic of souls and, in any case, she was not in the habit of verbalizing her likes or dislikes willy-nilly to the general population. Then it struck her, it wasn't that she wanted to dance, exactly. It was that she wanted to be held. By Hector. Faun turned puce at the thought, and tried to swallow both a giggle and the thought.

Completely oblivious of the turmoil to both his right and his left, Hector moved on. He wondered aloud, "A play and a cabaret. We should hold auditions next week, I think. Better get going. We'll ask the Vicar to announce them on Sunday during the service and see who turns out. Which is the best evening for you?"

Stanley struggled to catch up. He could hardly credit that his secret admiration for the long-dead English comedian George Formby had been taken so normally and his ears simply did not believe his spouse's statement concerning terpsichorean exertion. They would have to talk about it when they got home. Faun could hardly expect that she would dance with him — Stanley knew his limitations — and he could not envision that any other member of the congregation would be willing to trip the light fantastic with her. More likely to trip over the light fantastic, he thought rather smugly. The incident with the hem had rankled for years in their marriage and, although he admitted blame, it did not mean that he had to like it. Now here was Hector going on about auditions. Auditions for what?

Hector was in full flight. "If we have the cabaret in the first half, just six or seven acts — you, Stan, my boy, with George, and me, of course, and a couple of soloists from the choir and we'll ask for others, then we can have a short recess while we set up the stage. About half an hour, don't you think, Fan? The play shouldn't be more than about forty-five minutes. There's plenty of choice, and we'll have the oldsters out of there by, what, nine o'clock." He wasn't finished. "You'll produce, Stanley, which will leave me to look after the artistic side. Fan can do tickets, publicity, front-of-house, things like that, and you, my little Faun, you will look after refreshments and prettying up the auditorium."

Hector beamed at Faun as though he had bestowed a great gift upon her and was taken aback to see that she was violently shaking her head.

"Oh, I don't think I could," she said. Faun was not at all pleased to hear that she was being relegated to kitchen duties while the others were to have more glamorous theatrical tasks, but this was not the reason for her refusal. "I'm not in charge, you see. The Ladies of the Church wouldn't like it." Faun appealed to Fanny. "I'm just a helper."

Fanny nodded. "She's right, Hector," she said. "We'd have to get permission from the Ladies of the Church for anything to do with the kitchen, particularly of an evening. You won't be able to go round them."

"The Vicar will..." said Hector, but Fanny cut him off.

"The Vicar won't!" she replied, with finality.

"No, indeed," said Stanley, considerably winded and still trailing behind. The thought that the Ladies of the Church might obey the Vicar was an interesting idea, but it had been tested in the past and found wanting. "They are," he added with a dry cough, "a law unto themselves."

Hector looked at the three of them in turn. If the Ladies of the Church were not used to the idea of being interfered with, well, frankly, neither was he. In things theatrical, Hector Hammond did not brook opposition. A reasonable man in most aspects of his life, when it came to the theatre Hector could be way beyond a martinet. He preferred to be, and expected to be, an absolute monarch — a benevolent despot perhaps, but a despot nevertheless.

"Well," he said, mulishness edging into his voice, "we have to have sustenance between the cabaret and the play. Can't have the masses starve, can we? That's the way it is done. Who do they think they are!"

In unison, the trio answered him. "The Ladies of the Church."

Since Hector had found it necessary to ask the question, a word of explanation is in order.

It had been many years since the women in the congregation began to realize, dimly at first but, as time passed, with more clarity, that they were in a male-run bastion. The Vicar was, invariably, a man, the executive was men, the committees were all dominated by men, and even the janitorial staff was male. While it was true that many of these men were their husbands, the ladies still found themselves on the outside looking in when it came to church governance and even participation. Unable, even hesitant, to go up against tradition and authority, they looked round to find an area of endeavour over which they might exert control and a parallel domination. They came upon the kitchen. While it was true that they had been in the kitchen for years, their control there had never been institutionalized. Stealthily, and with tenacity, they began to lay down rules. Want tea and cookies served at the Men's Club? Ask the Ladies of the Church. Need to keep water in the refrigerator for choir practice? Get permission from the Ladies of the Church. Serve supper at a cabaret concert and a one act play? Definitely. But first, obtain a dispensation from the Ladies of the Church. And not just any old Ladies either.

If Hector Hammond was a benevolent despot in things theatrical, the Ladies of the Church were a totalitarian state. A state that came fully equipped with its own dictator. That dictator was one Mabel Grace Green. The rest of the Ladies were, as Faun had so aptly indicated, merely helpers. Of course, not everyone could even be a helper. Fanny had not been around long enough to be allowed to help. She might want to wash dishes or volunteer to slave over a hot stove, but her time had not yet come. Faun, long years into her apprenticeship, had, as we saw at the beginning of our tale, graduated to pouring tea after the Sunday service. In the fullness of time, she could expect to be promoted to cleaning the communion silver, although that was quite a way in the future unless disease were to carry off several of those ahead of her.

It took a certain amount of repetition before Hector was able to comprehend the intricacies of all this, and it was interesting that, as Stanley tried to explain it, he found himself more and more siding with Hector about their needs for the evening. Whereas he should have been using the recalcitrance of the Ladies as a weapon to pooh pooh the possibility of a cabaret, he found himself looking for chinks in the Ladies' armour that might enable Hector and himself to circumvent them. He began, if only by slight gradations at first, to buy into Hector's plan, to see in it not only an opportunity to belt out his favourite Formby but also to do something he had not even imagined himself wanting to do. It would be his turn to shine. More than that, if the evening came off, if the Ladies of the Church were successfully disarmed (deteapotted, if you will) Stanley Parkinson would have become a Theatrical Producer, too. With a capital P. Who knew?

It was Stanley, in fact, who came up with a solution to their dilemma.

"Perhaps we could have Mabel Green in the cabaret. Or in the play. You know, to act," he said, tentatively.

Hector stood. "By Jove!" he yelled. "You've got it!"

Grabbing Stanley by the shoulders, he pulled him to his feet and reached out to embrace him. Stanley found himself once more enveloped in Hector's aftershave, but, strangely, this time he did not seem to mind. He had provided a solution and he had pulled his weight in the planning of the evening's festivities. He could not imagine that Ms. Green would or could sing and he doubted that she would deign to read lines written by another human being, but it was new to Stanley to be surrounded by such effervescence and emotive camaraderie and he found himself liking it. Faun was beaming up at him and Fanny was essaying yet another of her hip twirling gyrations that, well, in and of themselves, almost made it all worthwhile.

"Excellent, Stanley, old chum," said Hector, slapping him so hard on the back that Stanley's upper plate was almost dislodged, "I'll approach her myself. Away from the church, of course. And get her on our side before we do anything else."

Meeting La Belle Mabel

Thus it was that Hector Hammond stood before Mabel Green's front door two afternoons later, ringing her bell. He did not go unarmed. A few quick phone calls to congregational acquaintances had provided a further gloss of information about the lady in question, although one of them had wondered why on earth Hector wanted anything to do with the woman. The results, as he admitted to himself standing there waiting for the door to open, had not been encouraging. Ms. Green had been described variously as formidable, indomitable, determined and, by a member not known for his timorousness, more than slightly scary. She had been christened at the church some sixty-eight years before, confirmed in it and it was the general opinion that she would, in the fulness of time, be buried from it. She was unmarried, which surprised no one, and it was generally accepted that she would stay that way. She lived, Hector was told, with a dog that was probably older than she herself and which had even worse breath. Anyone who wished to be in her good books, needed to endeavour to be in the dog's good books first. This advice came from the Vicar himself, but other persons did mention the dog.

When the door opened, Hector saw why they would. The ancient canine stood next to its owner, surveying him with rheumy eyes. Originally a large black labrador, the animal had devolved with age and overfeeding into a shapeless mass on four greying legs. Its tongue, an unhealthy looking yellow, lolled haphazardly from a drooling mouth and Hector immediately became aware that either the animal or its mistress was passing gas. He smothered a desire to laugh. Reaching out, nevertheless, to pat the ancient animal, he was met with a low growl. He turned his attention to the beast's mistress. Hector had not immediately recognized who Mabel Green was when her name was mentioned and it was only when Fanny described her after their guests left, that he realized which one of the church ladies she was.

"She's the huge one with the perm and the granny glasses," Fanny said, "You know her for heaven's sake. Lord have mercy, everyone knows Mabel Green."

Indeed, Hector did know her. Mabel Green was a woman of brobdignagian proportions who — almost — made the Vicar look like a sylph. Her two giant breasts made his own Fanny resemble the merest hermaphrodite. On the move, Mabel had the appearance of a Hummer maneuvering down a country lane, with all of its delicacy. Hector had once collided with her in a doorway and bounced off before he was able to steady himself. So corseted that she creaked when ambulatory, Mabel used a stick to keep herself upright and to hinder a centre of gravity that was forever threatening to tip her forward. Despite all of this, however, her identifying feature was her hair. Mabel Green had a perm. It was a perm tighter than bedsprings and shorter than the foliage on a Chia pet.

Stifling an ever greater desire to have hysterics on the spot, and listening to what he was now certain was a crescendo of flatulence, Hector decided that if he did not speak soon he would collapse against the doorpost. Unfortunately, and unusually for a man who had spent his life learning lines, he forgot what it was he intended to say.

"What an adorable doggie," is what he finally came up with. "What's her name?"

"Bruce."

Mabel Green frowned at him. "I know you. You're the fellow from the church."

It was an accusation.

"Indeed, I am," said Hector, recovering slightly. "I called to ask if I could drop round."

"That was for tomorrow."

"Well, er umm, no. For today. Thursday, we said."

Hector knew that he was correct, but it was not an auspicious start.

Once again, there was the undeniable sound of Bruce's intestinal unhappiness. Hector, who had made a career of appearing in British bedroom farces, had a finely honed sense of the ridiculous, but this was an entirely new experience. He was saved from paroxysms of laughter only because Mabel maneuvered her bulk sideways in the doorway, thrusting Bruce against the wall as she did so. She said, with a heaving sigh, "Well, you better come in. But it was Friday."

Hector chose not to argue the point and followed his hosts through to the parlour where he was directed to a hard-backed chair.

"Sit!" commanded Mabel.

Hector and Bruce sat.

Evidently, a woman of few words and inconsiderable social graces, Mabel peered at him for several long seconds. Bruce slobbered and Hector began to feel acutely uncomfortable. Not much discomforted him, but it was a toss up as to which of the two entities that were staring at him made him feel more off his game.

"Well?" said Mabel, eventually. As she said it, Bruce, who evidently had examined Hector as long as was deemed necessary, slowly sank to the ground and settled. As the animal did so, Hector heard the longest, lowest fart he had encountered in his entire life. He was suddenly terrified, not of the fart — although it really was of championship calibre — but of his certainty that he himself was about to have a fit and that if so much as one stray giggle were to escape him, it would be followed by others that would put a Feydeau farce to shame.

Hector stood up and, trying for nonchalance, leaned an arm against Mabel's mantlepiece.

"You knock anything off and you'll pay for it."

The words came from his hostess as calmly as if she were giving the weather forecast. Hector, totally lost, withdrew his arm, the cuff of his jacket catching a figurine in the process. He tried to catch the object, but, in doing so, only managed to swat it higher into the air before it began a descent that ended squarely on the belly of the dog, which now lay snoring rather uncomfortably on his back, next to his mistress. Bruce yelped in surprise and emitted an even more enormous fart. Hector did not dare look. He wondered whether the animal hadn't also voided its bowels in the process.

"Heavens to Betsy!" said Mabel, still completely without emotion. "Sit down, man, before you wreck my house."

Hector and Mabel sat in silence, the while listening to a declining scale of tiny toots as Bruce subsided again into sleep.

"What," repeated Mabel, "what do you want?"

"Well," said Hector, more than a little exercised, "we're going to put on a show." He stood up again. He always thought better on his feet. Waving his hands expansively, and at the same time trying to avoid the furnishings, he continued, "A Saturday in September when people start back at church after the summer. To build camaraderie."

In the dialogue Hector had composed mentally for how the conversation would go, Mabel was down to speak next. She would say something like, "What a good idea!" or "Marvellous!" In her own sitting room, however, she remained ominously silent, peering at him steadily through her spectacles.

"Er...," he began again, "fellowship, if you like."

He was beginning to sweat. Hector Hammond had played to all kinds of audiences in his career, including several at maximum security establishments, but this was going to be a tough one. He had not intended to do so, wanting to hone in on the evening's events alone, but he found himself expansively beginning with the police car and the scavenger hunt, leading up to the hamburgers and hotdogs and the picnic that would follow. He was gathering momentum as he went, adding hand gestures and facial expressions to his performance, when Mabel finally joined the conversation.

"Not in my kitchen, you won't."

"Errr... Excuse me?" It was not a line Hector had expected to hear and he had never been partial to ad-libbers. As he was wont to say, the best ad libs were always written down first.

"Not in my kitchen. No hotdogs in the kitchen. Hamburgers, neither."

Mabel seemed to be prompting him but he had lost his place in the script. Hector glanced over at Bruce for support and a possible explanation. Neither was forthcoming. It was possible the dog had died. Hector backed up.

"No, no, of course not. We'll do them in the parking lot. We won't bother you at all." He took a small breath. "Possibly the Ladies of the Church would like to help?"

"No."

"Oh."

Hector had acted in several two-handers in his career, but he was used to having some human connection with the other person. He was beginning to feel that he had more of a connection with the dog — even if it were dead — than he had with Mabel. He decided to get to the point.

"In the evening, we're going to have a social in the auditorium. The Vicar has approved it." This was true although only in the broadest sense.

Mabel harrumphed.

Hector sped on. "There'll be some singing. Members of the choir, you know. Maybe a skit or two." Behind her spectacles, Mabel had raised her eyebrows. "And then, we were thinking of a little play. To pull the evening together, you know, and finish it off with a wallop."

Like any actor of worth, Hector had learned to assess his performance while he was giving it. He cringed at the word 'wallop' and determined that in any rerun he would have to do better, although he was not sure what better would be with such an audience. He was also, he knew, being too florid and physical: he was all awkward arms and elbows, when he should have exuded a still confidence. Damn the woman! Worst of all, he had positioned himself wrongly. He was standing above her, not exactly threatening her — you couldn't threaten Mabel Green on a bet — but towering above her, even as gargantuan as she was, wouldn't allow her to relax. She had to look upwards to see him properly and, since the windows were behind him, his face was in shadow. Which was a bloody good thing, he chided himself, since he seemed unable to remove an unholy grin from his face.

Hector felt a drip of sweat rise in his armpit and begin to wend its way down his bicep. He decided to deliver his coup de grace.

"We wondered whether you wouldn't like to be in the play."

Mabel Green's eyebrows clamped together as though sutured. She did not speak.

Hector hurried on jocularly, going for broke.

"A little birdie told me you used to act."

Silence.

"In the church."

Deathly hush.

"Years ago."

"And which little birdie told you that?" The question was asked in a tone that implied that the little birdie in question would be hunted down and throttled without fear or favour.

"I beg pardon...?" said Hector.

The woman had no idea of how dialogue was supposed to go. "Who told you this?"

Hector had no wish to get the Vicar in trouble but he had a greater desire to get himself out of it. He had consulted the Vicar on how best to approach Mabel.

The Vicar's first response had been, "With a stick, if at all possible!" which, if illuminating, was not particularly helpful. Then the Vicar had remembered that when he was going through the archives of the church, he had seen photographs of an old church theatre company that had existed for several years sometime in the early sixties. The members had been quite ambitious, even putting on Shakespeare on one occasion. Moreover, he had a suspicion that Mabel Green had been involved. He and Hector had retired to the boardroom to see what they could find. What they turned up beggared description.

"Lord God Almighty!" said the Vicar, "I never thought I would see such a thing."

"Are you sure it's her?" asked Hector, peering at a fading black and white photograph.

The Vicar turned the photograph over.

"Well, it's her name written on the back."

"Good God, Vicar. Do, do really think so?"

"Well, she's put on weight..." The Vicar began.

Fortuitously, Hector glanced over at the reverend before he responded to this and he was able to remind himself who he was looking at.

"I suppose so," he said.

A gurgle of laughter began to erupt from the Vicar. He was well aware of both his size and his parishioners attempts to avoid the subject.

"Perhaps," he said, slowly, "she swallowed the rest of the cast after the last performance."

It was quite a while before either man could get back to the subject of their inquiry, but the end result was that perhaps an appeal to Mabel's past and to her vanity, if she had such an emotion, might be tried. Hector, of the opinion that there was not a person born of woman who, in their heart of hearts, did not yearn to tread the boards and to bask in the warmth of applause, was convinced that this was the way to bring Mabel to heel. True, it was difficult to envision what kind of actual applause she would be able to evoke from even the most sympathetic of audiences, but neither he, nor the Vicar, could think of anything else.

Sliding over the name of his co-conspirator, Hector raced on. "And your reviews were excellent. We, I mean I, turned up the newspaper clippings." He closed his eyes as if trying to recall a piece of great literature, and held his hand up, palm outward, to forestall interruption. "The sweetness and conviction of Mabel Green's graceful Viola, whether in disguise as a boy dealing with Olivia's infatuation or herself falling in love with the handsome Orsino, is the standout in an almost professional cast that had the audience on its feet at the end of this accomplished production of Shakespeare's beloved 'Twelfth Night.' We particularly look forward to seeing the attractive Miss Green again in the future."

This last sentence was solely of Hector's invention, but he was betting that Mabel would not remember and its purpose, of course, was to add weight to his argument that she appear in his play. Opening his eyes after a beat, he examined his objective. Unless he was mistaken, there was the slightest upturn to the right side of her upper lip. Either Mabel was about to have a stroke or she was endeavouring to smile.

Hector pressed on.

"It would be wonderful to include you among the company of players we are putting together. To have you back treading the boards! To see such a talent to amuse in the lights. To know that you would be with us when the curtain..."

"I'm too old."

Was Hector wrong or did Mabel's response have within it just a smidgen of the coquette?

Suppressing a shudder, he pressed on, more hearty than before.

"Nonsense, my dear! You're in your prime and I always say that a well lit stage will take ten years off even the most wrinkled of faces." Immediately, and horribly, aware that this had not come out right, Hector added hastily, "Not that a woman with your bone structure would need it."

With a slight moue, and a smaller shrug, Mabel sighed, "I'm a little heavier these days."

Truthfully, what Hector thought to reply was that Mabel would be best suited to playing the Matterhorn in a production of 'The Sound Of Music,' but what he did say, lying through his teeth, was, "Nonsense!

You'll bring a sense of gravitas to what we are doing." The word 'bulk' appeared unbidden on the tip of his tongue, but cleverly he replaced it, adding "And believability, too. How could you not?!" Whether Mabel took this last as a question or a statement, Hector realized that she was, at that moment, on the fence and only in need of a slight push. He determined to give her a good shove.

With a flourish, Hector executed a deep bow, sank down on one knee in front of her, grabbed hold of a claw-like hand and, resembling d'Artagnan before the evil Milady de Winter, kissed it.

"Please, dahling!" he said, gazing up at her from the far side of her knuckles.

Whatever else one might say about Hector Hammond, he was a good actor. Mabel was enchanted. Beyond that, it may have been the 'dahling' that did it. No one had called her that since the Duke of Orsino had tried to get into her undergarments backstage, oh, so many years ago. So, yes, it was against both her better judgement and her principles but as she prepared herself for bed that evening she was still able to give a little hum and ask herself, "Why not?" As he prepared himself similarly that same evening, Hector was still essaying, to Fanny's great amusement, little flamenco steps of satisfaction. He had hooked, lined and sinkered Mabel without having to say what part she would play and even what the play would be. He hadn't the vaguest idea what he would do with her and, in a sober moment, he had his doubts that Stanislavsky himself would have been capable of doing anything with her, but, Holy Tallulah, he had her.

"Of course," he had said, when he had finally untangled his hand from hers — for some reason she continued to hold on to it — and hauled himself upright, "you will have to let the other Ladies look after the refreshments while you are backstage getting ready for your performance..."

Mabel never even blinked. "Don't you worry about that," she said. "It will be managed."

Long exposure to the vagaries of theatrical ambition and the concomitant call of the greasepaint ensured that Hector knew when he was on a roll. He was on one now.

"Of course," he said, almost as an aside and possibly only to himself, "I should meet with the other ladies as well…"

Mabel's response was prompt and possibly even grim. "You'll do no such thing. You leave them to me."

Mussolini would have been a pussy cat compared to Mabel Green.

Cappuccinos...

If Hector had cause for congratulation when he contemplated his day as he relaxed with his feet up on his recliner, Stanley, on the special hard-back chair bought the better to coddle a back prone to spasms of lumbar pain, was less at ease. A jubilant telephone call telling of Hector's triumph over 'La Belle Mabel,' as he called her, left Stanley with a sense of unease that would not go away and which, indeed, grew the more he thought about it. If Mabel Green could be brought to heel, there was no end to what Hector might accomplish. Stanley's rational side knew that to attempt so much was ridiculous. And to what purpose? There were not the numbers among the congregation to carry through the day-long event that Hector was proposing. If they tried it, convalescent homes across the city would be wheeling the fellowship through their doors before anybody knew what had hit them. Funeral homes would see an influx too. He was prepared to bet on it.

Stanley was also half aware, as well, of a niggling, irrational feeling that the day was being taken away from him, that his idea was being hijacked, and while it had never been his intention that the congregational social evening be to his glory, he found it just a little unnerving that it might be to the glory of someone else. By the time he set his denture in the glass of water on his bedside table, he was in a considerable state of umbrage, a state that gave him a restless night with an uncomfortable day to follow. Stanley would not have called himself a jealous man, but a feeling of virtuous annoyance would not go away. The people who worked with him at the bank suffered for it.

"Miss Tilsley. You were late back from lunch."

"Morrison, I need that report before close of business. And please remember to proofread the document before you print it, this time."

Stanley even found he had cause to leave a note for the cleaners: 'The top of the large cadenza is covered in dust.' Normally, he would have merely drawn an index finger through the dust and left it at that, but, really, it was too much. His secretary, the said Miss Tilsley, a woman of indeterminate age, not modern enough to demand to be a Ms., but surely too old to be any kind of 'Miss With Prospects,' began to warn people off. She was not very fond of her boss, but she was well aware that the bank offered far worse, and she was used to Stanley's foibles. It was she who, on a busy Thursday morning, informed him via the intercom that he had a telephone call from a woman.

"A woman," said Stanley, without punctuation. "Who is it?"

"She didn't give her name." Miss Tilsley knew she should have asked for it, and bit her lip. "She sounded foreign."

Stanley did not normally take up the cudgels with his secretary. He was well aware of her value, and, a rigorously fair man, he knew it was rare for her to fall short of the standards that he had both set and insisted upon, but he was, as we have said, just a little bit on edge and that can cause the most placid of souls to be jittery.

"Miss Tilsley, half of the women in the city are foreign these days," he declared. "Please ask what her name is. And her business in calling."

The intercom buzzed again.

"She says the nature of the call is," and here Miss Tilsley paused momentarily, perhaps unconsciously, for dramatic effect, "personal." She paused once more before adding, in a voice that evidenced both doubt and wonder, "She said her name is Fanny Hammond."

For several seconds, Stanley sat at his desk destitute of words. Then, managing a strangled cough as he cleared his throat, he said, "Thank you, Miss Tilsley. Put her through."

Stanley Parkinson's mind was not what one might call naturally quick, but the thoughts that managed to speed their way through it before he heard the click in his ear indicating that the call had been transferred, were myriad. There is no need to go into all of them here but when he found himself rising out of his chair to welcome her, some residual clarity persuaded him to sit back down again. His main and overriding thought was that he must clear his throat, the better to be able to speak to his caller, and, consequently, the first thing that Fanny heard on her end of the line was an enormous, lengthy and most unlovely hawking sound, rather like someone suffering from a virulent strain of bronchitis.

"Stanley?" she essayed the word tentatively.

It was music to his ears.

No response forthcoming, Fanny spoke again. "Stanley?" she inquired. She could hear breathing. "Is that you?" she added. "It's Fanny Hammond."

A full orchestra of violins was playing Viennese waltzes in his head, but eventually Stanley managed speech. Of a sort.

"In! Deed!" he said, "Hell hell, hello! Fan Fan Fanny. How are you?"

Fanny heard both the words and the message behind them and relaxed. She had been in two minds whether to make the call and she had had, of course, to leave the apartment to do so. She was not used to making telephone calls from pay phones and had trouble finding the requisite change, but a more than passing acquaintance with Mills and Boone also meant that she knew she had to be careful. She had no intention of doing anything that could come back to bite her.

She, in her turn, was temporarily at a loss for words.

"I was wondering," she said at last, remembering the script she had so carefully prepared in bed last evening next to a gently snoring Hector, "if we might not get together for coffee to discuss things."

The last word lingered, as Fanny, her breath honeyed and warm, spun it out into a fine gold. Stanley heard what she said all right, but he did not quite believe it. He could not think. It would have been easier to do so had not the thump of his heart been pounding away in his chest loudly enough make him wonder whether he was about to keel over.

Fanny spoke again. "Just you and I," she said.

Again, Stanley had difficulty processing what she was saying, and he did not notice the grammatical infelicity of her phrasing.

"Soon."

The word was a long lullaby in his right ear. It drowned out the throbbing at his temples and the rasp at the back of his throat which seemed to have suppressed speech.

"There are things," there was that word again: it was the sweetest word he had ever heard, "we need to talk about…"

And with this, Fanny was silent. She let the words percolate gently while waiting for a response. Unfortunately, she did not receive one. Stanley found himself covered in sweat and he was busy mopping himself with an increasingly damp tissue that stuck to his forehead. At this juncture, Miss Tilsley, all smiles and apparent business, swept into the room, mouthing that she would just leave these three documents on his desk for when he had time to sign them. Stanley blushed magenta. Miss Tilsley recorded the tableau for future reference. Fanny, still attached via Ma Bell and beginning to worry whether she might have overdone it, frowned.

There was no need to worry. Just then, Stanley would have followed Fanny Hammond to the ends of the earth and certainly to the Starbucks at which they agreed to meet. It was not long before his carefully arranged schedule had been cancelled, and a lone three o'clock appointment appeared on his calendar, indicated, as Miss Tilsley happened to notice when she was able to inspect it, by a single word. Miss Tilsley found the word incapable of interpretation. However, as she explained to one of her peers at lunch, she thought that the smiley face which followed his chicken scratchings spoke volumes.

By the time Stanley, ten minutes early, sat down in a crowded cafe that afternoon, he was beginning to have second thoughts about the whole endeavour. To be accurate, he had been having them on and off ever since the assignation had been made — and there was no way around the fact that it was an assignation. There in the crowded coffee shop, visible to everyone since the only place to sit was at a tiny, round table on a raised bar stool, he felt exposed. Two banking acquaintances had already acknowledged him and the noise in the place was appalling.

Stanley scanned the room and set his eyes on the door. It was a warm summer's day and the clientele seemed to be either from the financial services industry, dressed in what he liked to call 'Business Shabby,' or holidaying denizens in from the suburbs, who were dressed in not much at all. Stanley, all suited up, felt just a little out of place, although the better part of him knew there was no reason why he should. He was squaring his shoulders and adjusting his tie, when Fanny appeared in the open portals of the establishment. The outside light framed her as she paused, one hand raised against the door jamb, to look around. She had dressed for the occasion, in an outfit that if it left little to the imagination still did much for anticipation. A colour to complement her complexion, the mocha ensemble was high above her knee and tight everywhere. Stanley could not have been expected to describe it properly, but it seemed, from a distance, that the material stopped just underneath the line of her bosom, whence it was replaced with what looked like a totally improbable black netting that hardly hid the areola of her nipples. Not that Stanley would have stated it in quite these terms, but just about every other male in the establishment did. Conversation in the coffeehouse ceased momentarily until Fanny, spying Stanley across the crowded room, called out to him. "Stanley," she trilled, "I'm here." Having stated the self-evident, she moved towards her quarry, the jostling crowd in the room separating more completely in front of her than the Red Sea when Moses led the Israelites across it.

Stanley was entranced and it was several minutes before he became calm enough to think coherently. He stumbled through the ordering of their refreshment and was loath to leave her side to do it. He spent so much time looking back at her — to make sure that no one stole his prize — that the server had to tell him twice how much to pay, and in the end Stanley dropped a ten dollar bill into the man's outstretched hand and turned away. It was most unlike him. When he arrived back at their table with their two cappuccinos, he found that Fanny, coping with the crush all round, had pulled her stool forward and appeared to have deposited both breasts on the tiny table top in front of her. He set the coffees down next to them, and croaked, "I didn't know whether you wanted sugar."

Fanny's immediate putting of her hand over his and pulling it towards her, took his mind off her sweetness preferences, however, as did the statement that followed it.

"We mustn't let Hector know about this," she said.

For one instant in time, Stanley could not remember just who this Hector might have been, but then it hit him like a thunder clap and he said, in the strangulated voice of a harem eunuch, "No, indeed not!" and, finally able to tear himself away from his companion's mammary display, he looked into her eyes. What he saw there surprised him. Tears appeared to be forming among the lush forest of mascaraed lashes that even Stanley recognized as being adhesively attached.

Fanny dabbed delicately at the corner of one eye with a square of lace handkerchief slightly larger than a postage stamp, and sighed.

"We don't want to hurt him."

"No, indeed not!" Stanley repeated the words, this time more naturally, even managing to invest them with the patina of regret.

"We'll have to be very careful how we do it."

Fanny squeezed his hand and Stanley squeezed back.

"It won't be easy..." he said, pondering the issue.

Fanny drew his captive hand towards her, pulling it absently forward between both the two so far untouched cappuccinos and also her two, so far untouched, breasts.

"We'll have to tell him together."

This statement rendered Stanley mute. His imagination had conjured up a great deal since Fanny's telephone call that morning, and, indeed, truth to tell, quite a bit before it too, but it had never included speaking to Hector about anything.

"Do you really think so?" he said, hesitantly. Stanley was not a man who enjoyed confrontation and it did not seem to him that Hector was the kind of person who might accept his spouse's peccadilloes quietly. He did not seem to do anything quietly. And speaking of "quietly," there was also Faun to think of. Well, truthfully, he hadn't been thinking of Faun at all, but now, suddenly, she began to edge into his consciousness like a knife between his ribs. Fanny and her bosom might represent romance but, by Jove, Faun was comfort, and familiarity, and, not to stray too far from the point, food to him.

"Must he know? Must anyone know?" Stanley asked his questions plaintively as he looked across at Fanny, his voice edging to hoarseness. He was a little surprised at the expression on her face. She seemed puzzled by what he was asking.

"I mean," he said, pausing, "I mean, everyone might have to know eventually." He shrugged a little. He was not used to this kind of undertaking and it was necessary to feel his way. Somewhere down the road, they might have to tell people as they went off into a rosy sunset, but they hadn't got that far yet. "But not just now, surely. It would be our little secret. Don't you think?"

For the past several moments, the index finger on Stanley's right hand had been wedged between Fanny's décolletage and he was more hot and really bothered than anything else. The one thing he was certain of, and it was with a blinding kind of certainty, was that he couldn't believe his luck. He was not a man given to self-delusion. Stanley Parkinson was quite capable of looking in the mirror and being able to recognize the rather plain man of late middle age who stared back at him for what he was. It was entirely possible too that, if events had not been galloping along at the speed of light, he might have looked across the table and seen his companion for what she really was: an attractive, if rather blowsy woman, also in late middle age, whose better days were, like his, receding daily further into the past, but, at this point, none of that seemed to matter. Stanley was agog — agog with the possibilities of his situation and indeed at the declaration he thought he had just heard. And he was not about to let the opportunity escape him.

He smiled. He would have smiled more widely but for the expression on Fanny's face that had changed from puzzlement to what he could only interpret as a look of complete failure to comprehend what he was saying. Dislodging his index finger from its comfortable crevasse, Stanley squeezed Fanny's hand. He would have done more, but, at that moment, he felt a firm tap on his shoulder and the cooing voice of Miss Tilsley just above his head.

"Oh, Mr. Parkinson," the voice said. "I saw you sitting there and thought I should tell you that Mrs. Parkinson telephoned to ask you to bring milk home when you come."

Faun had, indeed, made such a telephone call, a call that Miss Tilsley had answered just before she absconded from the office shortly after Stanley left it. It may have been against her upbringing, but it was not against her inclination, and Miss Tilsley had decided to see what or who the smiley face on his calendar represented. She had spent the previous minutes peeping through Starbuck's plate glass window. Unable to interpret what she saw to her satisfaction, the redoubtable Miss Tilsley had determined to beard the lion in his den. As might have been expected, her appearance put Stanley completely off his stroke. Actually, to say this is somewhat inaccurate. Her appearance just about caused him to have a stroke rather than to merely put him off it.

Dimly aware that the social amenities would have to be adhered to, Stanley stood and turned to face his secretary, the better to be able to introduce her to his companion. The better also to, he hoped, to express, through the sternest of expressions, his disapprobation at the interruption. Unfortunately, his complexion continued to be an unbecoming shade of ruddiness and his expression held more of the teenage miscreant found with his fist in the cookie jar than anything remotely managerial.

"This," he said, waving in Fanny's general direction, "is Mrs. Hammond." Balking at using her sacred diminutive in front of the help, he added, "Mrs. Hammond is a lady from church."

Miss Tilsley's own expression clearly said, 'In a pig's eye she is,' but before she could say anything at all, Fanny, who had immediately sized up what was going on and was far from loath to having a little harmless fun with it, spoke up for herself.

"Hello, dahlin'," she said, rather coyly. "Are you one of Stanley's little friends too?"

Stanley and Miss Tilsley were so eager to clear up any misapprehension on this subject that they both spoke at once and it took a minute or so to sort things out. It was Fanny who put them out of their considerable misery and explained what was going on.

"And I thought," she said, coming to the convoluted conclusion of a story that had been long enough to cool their cappuccinos, "that Stanley and I had better meet and sort out this whole business of a day long event." She turned to Stanley and continued. "You see Stanley, Hector has a heart murmur and I do not think he should be doing so much. I don't know what you think, but I should be so grateful if you could just talk him out of the police in the morning and the games in the afternoon and the jazz and the tea and let us concentrate on the one act play in the evening." More to herself than to anyone else, she added, "And the variety show, of course. He's already looking for people for that. I know we'll never be able to talk him out of that."

"Well," said Miss Tilsley, still intrigued but considerably disappointed as well, "I guess I'll leave you to it." She began to move away. "Nice meeting you, Mrs. Hammond. And Mr. Parkinson, don't forget the milk..." Here Stanley's secretary paused and turned back to face Fanny. "I wonder," she said, "I don't suppose that Mr. Parkinson might have told you, but perhaps I could mention it myself. I do recitations."

Stanley had not the slightest inkling that Miss Tilsley did recitations, and, at this point, he could not have cared less. He was far more concerned with Fanny's explanation that Hector had a heart murmur and that this was why he and she had to meet in private to discuss the day of festivities. Fanny was hiding the real reason for their meeting, he was sure, and it was a sign of her genius that she had thought to do so so quickly, but, if they followed through on it, it really did give them a wonderful excuse to cancel many of the events of the day and to concentrate on those that would bring them back to his own original nice social evening.

Just as he wished! A heart murmur! She was inspired!

And the two of them could still be together. In secret.

Stanley hardly paid attention to the rest of the conversation going on between the two women.

"You do recitations?" exclaimed Fanny.

"Well, yes, I do. At elocution, we always used the recitation form to, you know, hone our skills," replied Miss Tilsley.

"Elocution, too…" Fanny clapped her hands in delight. "Stanley," she said, "Miss Tilsley does… Wait a mo', m' dahlin' I can't go on calling you that."

Miss Tilsley simpered. "It's Lavinia. But everyone calls me Vera."

Stanley certainly did not call her Vera, and he was beginning to realize where the conversation might be going.

"I'm sure Miss Tilsley has absolutely no desire to be part of our little evening, now do you, Miss Tilsley?" he declared with what he hoped was an authoritative frown.

Miss Tilsley was made of sterner stuff. "Oh, Mrs. Hammond," she said, aspirating carefully, "I should be delighted."

"Wonderful!" replied Stanley's muse, "And I'm Fanny."

By the time Stanley sorted out everything that had gone on at Starbuck's that afternoon, it was half past midnight and he had been in bed for two hours brooding about it. Initially, he had decided he would inform Miss Tilsley that since she was not a member of the congregation she was ineligible to perform at the festivities. And that it really did not become her to interrupt people's private conversations. Further consideration caused him to change his mind. It was his intention to have his secretary design the tickets and the posters for the event, and there was also the programme to consider, so it might not be a good idea to upset her before he had even broached the subject. Then he began to wonder if the dratted woman might not have some suspicion that he and his wonderful Fanny were really meeting for another purpose. The way to throw her off that particular track might well be to let her see that there was nothing going on between them when everyone met, as they would, at rehearsal.

As for Fanny, how clever she had been. She had, he hoped, defused Miss Tilsley with a great story and she had, moreover, given him hope that somewhere down the road he and she would be what in his day had been called an 'item.' Stanley, a good Christian man, had early on pushed the thought that a heart murmur might lead to other things into the furthest reaches of his fevered brain. Yes, they would have to be cautious and play it safe but the social evening would give them time together, allow them enchanted evenings when they could feast their eyes on each other across any number of crowded rooms, so to speak, and be safe in doing so. And, of lesser importance than that, but not without its own place in the overall scheme of things, he had found an ally in his determination to cut back the dreaded Saturday to something more like he had envisioned in the first place. Fanny and he had already arranged that she and Hector would come to tea with Faun and himself on Saturday afternoon to deal with that. He had told Faun about it at dinner. He had been surprised by her obvious delight. She hadn't even complained about him forgetting to bring home the milk.

...And Cucumber Sandwiches

The Parkinson's tea seemed destined for disaster from the start. Stanley, nothing if not consistent, again forgot the milk when sent off to do the groceries on the Saturday morning, and Faun was forced to offer the evaporated kind. This offended both her sense of propriety and her sense of taste. She had determined that everything must be just so for the Hammonds' visit. The cat throwing up a fur ball on the front room couch fifteen minutes after their arrival did not help matters, particularly since Hector, who truth to tell, despised cats, had just spent several minutes declaiming the whole of William Blake's immortal poem by heart, having misheard Faun when she told him that the animal's name was Tigger from 'Winnie the Pooh' and not the Tyger of fearful symmetry fame.

Fanny arrived somewhat subdued. Stanley did not immediately notice this, however, since the first thing she did after the ritual hellos was to take him by his underdeveloped bicep and whisper something into his ear. He was not certain about what she said, and hardly cared, but the gesture of familiarity allowed him to sweep aside any doubts he had being having about the strength of her feelings. It was a good thing that he did not hear her since the gist of what Fanny said was that he was the dearest man and they must make sure that they didn't hurt him, that she would rather die than disappoint him. Stanley got his 'hims' all mixed up and squeezed Fanny's arm in what he intended as conspiracy and she took as sympathy.

By the time the crustless cucumber sandwiches had been devoured, tea served and the presence of evaporated milk explained to Faun's satisfaction, Stanley's annoyance, Fanny's understanding and Hector's fulsome forgiveness, the tension in the room was becoming manifest. The cat had decided that it reciprocated Hector's dislike, and seated itself in front of him, looking up with a beady and contemptuous eye.

Hector found this disconcerting, as he did the fact that his companions seemed to want to converse on any other subject under the sun than the entertainment they were there to discuss. He was about to take them to task when Faun rose from her position on the edge of the couch next to him and asked archly, "Now who would like some trifle?"

If there was one thing that Hector Hammond disliked more than cats, it was trifle. It was Fanny, however, who alone knew this, and who, even in her worry about her spouse's overtaxing of himself, couldn't help but see the humour in the situation. She spoke first. "Umm, dahlin'," she said, "that sounds so good. What do you think, Hector? Trifle! Umm."

Hector turned a jaundiced eye on his spouse, but, gentleman that he was, he turned next towards Faun, smiling warmly. "Wonderful! Just a tad, m'dear, for me though. Got to watch the waistline, eh? It wouldn't do to put on the pounds when we're all going on the boards come September!" To Stanley he added, "How lucky you are, Stan, my boy. She's a treasure indeed. A treasure!"

Stanley accepted both the accolade, as though Faun were some kind of chattel, and also a large dollop of the trifle to which he was extremely partial. With the single exception of her trifle, Faun, as I have pointed out before, was not the cook Stanley's mother had been and the thought flashed across his consciousness that he rather hoped Fanny would be an improvement. This thought, however, reminded him of the purpose of the get-together. He glanced over at Fanny who saw him looking and lowered her eyes demurely. Stanley's breath caught at the back of his throat. There she was! A veritable madonna sat before him. He was a little taken aback when Fanny lifted her eyes, frowned and almost glared at him with a look that clearly said, "Get on with it, man."

Thus it was that Stanley rather than Hector raised the subject of the September social. That he did took Hector aback since he himself had been chomping on the bit and ready to go. It did not help that Stanley, as always, spoke to his companions as though he were addressing a public meeting.

"I have been thinking," said Stanley, standing up as he began, "that we should really determine whether we will be able to carry through all the events of September's social that we have been talking about. Really, the weight of these combined activities might cause us to spread ourselves too thin. Wouldn't it be better, more advantageous to a satisfactory outcome, to decide on one or two of the most promising of what we have been contemplating and concentrate our efforts on them?"

He raised his hand to forestall comment. He was not finished. Fanny was looking up at him with — what was it in her eyes? — he could not quite make it out. Could it be adoration? (For a more complete assessment of Fanny's expression, it might be worth adding that Faun's crustless cucumber sandwiches had given her gas — not Bruce-type gas, thank God, but gas nevertheless.) Faun, who had, of course, known what Stanley was about to say, looked towards Hector hopefully. Hector frowned darkly.

"The point of the day is to bring people together, for it to be an occasion of fellowship. We cannot allow the events of the day to overpower the day itself." Stanley did not know exactly what he meant by this, but he had rehearsed it and it certainly sounded good. He looked at Hector for affirmation. What he saw on his face seemed more like anger leavened by stubbornness. Stanley averted his gaze. To his surprise, he heard Faun speak.

"Stanley is right, you know," she said, reaching over to squeeze Hector's knee. "We're none of us as young as we used to be and we don't want to wear ourselves out. Wouldn't it be far nicer for you to do the things that you do best, Hector, and to concentrate on a wonderful evening of entertainment? I do so look forward to that."

There was both sincerity and flattery in Faun's words and Hector reacted to them. He laid his hand gently on top of hers and patted it. Before he had time to reply, however, Fanny joined the hunt.

"I've been telling him just that. Dahlin'," she said, "you can't do as much as you used to." Fanny's bosom rose as she turned towards Faun and Stanley. Emotion pulsed through her voice. Her childhood in Jamaica was not far behind. "It's 'im 'eart, yuh see. 'Ee cahn't do what 'im used to do. 'Im hav tuh pace imself. 'You have to pace yuself,' Hi told 'im, 'Ector man, hor 'eaven will know what will 'appen.'"

Stanley was entranced. He was moved. That Fanny would put on such a performance! Sure, a little corner of him wondered at the lack of grammar, the confusion of "aitches" and the preponderance of a barely intelligible dialect, but the tears appearing at the corners of her eyes — he had never seen anything like it!

Hector, on the other hand, was neither entranced nor moved. He had planned a whole day's entertainment and he wasn't about to give up without a fight.

"Well, of course, I don't intend to do it all by myself. There'll be all kinds of people to help," he said, pointedly appealing to Faun, the individual he considered to be the weakest link in the chain of opposition that had so unexpectedly sprung up against him.

To his surprise, Faun, removing her hand from underneath his and retreating further onto her seat, shook her head. "Oh, Hector," she said, "I wish that were true. But don't forget that we almost had to give up having a rummage sale last year because there weren't enough people to help out. And it used to make money too."

Fanny knew that comparing Hector's dream of a day of sparkling entertainment to a rummage sale was not likely to achieve their desired result and she frowned severely at Faun. Stanley caught the frown, but he liked the argument and decided to stick with it.

"No, indeed, such a day-long event would not only wear everybody out, it might also send us further into the hole financially, and we can't expect to make money from theatre," he said, nodding his head solemnly at each person in turn.

Fanny could have slapped them both.

"That's not the point at all," she said, "Of course, Hector could do it, and make it a tremendous financial success, too." She bristled and gave Stanley a look so severe that he almost cringed, before turning to her husband, all sweetness and light. "But what would happen if you got sick, dahlin'? You know how you tire easily. Who would take over and run everything? Who could replace you as the star of the show? Stanley? I don't think so."

Stanley didn't think so either but he really didn't like Fanny's tone. There was no need to be quite so scornful. Faun didn't help. "No indeed," she said, "Stanley wouldn't be any use at all." Then, realizing that she might, at a later hour, be accused of disloyalty, she moved quickly to ameliorate her statement slightly. "Well, not much use anyway. And certainly not as part of the entertainment."

So much for the idea of me doing my George Formby, thought Stanley bitterly, but he decided to press his advantage.

"Why not let us concentrate on the evening and make it a walloping great success?" Stanley had never before used the word "walloping," but he pounded his fist on the arm of his chair as he said it and it seemed to have an effect.

What Stanley didn't know and what Hector was not about to tell him — or anybody else, for that matter — was the fact that Stanley Parkinson was not the only one who had been having palpitations lately. Just that morning, Hector had been shaving at the time, his heart had gone bump diddy diddy bump when it should have been going bump bump bump. It wasn't the first time and it scared him a little. Plus the fact that for a split second he hadn't seemed able to take a breath. In his heart — now there is irony — he knew it was nothing and, even if it was, no one was going to rip him open and fiddle about with his insides if he could help it, not at his age they weren't. But perhaps a whole day was a bit much, particularly when Fanny seemed so worried and, yes, he knew she was right when she said that he would end up doing everything. He always did. He smiled wryly to himself. He did like to be in control. But somebody had to be, and he was good at it, he knew it.

"Weeelll," he said, stretching out the word, still seeming to give it some thought, still wanting to be 'on' and centre stage, "It would give me more time to pick out the play and put the cabaret together."

Stanley's little social evening had suddenly morphed into a cabaret and a play and he didn't much like the beaming look of affection that Fanny was directing at her spouse, but he could feel a certain satisfaction with the outcome of the conversation overall. What did Stanley expect her to do anyway? Leap into his arms and then turn round to tell Hector that, oh, by the way, she and Stanley were off hand in hand to clouded cuckoo land? What would Faun think if Fanny did that, anyway? What a mess it was!

Stanley was about to sigh when Fanny winked at him.

It was a gigantic wink, a wink of stupendous complicity and it buoyed him tremendously — which was just as well given what Hector said next.

"Stanley me boy, by any chance do you have a top hat?"

"A top hat?" Stanley hadn't any idea what Hector was talking about. "No, I, er, no I don't," he replied, clearly at sea. "Why?"

"No worries, my boy!" said Hector, reaching over to squeeze Stanley's shoulder. "We have a bowler somewhere, don't we, Fan?"

"A bowler? Umm, I'm not sure what you mean." Once again, Stanley found himself not having the vaguest idea what Hector was on about.

He remembered that Charlie Chaplin had had a bowler but he was pretty sure that George Formby did not. If the working class George had any kind of a hat, it would have been a cap, never a banker's bowler. Anyway, banker or not, he had no bowler.

Puzzlement gave way to incredulity as Hector continued. "We'll let everyone know about the cabaret and the play during the Announcements tomorrow morning at church. Yes, indeed, we'll begin tomorrow. It's time to get the show on the road." It annoyed Stanley that Hector pronounced the word 'shew' like he was Ed Sullivan or something. His annoyance was quickly pushed aside, however, when Hector went on. "You can tell them about the plans for the evening, while I'll let them know about the auditions." He was grinning beatifically at Stanley. "How about that, my friend, eh? The two of us. A little soft shoe shuffle and away we'll go."

And with this, Hector did just that. He essayed a little dance, humming along as he went, finishing with the tightest pirouette possible and what anybody else would have known to be jazz hands. Stanley, however, had never heard of jazz hands. He was convinced Hector had lost his mind.

Soft Shoes In The Sanctuary

Stanley heard nothing further from Hector until approximately three minutes before the service was due to begin the next morning. He had begun to think the idea of making an announcement had been abandoned, or, alternatively, that Hector must have decided if one was to be made, he would make it by himself. Contrarily, Stanley was not pleased with this idea: he did not want an announcement made, but he found the idea of not being part of it, when he, after all, was the genesis of the whole thing, unfair. Only the thought of not having to wear a bowler was able to bring him back towards a state of equanimity. Stanley had a banker's distaste of making a fool of himself.

When, therefore, he felt something being placed on the top of his head, and a tap delivered to it to hold it in place, it would not be too far off to say that Stanley flinched. He did not, of course, immediately know what the object was, but the voice hallooing into his ear soon clarified matters.

"There you go, old chap," it said, brimming with bonhomie, "A good fit and all ready to go."

Stanley twisted round to look up. Hector's bow tie was slightly askew and his head was bare. He seemed to know what Stanley was thinking. "Fanny has the topper. Don't want to give the game away too quick," he said, grinning down broadly. "Actually, you may want to take yours off. People will see."

Stanley grabbed hold of the brim of the bowler and ripped it from his head, bringing it to an abrupt rest over his genitalia. He was gazing down at it as though it represented some awful kind of public erection when Hector continued.

"I'll begin," he said. "I'll tell them what we're here for. If it's going good, we can do a little soft shoe shuffle and then you tell them about the events of the evening, with me finishing off by announcing the auditions for Tuesday and Wednesday." Stanley remembered that Hector was insisting on separate audition evenings for the play and the cabaret, but that was about the only portion of this sotte voce speech which made sense. He opened his mouth to reply but Hector was not finished. "Then I thought we'd twirl our canes and just sashay off in a two step." A silver topped cane appeared in Stanley's line of sight and was thrust towards him. "Good, eh?"

Had a king cobra materialized in front of him, Stanley could not have recoiled further.

He blinked plaintively up at Hector. "What am I supposed to do with this?" he asked. "I don't do this kind of thing."

"Oh, Hector, Stanley's quite correct. He can't dance." This was Faun, seated next to him on the pew.

For reasons he did not understand, Stanley found himself objecting to what was given as an uninflected statement of pure fact by his spouse, who, as she spoke, leaned across him to make her point more strongly and inadvertently crushed the bowler further into his groin.

"Watch out," he said, gruffly. "Mind the hat!"

Part of Stanley realized that a crushed bowler might provide a partial solution to his difficulties. Another part, an infinitesimally minute and certainly secret part, was determined to rescue it.

"It's not that I can't dance," he tried to explain, with a frown in the general direction of Faun, "it's more that I have no experience at this sort of thing."

Hector continued to beam down on him. "Just follow me and we'll give it a whirl," he said. "And remember what we always say in the theatre. A bad rehearsal portends a good performance."

This answer was not satisfactory, and to Stanley's mind did not even make sense. There had been no rehearsal: they were going straight to the performance. Before he could question the logic of what was said, however, Hector thumped him on the shoulder and moved away to sit in his own pew. Stanley followed his retreating figure and saw Fanny smiling in their direction. When she caught Stanley's eye, the smile widened into a rather toothy grin and, rather cheekily, he thought, she gave him the V for Victory sign. Without even thinking about it, Stanley, a banker to the change purse he kept in his trouser pocket, half rose from his seat to doff an entirely imaginary hat at her. Only after a moment or two of delightful reverie did he come back to the realization that he was going to make a complete cake of himself if he did not sit down immediately.

Stanley heard almost none of the service and could not have repeated either the title or the content of the Vicar's sermon had his life depended upon it. A corpse laid out in the sanctuary would have been more aware of its surroundings than Stanley that fair summer morning. Words flickered into his consciousness but he discarded them. With what little brainpower he still possessed, he waited to hear that one dreadful word, 'Announcements'. At last, of course, it came. He remained unaware of the ritual telling of a Thursday choir practice, the weekly bridge club for seniors and the reminder about the women's bi-monthly sewing circle that would, in fact, not be held this week since there was the coming outing to Niagara-On-The-Lake on Friday.

Then the Vicar got down to business. Stanley's business.

"And now, my brothers and sisters, I would like to call on Stanley Parkinson and Hector Hammond who have something exciting to tell us." The Vicar said this archly and, dressed in vestments that made him appear even more voluminous than nature intended him to be, the effect was not a happy one. Long accustomed to the failure of every diet known to mankind and happily confident that his charm superseded any doubtful mannerism that might blithely erupt during his speech, he continued, delighted both with himself and the knowledge of what he was about to say. "Hector! Stanley!" he cried, in a voice trained to reach the back-most pew and every sleeping parishioner seated upon it, echoing his favourite television game show, "You two, 'Come on down!'"

Stanley was slowly rising from his seat when he felt himself hoisted up and manhandled forward as Hector thrust a good left hand under his compadre's armpit and refused to let go. Before he knew it, Stanley found himself practically levitating up the chancel steps. He almost dropped the cane in the process. He could not have dropped the bowler if he had tried: it was clasped in a death grip still, for reasons known only to himself, in the general direction of his private parts. He was in a state of shock when Hector spun him around to face an intrigued and eager audience.

They did not have to wait long.

"Vicar! Ladies and Gentlemen! Friends!" Hector's exhortation was modelled on Marc Anthony's address to the Roman mob. He may have lacked the toga but he was not short on dramatic effect. "We are here today, Stanley and I are, to spread the good news," he said. As he declaimed these words — words surely dear to the heart of every Christian — Hector withdrew the topper which had been hidden behind his back and plonked it rakishly on his head. Stanley, taking this as a sign that he must do similarly with the bowler, finally removed it from in front of his nether portions and set it uneasily likewise. Not wishing to drop the cane, 'the blasted cane' as he was already calling it, he hefted it with the hat and, swinging it through the air, almost maimed Hector in the process. The congregation, unused to slapstick during their Sunday worship, was beginning to stir uneasily when it heard Mabel Green guffaw from the front pew. Hector, a farceur of note, reacted to the cane by cowering away from Stanley and the congregation began to titter.

"Careful, Stanley, old boy," said Hector, as though addressing parliament, "it's for walking, not for murthering — me or anybody else."

Stanley, beet red and breathless could have 'murthered' Hector with his bare hands. The congregation was delighted, however. It was used to a Stanley Parkinson so dry and dismal that when he read the financial statements at the Annual General Meeting, the occasional bi-polar member had considered climbing the steps to the steeple and flinging himself from the window at the top. This new, never before imagined, Stanley was — who would have thought it? — funny. The man was a comedian. The proof was that when Hector proceeded to fling his arm over Stanley's shoulder and in his usual stentorian tone declare to the assembled throng that they were not to worry, since he and 'Stan' were, in fact, the best of friends and, in any case, were a little long in the tooth ("or should that be teeth" he added, mock perplexed) to be fighting duels, Stanley flinched a flinch of seismic proportions and dropped both the cane and the bowler.

The congregation howled.

The Vicar, shaking in the pulpit like an enormous yellow blancmange, bawled the immortal words, "Order, Gentlemen, please!" but the last of these words became a shrill giggle when he noticed that Stanley, determined to retrieve the bowler which had rolled down the steps towards the pews, was bending between Mabel Green's legs to reach under her seat where it had come to rest. The Vicar was unable to continue. Stanley was unaware of the Vicar's laughter. It was imperative to retrieve both his dignity and the bowler — just as he had retrieved the cane before it too had reached the safety of the sanctuary floor. Finally finding a use for the silver topped stick, Stanley moved into Mabel's splayed legs and began to fish between them for the hat. He became vaguely aware that she was wearing knee-high stockings and what he would later, when he had time to think about it, remember as pale blue bloomers, before Ms. Green slammed her thighs together and caught the cane tightly between her knees.

The Vicar, who had a bird's view of this from his elevated perch, sat down abruptly and turned a most unbecoming shade of purple. Hector too sat down, on the chancel steps, resting his head against the marble of the font, tears streaming down his face, top hat askew.

It was some time before any kind of order could be restored. Those sitting in the back pews demanded to know what was going on from those further down front. Members of the choir, most of them paid agnostics, all of whom had a great view of the entire event, were delighted with what they were seeing, regretting only that they had left their iPhones in the cloakroom and were unable to record the scene for posterity. Mabel Green, totally bemused at finding a man in apparent supplication before her, not to mention in such proximity, initially refused to loose the errant cane from the Scylla and Charybdis of her knees, and then, when she finally did, refused to budge, even as Stanley, more determined in this than he had ever been before in life, sought to locate the bowler and pry it from its hiding place.

It took time for order to be restored and more still for their announcement to be completed. In this, neither Hector nor Stanley helped matters — Hector because, when he finally did begin to speak, he tipped his topper to the congregation, spun his cane round with one finger and insisted on entertaining them; Stanley because when it was his turn to speak, he stood stock still, the words escaping through a mouth that opened and closed like a ventriloquist's dummy. His statement that there would be both a play and a cabaret was met with oohs and ahs, and his comment that all proceeds would go to the Steeple Fund elicited applause. This was replaced by laughter when Hector linked arms with him and more or less dragged him through an approximation of a tap dance in which Hector pointed his toes with alacrity and Stanley, when he finally caught on to what was expected of him, shuffled around like a zombie. Stanley did his best but he remained two unfortunate beats behind Hector, lacking both his partner's finesse and his vivacity. This was most evident when he fumbled to raise his hat several seconds after Hector had raised his and then, dropping the bowler a second time, had to go chasing after the errant object all over again. Hector's double take at his scrambling colleague was generally reckoned to be a highpoint of the service.

When Hector did, finally, begin to tell the congregation about the two nights of auditions, he had them in the palm of his hand.

"If you have ever thought to be an entertainer," he began, "this is your chance. Your chance to put on the greasepaint and the powder, to tread the boards, perhaps to trip the light fantastic, to be a songbird in full flight. You know who you are: you know your talents, your desire to shine and to galvanize us with your theatrical ability. We would love to have you come out and tell us what you have to offer. Bring us your party piece! Sit in on our little play reading. Put on your dancing shoes."

Hector paused to take a breath and saw Fanny gently shaking her head at him. He knew he had said enough.

"So there you are, my friends, we will be reading for our play on Tuesday evening at seven o'clock in the Latimer Room, and auditions for the cabaret will be on Wednesday, also at seven. We hope you will come out. We are depending on you," he said, placing a hand over his heart with a pleading look on his face. "And now, folks," he added, bending from the waist and pointing with his cane in the general direction of Stanley, who was standing in what appeared to be the definitive imitation of a man in a coma, "my dear friend and colleague will perform the highland fling. Please give a hand to Stanley Parkinson."

The fact that Stanley was not a man given to irony made it all the more ironic that he, by common consent, was reckoned to have been the star of the show that morning. Since no one could imagine that how he had behaved had not been an act, the plaudits on his performance began even before he left the church. The Vicar, who knew better, acted as a catalyst to a series of congratulations that began when he embraced his parishioner, who was only then beginning to emerge from an almost total fog of embarrassment, and declared, "Splendid, Stanley. Kudos!

I have never seen anything like it in my life." Indeed, he had not. The congratulations came so thick and fast that Hector began to become jealous. Fanny, well experienced in recognizing the warning signs, took him off home as soon as she could. There, she was able to jockey him out of a slight petulance with empathetic words and a languorous foot massage that always managed to relax him in moments of stress.

It was Faun who saw Stanley's performance for what it actually was. She saw it so clearly that she had been moved to tears watching him five rows back — just far enough away to preclude her from offering any kind of support. Her annoyance with Hector began when she saw the two of them on the chancel steps: the one all eager bonhomie, the other clearly at a loss and wishing to be anywhere else than where he was. It took a while for her to become aware that people were, in fact, laughing at what they thought was an act. This had the effect of making her even more annoyed, however, and more protective, too. Her Stanley did not deserve this. It had been many years since Faun had thought of her spouse as 'her Stanley,' if, indeed, she ever had, but that was how she thought of him now. A sob choked the back of her throat and her chest heaved. What, she wondered, had he ever done to deserve this?

The marriage of Faun and Stanley Parkinson had never been what could be called passionate. Over the years, it had meandered from pleasurable to companionable. Both of them had accepted this with equanimity and if they had thought about it, they would have said that it could have been far worse. Faun gave in to her husband, and he liked that. Stanley led and Faun happily followed. He gave her a reason to be the person she was; she provided the support necessary to cope with the vicissitudes of his chosen profession. Like most married couples, perhaps, neither of them verbalized these things, but the truth lay upon their marriage like the down comforter that was spread neatly over their double bed on a cold winter night. Faun suddenly felt as though someone had ripped that warm blanket away and exposed her marriage to ridicule.

As the congregation continued its spontaneous applause at what it perceived to be the performance on the chancel step, Faun had bowed her head. The tableau presented there was too much to bear. She did not want to see it. She looked down at her hands as they twisted together on her lap. The stray thought that this is what wringing your hands means went through her head, but it was soon followed by another. I'd like to wring your neck, Hector Hammond, was what it was and Faun glanced up sharply. There he was, bowing and scraping to his audience.

"How could I have been so stupid?" she asked, unaware that the words were spoken out loud. "How could I?"

And this was Faun's second revelation on that summer Sunday morning for, until she asked the question, Faun had never been aware, not in any clear sense anyway, of her infatuation with Hector. Oh, he was an exciting man and, oh, what bliss it would be to dance with him, but further than that she had not gone, had not permitted herself to go. Now she knew it for what it was: infatuation. A stupid, unthinking desire for something who was not worth having and who could never replace what she had with her Stanley. So what if what she had with Stanley was safety and the familiar and the routine of her life? It was hers and how dare Hector Hammond interrupt it?

Then, into the jumble of all these thoughts tumbling through her mind, a mind not used to such passion or even opinion, there was born another thought.

Faun slowly raised her eyes, again seeking out Hector. He was leading a clearly comatose Stanley down the chancel steps, nodding affably to the people in the front pews, doffing the topper as he went. Biting her lower lip until it began to hurt, she saw the two men come towards her. Hector was bringing a shell-shocked Stanley back to her — and still the applause continued. She looked at Hector and he beamed.

"Oh no, you don't," she said, silently. "You can't do this to him. Not to my Stanley, you can't. Just you wait. I'll have my revenge on you. You just see if I don't."

Faun assisted Hector as he lowered Stanley onto the pew. She rubbed her husband's cold and clammy hand, trying to get the circulation going again and for the first time in many years, she was aware of wanting to hold onto it and to not let it go. And she did precisely that.

Casting A Net And A Play

Stanley and Faun arrived at the church early on Tuesday evening, only to find that Hector and Fanny were already there. Stanley did not see a need for his being there at all, but Hector had insisted, pointing out that as a co-producer he should be involved in picking the cast for the play as well as in all the behind-the-scenes activities that he was expected to carry out. Stanley didn't have an inkling about what was expected of him, but he did like the idea of being part of the choosing. Faun, unknown to anyone, intended to audition for the play and, in any case, as Fanny told her on the telephone, she should be there. The four of them were a team.

Hector had given Stanley copies of three one-act plays he considered suitable for the event, but Stanley had had neither the time nor the inclination to read them. When they arrived, however, Hector announced that he had already chosen A. J. Archibald's 'The Intruder' because, although all three plays were limited to a one-room set, Archibald's play had a lot of fun with a corpse on the stage. Stanley hadn't even thought about such a thing as a set and was taken aback when Hector pointed out that he, Stanley, in his role as producer, would be in charge of building it. Another plus for Archibald's play was that there was a cast of nine — five men plus the corpse and three women — although Hector did admit he was worried whether they would be able to find people of the right age to play the different parts. The characters in the play were in their thirties. It worried Hector that he would end up directing a geriatric version of the playwright's well known whodunnit.

Stanley and Faun found that the chairs in the Latimer Room had been arranged in a circle. Hector explained that Stanley and he would sit in and listen to a reading of the play. Fanny and Faun would serve refreshments at a suitable point in the evening and supervise the completion of biographical information sheets.

Turning to Faun, Hector smiled widely and said, "You better be coffee lady and let Fanny deal with the bios. She'll know what to look for."

Whatever this meant, Faun was not about to find out. "Oh," she said, taking a deep breath, "I'm afraid I can't. You see, I am going to audition for the play."

"Faun, you never told me anything about this," said Stanley, frowning. "Are you sure?"

"Oh, yes, I've been thinking about it and it might be fun," Faun replied.

"Well, good for you, my dear. I'm sure you'll be splendid!" This was Fanny, sounding more amused than convinced. "Who do you think she could play, Hector?" she asked.

Hector appraised Faun as if she were a side of beef. Quite simply, there was no part in the play for a rather bland, self-effacing female of not quite pensionable age. Fanny knew it, and she knew her husband knew it as well.

"You'll just have to wing it," Fanny whispered, taking him aside. She knew Hector hated to cast wrongly, but she suspected Faun might be the least of his problems given the other candidates. As if to prove her correct, the door to the Latimer Room was flung open and Mabel Green hove into view, panting. Bruce trailed behind, panting likewise.

Mabel sailed straight towards Hector. "I've read the play. Think I saw it years ago. I'll be Mrs. Knowles." Mrs. Knowles was the mother of the play's heroine, a flighty female just beyond menopause. Mabel's menopause was lost in the sands of time and flighty was not an adjective with which even her worst enemy could have reproached her. For once, Hector was speechless. Faun, who had always been scared of Mabel, giggled. She had read the play and thought that she would try out for the same part. She had no intention of butting heads with Mabel, however.

Before the conversation could go further, the door opened again and Roger St. John Mountjoy entered. If ever a man were badly named, Roger was that man. Round-shouldered and slight of build, his name was the most impressive thing about him. A taciturn fellow with a voice that sounded as though he was speaking into a bottle, Roger lived alone and participated in every possible church activity. This was a new opportunity and here he was.

"Evening," he said, "I thought I'd come out and see what it is all about."

Hector sighed inwardly. If this were to be the calibre of readers, A. J. Archibald would be spinning in his grave before the evening was out.

In the next twenty minutes or so, twelve more members of the congregation came into the room, as well as the Vicar who had adopted a proprietary attitude to the whole enterprise. They were a motley crew. None might be said to have had talent, and not a few were totally unsuitable for public performance of any kind. Most of them were women: only four were men.

In due course, Hector called the room to order.

"Thank you for coming," he said, expansively, "It's great to have you on board. It looks as though we can get started. Let me tell you something about the play we have selected."

Stanley wondered who the 'we' was, but listened to what Hector had to say. "'The Intruder' is one of A. J. Archibald's best known short plays. It was written in the 1930s and is set in an upscale Bed and Breakfast in Bournemouth. The plot concerns a burglar who enters the house late one evening and steals the landlady's silver candlesticks while everyone is asleep. It thickens when it is discovered that one of the five paying guests must have let the intruder into the house as all the doors were locked at the time. Pre-shadowing Agatha Christie's Miss Marple, one of the guests helps a very young and callow policeman to investigate and she announces that she knows who carried out the crime. Before there is time to tell anyone, however, she disappears and a body, not hers, is found murdered in the living room. The play ends with no one knowing who the body is or who the murderer is. Only the intruder is exposed. In many ways, the play was way ahead of its time. There was even talk of the Lord Chamberlain banning it and Archibald made a great deal of money out of never telling anyone who his villain was."

"So you see, we can have fun with it," said Hector in conclusion. "Everyone will have a guess while we have refreshments and then we will move on to the cabaret."

It was Mabel Green who interrupted. "I thought we would have the play last," she said. "It should be at the end of the evening. Put it there."

Hector had no intention of having the play last. He had thought about it and had decided that the cabaret would be more festive, have something for everyone, and also, not quite coincidentally, he would be in it. Mabel's suggestion and the tone in which it was made, startled him.

"It seems to me that Ms. Green is correct." This was the previously noted Mr. Roger St. John Mountjoy. "We should finish with the play."

Hector frowned. Both Ms. Green and Mr. St. John Mountjoy had used the first person plural pronoun. Hector had noted the usage and he was not amused. The only pronoun he intended to countenance was, yes, of the first person, but definitely singular. He was opening his mouth to respond when Roger, most unusually, spoke again. "What does everybody else think?"

During the next five minutes, the placement of the play was discussed vigorously. No one had any idea what he was talking about, but everyone had an opinion. Fanny was becoming alarmed that Hector might lose his temper at the thought of someone hijacking his vision of the evening and rolled her eyes at the Vicar for help.

Slowly hauling himself to his feet, the Vicar called for order. "I think," he said, in a tone that brooked no discussion of the matter, "that we really should let Hector and Stanley decide these things. They are our producers and they know how they want them to go. Hector is, after all, a professional." Not wanting to leave himself open to the future wrath of Mabel Green, he added, looking directly at her, "For myself," he said, "I see the play as the highpoint of the evening, but we must not forget that while a great number of the older heads will want to stay on for the refreshments, some may go home before the cabaret. The whole evening would be too long for them."

Having thus given his imprimatur to Hector's plan, the Vicar shook his head sadly, winked at Fanny and crashed back onto his chair. Not giving anyone time to interrupt again, Hector continued.

"There are nine parts. We'll run through the play twice so that everyone will get a chance to read. Please come forward and take a seat in the circle when I call your name. Now then, let's have fun!"

The readings did not go well. At the end of the first go round, Hector leaned over to Stanley and whispered the words, "Lord God Almighty!" in his ear. At the end of the second, he leaned over again and said, even more succinctly, "Jesus wept!" Stanley, who had no experience at this sort of thing, thought that both readings sounded more like a bunch of pre-schoolers sounding out their letters than a group of adults auditioning for public performance. Indeed, he decided, we might be better off with first graders. To his surprise, Faun had been about the best of a bad lot, managing to be both animated and coherent. Roger was the worst, somehow sounding as though he was calling out his lines from a bathysphere in the ocean depths.

Mabel Green did not so much read her lines as recite them, having, apparently, decided that an approximation of iambic pentameter suited her character. She had not recovered from the Vicar's rebuff. As a kind of Greek chorus to Mabel's reading, Bruce wagged his tail once each time his mistress began to speak and farted each time she finished. This had the effect of mesmerizing the other persons in the circle. It might, when you come think about it, have affected the quality of their reading as well. It did drive Fanny to retreat into the kitchen where she pushed a dish towel into her mouth to stifle screams of laughter. Hector had told her about Bruce, but she had not believed him.

After the two readings, and the light refreshments between them, everyone left. Only our four principals remained. Hector sat with his feet stretched out before him looking at his copy of the script as though it were a bucket of eels. He shook his head. Eventually, he erupted in rueful laughter.

"Who would have thunk it?" he said, slowly shaking his head. "How did we ever manage to get such a hopeless bunch of clods into one room at one time? The damn dog had more talent than all of them put together!" Realizing that Faun was hanging onto his every word, and that he had not meant to include her in his blanket condemnation anyway, he turned to her and continued, "Of course, dear girl, present company excepted. You were a shining star!" This was stretching the truth more than a little but in such company an approximation of competence resembled a supernova streaking across the night sky.

"Oh, do you think so, Hector? How nice of you to say so." Faun said this shyly, but got to the point. "Which part shall I play then? The maid?" She asked this demurely, "I think I could do that."

"The maid!" responded Hector loudly. "Not at all! You shall be our landlady!"

The landlady was one of the biggest parts in the whole play and Faun was glad to have it. She would learn every word, she would attend all the rehearsals and then, on the night of the performance, she would have her revenge on Hector. Indeed, she would.

Faun clapped her hands in delight. "Oh, Hector," she said, "do you really think I can do it? Stanley, what do you think?"

Stanley, unused to seeing his spouse so front and centre, did not quite know what to think. He was proud of her, of course, but, at the same time, perhaps a little jealous. Now, he would have to be in the cabaret. Yes, indeed, if Faun was going to make a name for herself as the landlady, he would have to work on his George Formby. It would be hard but he could do it. He nodded to himself in silent affirmation. The ability of a man to fool himself and to believe what he wishes to be true was working overtime in Stanley that Tuesday evening. The compliments heaped on his shoulders on Sunday morning had come home to roost. Initially, he had scorned them, knowing full well that terror and talent are two very different things, but, as time passed, the memory of his fear began to fade to be replaced by the far more pleasant remembrance of the accolades he had imbibed afterwards. He knew that his was not a big talent but by Tuesday evening he had convinced himself that it was big enough to carry him through two verses and a couple of the choruses of his favourite tune. Moreover, Fanny had urged him to sing that very afternoon when she called him at the office just, she said, to say hello.

Stanley repeated Fanny's words to Faun in response to her question of him. "You will be very good, my dear," he said. "Very good indeed. But, Hector, who will you cast in the other parts?"

"God only knows," replied Hector, gloomily.

"Well, you had better decide, Hector, my love," said Fanny, "because you told everyone you would telephone them in the morning with the news."

Hector moaned. "Well, not here and not now. Let's get out of this place." He turned to Stanley. "Thanks for coming, Stan, old boy. We'll see you tomorrow evening for the cabaret. I'm sure we'll have a much stronger turn out for that. At the very least, there's you and me! And I have a couple of people in the choir coming along so we should be in good shape there. Let's just hope Roger St. John Mountjoy doesn't want to be in the cabaret too!"

With that awful possibility in mind, our four principals took themselves off and went home.

It was two in the morning before Hector finally decided who should be whom and assigned the parts in the play. It was no easy task. The overriding factor was that he had a surfeit of women and a paucity of men. His solution for this was not to be entirely successful when the play was finally performed. Having minimal room to maneuver, Roger St. John Mountjoy became the callow young policeman. Hector decided that the stage directions for the character would have to be severely rewritten to accommodate the thirty extra years Roger was would bring to the part but he was still marginally younger than the other males who had shown up for the audition, one of whom was completely bald and another of whom had a nervous tic.

Hector knew that he had no choice but to give the Miss Marpleish role to Mabel Green. She was of the right age and, remembering Margaret Rutherford in the films, roughly the same shape. God only knew what she would do with the part, but there was one advantage to her playing it: she would disappear before the end, never to be seen again. Perhaps, he thought as he lay tossing in his bed, we can have the damn dog asphyxiate her.

It was in the casting of a woman in a male part that Hector, in retrospect, went awry. In Archibald's version of the play, a young, newly married couple is staying at the Bed and Breakfast. They arrive, very embarrassed at being on their honeymoon, and are very much in love. It was Hector's decision to turn the male half of the couple into a female and have them portray two women traveling together on a golfing holiday. The dialogue, as he read it, seemed to support this interpretation with very little need for change. Two kisses could easily be excised, as could a couple of 'darlings'. Hector had two women not completely beyond child-bearing age among his readers and they became the couple in the script, no longer young but passable in a dim light, so to speak. Unfortunately, Hector was a man of his generation and, for all his years in the theatre, he had managed to maintain a certain innocence about the more, shall we say, liberal elements of modern society and the new frontiers of its sexuality. What to Hector were two female friends happily vacationing together would play out just a little differently in reality. Fanny thought to warn him, but, when Hector took on a director's role, he could be quite the martinet. She decided to hope that everything would turn out all right on he night, but it gives nothing away to say that, alas, it did not. An audience supposedly trying to deduce who the intruder was found itself instead hanging on the antics of the two ladies, and spent a fair amount of its time trying to determine which one of the two was supposed to be butch.

Life Is A What Again, Old Chum?

Vera Tilsley arrived before anyone else on Wednesday evening. She thought, she declared, that she could make herself useful if there was any setting up to be done or coffee to be made. Stanley frowned when he saw her, but there was not much he could do and Faun had always liked the woman anyway.

"Shall I pour one for you, Mr. Parkinson?" Vera asked when the coffee was ready.

"Wait a mo' dahlin'" said Fanny, laughing. "You can't go round calling my Stanley 'Mr. Parkinson' now can she, Stanley? It doesn't seem right."

It seemed entirely right to Stanley, but Faun was nodding and he had rather liked Fanny's 'my' Stanley.

"I suppose not," he replied jocularly, adding quickly, "We'll save the formality for the office, eh, shall we!"

Vera, not fooled for a single moment that her boss liked it, looked down demurely and said, "Oh, of course, sir."

Faun and Fanny both laughed at the 'sir,' just as Vera had intended, but Stanley was not a happy man. Fortunately, before he could say anything further, an influx of people began and there were other things to think about. For one, Faun had to be sent down to the church office to xerox several more 'bio' sheets. More than twenty people had turned out to audition. Hector arranged them in rows and had them put their hands up as he divided them into categories: singers, dancers, and speechifiers. Speechifiers, as Hector explained, was a catch-all name for those who did monologues or read poems or recitations like 'Albert and the Lion' and 'The Shooting of Dan McGrew.' Strangely, mimes were to be counted among the speakers; Hector hated mimes.

Hector had secured the services of a friend who had lived until recently at a home for retired actors and musicians downtown to accompany the singers and to provide music for dancers if they did not bring their own, so he announced that he would have the musical people go first. Vera, now very much in her element having handed out the bio sheets and collected them when they were completed, rolled her eyes at this and sighed theatrically to Faun, "It looks as though I'll be here all night."

"Don't worry, my dear. Stanley won't mind if you are a few minutes late in the morning."

Vera was well aware that he would mind quite a bit, but she smiled, and changed the subject. "Isn't this fun?" she said. "Let's find a seat and listen, shall we?"

Hector's accompanist, Laddie, was one of those people who could play anything with, or without, music. "Just give me a couple of bars," he would say, and off he would go. Well into his sixties, and even a little deaf these days, he had played for Hector so often in the past that they required little rehearsal, Laddie having the nous to anticipate Hector's eccentricities and those occasional but dangerous times when he left the rhythm to its own devices. Even so, some of those auditioning would put Laddie's abilities to the test on this particular evening.

The first two candidates were young girls from The Fairchild School of Dance which rented space in the church hall four afternoons a week. The school's students were mainly neighbourhood children and ranged in age from five to seventeen. There were also a few overweight women who danced for the cache it provided and for the weight loss they hoped might go long with it. The two girls were a very talented eleven-year-old Chinese girl with a mouthful of metal braces, and a seven year old French Canadian lass who was dressed to resemble a dancer from the Bolshoi Ballet, but who had no talent whatsoever and would not have been able to keep time with the music even if Laddie had used a bass drum to help her. He eventually gave up playing and was yelled at by the child's parent for being so uncaring about her little Anya. It didn't help matters when he responded by announcing, "You don't like it, eh, so take me out and shoot me!" Unfortunately, he then amended his statement. "Or better yet, take the kid out and shoot her!" Little Anya became hysterical but was calmness itself compared to her mother who threatened to sue Laddie, Hector, the church and the little Chinese girl who she saw smirking at her baby from behind the raft of steel girders she had in her mouth. It was Vera, well versed in ushering irate people out of Stanley's office, who eventually persuaded the woman to leave. Everyone listened to her imprecations as she went down the hall and out the big oak doors.

Fanny had a quick word with Laddie about the fact that he should remember the performers were amateurs, and Hector thumbed through his sheets to see who was next. In fact, the next two performers were both excellent. They were both from the choir. The soprano sang an aria from Puccini's 'Butterfly' and a young tenor sang, with a dash of brio, the Major General's song from 'Pirates of Penzance.' Hector was delighted and knew that they were on their way. Unfortunately, they were followed by two older female members of the congregation who sang 'Ave Maria.' Both of them. The same version. Separately. Laddie was not a churchgoing fellow and if he did not like to have to play such a hoary old chestnut once, he certainly didn't want to have to play it twice. The second singer found herself racing through the Gounod trying to keep up with the Laddie's riffs on the piano. Later singers varied from the merely competent to the godawful, and everyone was hoping for a break when Hector turned to Stanley and asked, "So, Stan, what about you?"

Stanley had been miles away for the last several minutes: well actually it hadn't been miles, it had been across the room in the embrace of Fanny's open arms. He had been watching her as she brought out the cookies to go with the coffee at refreshment time. One unfortunate little biscuit had slipped off the plate and Fanny had hitched her skirt higher to be able to squat down and rescue it. Stanley was enchanted. There was not a great deal of skirt to be hitched and Fanny had looked around the room to make sure that no one would be examining her while she was on her haunches. Stanley caught her eye and they gave each other what he took to be a look of complicity. What Fanny took it to be is anybody's guess.

It was at this precise moment that Hector spoke to him. He jumped.
"Sorry," he said, "What about me?"
"Your song, old boy. Formby."
"My song?" Stanley repeated the words, "What about it?"
"Well, are you ready to sing it?"

"Me?!" Stanley was appalled at the very thought of having to sing it right then and there and his voice rose exponentially. "I don't have to sing, do I?" It had never crossed Stanley's mind that he might have to audition. It had never crossed his mind that, at some point, he might have to practice the thing for, if he were to be honest about it, the idea of him singing the song on an actual night had never been considered in any realistic way either.

"Everybody has to audition, Stanley." Hector said this expansively. "Even me! It gets the juices flowing and we can see where we are."

Stanley could see quite clearly where he was and he was not at all happy with the view.

"Oh," he said, "I didn't bring the music along."

The truth was that Stanley didn't have any music, and he doubted he could have read it even if he had it, but he was aware that that would not go down with the professional in Hector.

"Don't worry about that, old chap" beamed Hector, "Laddie can play anything you like. Just give him a key and away he'll go."

A flustered Stanley had no idea why Hector would want him to give Laddie a key and even less which key he was supposed to give. He had no intention of asking.

Faun tried to come to his rescue. "Stanley knows the song, Hector. I really don't think he needs to sing it here."

Had anyone been listening carefully, they might have caught a certain coldness, even a warning, in Faun's voice, but Fanny spoke so quickly after her that it was easily missed.

"Why of course, Hector, we'll hear Stanley sing," she said, "but let's do it later. Look at the time. We've still got a long way to go to get through the rest of these nice people. We don't want to keep them here all night."

"But what about me?" asked Hector, slightly put out. "I should sing too."

Like most of his profession, Hector loved to perform. It could be on the stage, in someone's living room or even in a broom closet if needs be, just so long as he could get up there and do it. He had been thinking about which of many party pieces he might perform all afternoon. Of course, he didn't think of it in terms of an audition, but he did think it would be a nice treat for everyone there for him to do a couple of songs — three if they asked for an encore — and it would show them how it should be done if nothing else. He and Laddie had discussed which pieces he would do over the phone earlier that evening.

Hector decided to press further on the matter of Stanley's singing, the better to have a reason for he himself to sing.

"Just a short run through to make certain of the words, then," he suggested.

He looked at Fanny for support but it was Faun who cut in to settle the issue.

"I don't think Stanley should sing tonight. He has the beginning of a sore throat. I noticed it at dinner tonight. He should be careful with his voice."

There was nothing whatsoever wrong with Stanley's throat and he was not used to having Faun as so vocal a supporter, but he was thankful for her help. He decided to underscore the idea of a sore throat by giving a little cough. Taking a breath caused him to swallow the remains of a breathmint he had been sucking, however. The errant mint went halfway down his windpipe before being blown back up and Stanley collapsed in a paroxysm of coughing that brought tears to his eyes and provided the solution to his problem. Faun led him to an armchair and it was decided that the company would break for refreshments.

It was during refreshments that — if one is permitted to say this of events taking place in a church hall — all hell broke loose. Hector was regaling the company with tales of his theatrical past when the Vicar arrived. He had not been expected and he stood in the doorway gazing at his assembled flock.

"Evening, Vicar, we didn't expect to see you here." Hector called out to him. "Come on in."

Hector was surprised to see the Vicar. They had talked that afternoon and nothing had been said about him being there, but he was even more surprised by what the Vicar said.

"I've come," the spiritual leader declared jocularly, "to audition." This simple statement had the effect of flummoxing his audience, and neither they nor Hector said a word. The Vicar, sensing that he had scored a small coup, continued, "I thought I'd give it a whirl!"

His coup, however small, was to be short lived. Hector, responding expertly as if an unexpected ad lib had been flung at him during a performance, moved forward to greet the Vicar saying, "Wonderful!

Wonderful! Such an addition to our company!" Initially thinking to embrace the enormous figure in front of him, he decided that it would probably be easier to hug one of the smaller species of whale, and grasped the Vicar's hand instead to shake it. He was still shaking it when the door behind the Vicar opened again, this time with a smart shove. The unfortunate clergyman was propelled forward, the prow of his enormous belly striking a blow to Hector's own more sedate midriff that would have knocked the wind completely out of both their sails, had they had any. No one was to know whether the far from balletic sight of Hector and the Vicar trying to maneuver round each other, each trying to maintain some iota of dignity, would have succeeded, however, for they were in the process of being upstaged by a completely unexpected scene stealer. Framed in the open doorway stood Mabel Green.

"Move!" she barked. "You're in my way."

The Vicar, glancing hurriedly over his shoulder, practically pirouetted out of her way leaving an incredulous Hector exposed in front of her.

"Mistress Green," he said. He had taken to calling Mabel this behind her back since, as he told Fanny, the likelihood of her ever having been anybody's mistress (except Bruce's, of course) was minimal and he believed that everyone should have the chance to be a mistress at least once in her life. "How are you? What are you doing here?"

"Where else would I be? Here to read poetry. I'm late. That damn dog has diarrhea. When do you want me?"

Hector didn't want her, not even remotely, and he looked around the room for help. The Vicar refused to catch his eye and Faun had her back to him. Fanny and Stanley were nowhere in sight. He took a deep breath. "Well, we've just been listening to our singers and haven't got to our readers yet, but, in any case, if you are in the play, we couldn't possibly expect you to be in the cabaret as well. It wouldn't be fair to put you to all that trouble." He took another breath and hurried on, "And we already have two or three people who would like to do readings." The smile Hector turned on for Mabel would have been worth the price of admission in any other venue, but this evening it was a signal failure.

"Nonsense!" declared the redoubtable Ms. Green. "Can't have too much poetry. I'll do 'The Lady of Shallot.' They'll lap it up."

Where Mabel Green had picked up such a colloquial expression the assembled company did not know, but not a single person challenged it, and Hector, mouth slightly open, said not a word. He was not quite certain what to say and looked around for Fanny who, at the very least, should be able to provide some kind of succour. He saw Faun who, he thought in passing, had a most peculiar look, almost of satisfaction, on her face, but his spouse was nowhere to be seen. He was beginning to frown at Fanny's absence when Mabel, apparently not content to stop at the thunderclap she had introduced into the proceedings, proceeded to unleash a tornado. "Or," she said in a voice resembling a drill sergeant's, "perhaps something biblical."

The absent Fanny heard none of this. Busy in the kitchen getting ready to do the washing up, she had been humming along with a general contentment at life, when she glanced round to see Stanley standing in the doorway staring at her. She was well aware that he had what she called a 'tendre' for her, but, for the first time, the expression she saw on his face alarmed her slightly. Fanny liked a good flirtation, as she would have been the first to admit, but her devotion to her husband was total. Had she, she wondered, gone too far with Stanley? Surely not? And, even if she had, she still needed his support, didn't she? Hector might think he could do everything by himself, but the truth was he wasn't up to it. He loved the idea of the evening's entertainment and, even if it was to be his swan song, he would do it, and make a success of it too, but Stanley being there would be an absolute help. Stanley might be no use on the artistic side of things, but he could take over the organizational stuff and deal with the finances. She wouldn't have allowed the whole thing to get started if she hadn't believed that. Stanley would be there.

"Hi, there, Stan, dahlin'," she said, rubbing the back of a soapy hand over her forehead, "I was so hoping you'd come in. I hope you're not going to leave a girl to do all these dishes by herself are you?" She gave a little pout and pointed at the dirty crockery in the sink in front of her. "You're just what I've been waiting for. A big strong man to do the heavy lifting."

The Summer of Stanley's Discontent

Had Stanley been the kind of man who attached labels to things, he might have said that the Sunday on which he and Hector made the announcement about the September social marked the beginning of the most uncomfortable summer of his life. Hector's decision to hold weekly breakfast meetings to obtain progress reports only added to the pain. Stanley, who never ate breakfast, arrived at the first of these, held at a local family restaurant, to find the Vicar, the church janitor (of whom more later) and a member of the congregation he vaguely recalled as being of Greek extraction in attendance. Hector declared that the Greek gentleman was going to build the set for the play. That, at least, was a comfort. Far less so was the fact that Fanny did not attend. Stanley had hoped he would be seeing her and was desolated when Hector hooted at his query about where she might be, declaring, "Fanny? She'll be abed till ten!" The image was enticing; her absence was not.

Worse was to follow. They had hardly seated themselves when Vera appeared.

"I thought I'd ask Vera to come along as our amanuensis," Hector announced airily as he introduced her. Stanley didn't know what an amanuensis was, didn't care, and was too furious to ask. Vera refused to catch his eye and Hector merely beamed broadly, adding "You can take the subway together when we get finished. What do you say, eh!" Vaguely aware that the congealed expression on Stanley's face did not evince contentment, he hurried on. "So Vicar, what are you having this morning?"

As Vera explained to Stanley on their ride downtown later that morning, Hector had called her at home the previous evening requesting her presence and she had not liked to call Stanley so late at night to see what he thought. Stanley was of the opinion that she knew damn well what he would think but before he could say so Vera had added that she was surprised Fanny hadn't been there to take notes. This put Stanley off his stroke a little and his reply, "Oh, Fan needs her beauty sleep!" sounded strange even to his ears. It elicited a wondering "Mmmm," from his secretary. The rest of the journey was spent in silence.

The actual breakfast, and each one that followed after it, did not help Stanley's equanimity. Hector invariably tried to persuade him to have a full meal and would particularly enjoin him to try the poached eggs, a speciality, he said, of the house. Stanley abhorred any kind of egg other than one that was hard-boiled and those of the poached variety he abhorred most of all. Almost as bad was the multi-grain toast Hector thrust on everyone: Stanley was a white-bread man through and through. Then there was the coffee. Hector instructed the waitress to provide a large carafe of strong black coffee to be delivered to their table. He himself took charge of replenishing everybody's cup after the merest sip, and waved the pot in their faces as he did so. Stanley only drank decaf.

The comestibles were one thing, Hector's directives were another. Every meeting added to what Stanley was assigned to do, and Hector expected a weekly report on what had been accomplished. It did not take long for Stanley to find out that he would not be allowed to procrastinate. At the second of the breakfasts, Hector asked whether Stanley had finished visiting the neighbourhood banks to solicit support and financial assistance, whether he had opened an account in the name of the 'September Soiree' as Hector had decided to call the event, and had he arranged with the church office to have full use of both the auditorium and the Latimer Room for three evenings a week for rehearsals. Since Stanley had completed none of these tasks, his responses were somewhat muted and the audience around the table looked on in frowning disapproval.

Apart from anything else, as Stanley complained pettishly to Faun, the breakfasts created havoc with his work day. Instead of arriving on the dot at eight, he was now wandering in around ten thirty, and with Vera in tow. Neither of them had done a stroke of work and Stanley was usually so agitated that it took him another hour to settle down. The only up side to the breakfast meetings was that Fanny got into the habit of calling him to find out how they went. About eleven o'clock after every meeting, Vera would call through on the intercom and say in a voice so sweet it could have caused type two diabetes, "Fanny's on the line. Up from her beauty sleep. Lucky girl."

Stanley thought of prohibiting Vera from attending the breakfast meetings, but not being a complete idiot, he realized that many of the tasks assigned to him could be sloughed off onto her during the subway ride downtown. Vera did not object. She knew that she would be having to do much of the work anyway, so she might as well get a good solid breakfast out of it. French toast and pancakes. The Greek turned up trumps when it came to the set and it was not long before the outline of a drawing room began to shape itself on the stage of the auditorium. There was a bit of trouble when all of the three doors opened outwards, as per Stanley's orders, when they should have opened inwards as per the stage directions (which Stanley did not quite understand) but, other than a bit of muttering in the language of the Peloponnese, the construction went on apace. There was nothing to complain about either with the janitor — a silent chap whose name you will learn in due course — for he turned out to be a complete whiz with things electric and knew how to install footlights and spotlights and house lights — all of them on dimmers — although, come to think of it, he wasn't exactly quick at doing the actual work. The Vicar did nothing. He read the enormous menu at the restaurant from cover to cover and seemed, week by week, to be in the process of ordering every item on it, but when asked to carry out a specific task he would invariably plead difficulty with his sermon or the need to visit some desiccated person — of whom there were, in truth, many— among the congregation. The one thing he did agree to take on was the cleaning of the stage's curtains. He then immediately delegated the task to the small group of elderly women in the church who, thirty years before, had purchased them from a nearby cinema and who had had a proprietary air over them ever since.

Stanley's visitation of bank branches came up, rather like punctuation, in every conversation Hector had with him. It was not something Stanley wanted to do and he put it off as long as possible. He knew the reception he would get — if only because it was the reception he would have given if the shoe were on the other foot. Not said, but clearly implied, was the question, Why should I give one thin dime to the competition? Stanley did eventually manage to pry a contribution from one neighbourhood manager on the understanding that the man's bank's logo would feature in glorious technicolor on the back cover of the programme, but it was not until Fanny suggested, in one of their post prandial chats, that Stanley tell the other banks' managers this that he made further progress. The final programme for the evening came to resemble a brochure advertising Canada's big five chartered banks, but the getting there had embarrassed Stanley no end.

Hardly less embarrassing was his visit to Mabel Green, Hector having determined that it was one of Stanley's jobs to put into place the actual organization of the evening's refreshments. It was one thing for Hector to have been told by Mabel not to worry himself about them, another entirely for the perfectionist that Hector could be to relax with those words as his only surety. The Vicar, scarfing down porridge, told Stanley that if Mabel told him not to worry, he should not worry, but Hector required reassurance and Stanley was to obtain it. Stanley blanched at the idea of bearding Ms. Green in her lair and was only shamed into it when Faun began to offer what he thought were snide comments touching on his masculinity. Stanley was having no doubts whatsoever these days about his masculinity but Faun could be passive-aggressive sometimes and this was one of those times.

Stanley dropped by Mabel's house one evening on his way home from work. Ringing the bell evinced no reaction and he had already turned away when Mabel finally came to the door. Actually, the words "Mabel came to the door" pale in comparison to what actually happened. The door was flung open, bouncing back against the hall wall and cracking one of the glass panes in the process. Mabel caromed through the opening into Stanley's arms. Using every ounce of his strength to hold her upright, he came, for a man who never swore even subconsciously, as close as he ever would to an exclamatory "What the fuck?" before managing a strangulated "There, there!" as he patted Mabel's broad back as though burping a 250 pound baby. The speed, however, with which Mabel had shot from the house accelerated Stanley backward and his knees began to buckle. Mabel had draped herself over Stanley's shoulders and he was going down. A short declaratory sentence came out of her mouth and Stanley collapsed. The two of them ended up horizontal on her front lawn, she on top.

"He's dead!"

These words were shrieked into Stanley's ear. "He's de de de dead." A paroxysm of sobs escaped Mabel. Then came silence. Complete silence. An iPodded jogger, catching sight of the two of them in his peripheral vision, ran into a fire hydrant. It was the man's scream of pain that brought Stanley back to a sense of his own predicament and he thrust Mabel off and found himself asking, "Who?" compulsively. His first thought was that the President of the United States had been assassinated again but then he didn't think that even such a calamity would have reduced Mabel Green to such a state. Next, he thought that perhaps she meant the Senior Vice President who was his boss at the bank. If it were he, he thought, they would be putting the flags out shortly, but how would Mabel even have heard of the man? Then, Stanley, his mind flitting about like an errant flea, wondered, with a dawning sense of horror, whether she might not mean Hector. Good Lord, he said to himself, let it not be Hector! Of course, if it were, it would be the end of this whole wretched business and they could all get back to normal and it might — the thought flashed through his head at the speed of light — also give him a chance with Fanny, but, oh my God, he never wished any harm for Hector, and it wouldn't be right!

Stanley was just about starting to pursue the ramifications of Hector's untimely demise when Mabel grabbed the front of his shirt, the better to pull herself upright, and bawled, "Bruce, you fool!"

Hoisting herself to her feet, Mabel looked down at the still prone Stanley. "Come quick!" she said, "You can do mouth to mouth!" Stanley, rightly appalled at the very idea, found himself dragged into the house and through to the kitchen where he found Bruce laid out — it is the most apt expression possible — next to his food bowl. There was no doubt that the animal was dead but, had he not been, the weight of Mabel who proceeded to prostrate herself on top of the dog would certainly have helped. Stanley, unnerved both at the sight and the situation, sat down heavily on a kitchen chair.

"What do you think you are doing?" shouted Mabel, glaring up at him from the dog's flank, "Get down here and help." Seeing Stanley shake his head rapidly from side to side, she continued, "He needs CPA. Get down here and give it to him. Now!"

Stanley was not about to explain to Mabel the difference between a Certified Public Accountant and CPR and he was even less about to perform the latter on an animal of any description. Considerably unnerved by the whole situation, it took him several moments to do anything at all until, bereft of any other idea, he pulled out his cell phone and called 911. During those few moments of uncertainty, however, Mabel went from thinking of him as a useless ornament, as she thought of every male she had ever met, to someone who would have to be dealt with. As a prelude to the dealing, a first step as it were, she stood up, marched over to where Stanley remained seated and boxed his ears.

Yet other events, some more insidious and all of them cumulative, added to Stanley's summer of woe. Faun, usually an oasis of comfort as she went about looking after his needs, became, inexplicably, almost pathological in that pursuit. 'Did he want this?' and 'Would he like that?' were accompanied by the fluffing of pillows and the dry cleaning, it seemed, of his entire wardrobe. His favourite slippers disappeared and were replaced by a new, and very uncomfortable, pair of canvas sandals. Worse was Faun's asking him, on a daily basis after supper, when he just wanted to sink into his armchair and peruse the Globe, to help her run her lines. In two weeks, Stanley knew every last thing her character had to say, and, moreover, every line that came before and after what she said, spoken by every single character in the blasted play. Even when Faun had memorized every last word in Mr. Archibald's script, she demanded nightly reassurance that she had not, somehow, forgotten any of them during the day just finished.

Then there was the whole business of George Formby. Stanley soon came to wish that he had never heard of the man. Hector, a professional after all, knew that practice — called rehearsal in the theatre — makes perfect and he wanted to hear Stanley sing. At first, Stanley was able to put him off by saying that he could not find the music. This was a reasonable excuse: he could not find it because he didn't look for it. And he didn't look for it because it did not exist, although he was not about to tell Hector this. Eventually, however, Stanley was forced to admit that it must have been lost and that it would be best if he dropped out and Hector found another soloist. Hector was in the middle of saying nonsense when Vera interrupted and declared that, if they left it to her, perhaps she could find a copy of the song somewhere. Stanley wanted to slap the woman, and he thought, in passing, that she had said this in a very arch manner, but, fortuitously, the issue was put aside when the Vicar accidentally knocked the maple syrup onto his lap.

Two days later Vera sidled up to Stanley's desk at work and dropped a large brown envelope onto it. "There you go!" she said. "Laddie transcribed it for you."

Stanley, his mind full of negative net worths and a possible corporate bankruptcy, hadn't the vaguest idea what she was talking about.

"Open it," prompted Vera pushing it forward, "you'll be pleased." Before Stanley had had time to process this information, she added, sighing moonily, "Laddie can do anything! We're dating!"

Stanley did not know which was worse: having the words and music to all five verses of his song at hand, or knowing that his secretary and his accompanist were, for all he knew, having it off nightly after practice. The very thought of such a possibility was the final nail in the coffin of his miserable summer for he, himself, was making no progress, absolutely none, in his pursuit of the divine Fanny. Yes, they talked after each breakfast and he was able to ogle her at play practice (he had stopped going to the cabaret practice in case he was called upon to sing) but that was about as far as it went. Sunday service was out as a time of assignation since he and Hector had become targets for every kind of suggestion on how to improve the upcoming event from members of the congregation who had absolutely nothing to do with it and knew even less. Apart from a couple of suggestively raised eyebrows and the occasional moue, it was difficult to make progress in church. The fabulous four, as Hector had begun to call them, went out for dinner together about once a week, but it was difficult too to flirt while Hector went rattling on about all the things everyone had to do and Fanny herself drooled spaghetti between winks in his direction.

It was the middle of the month before Stanley finally hit on a scheme to get Fanny to himself. The tickets for the evening's entertainment had been printed (at the bank, courtesy of Vera) and were about to go on sale.

"We need, you and I," said Stanley, as conspiratorially as possible over the telephone, "to get together to distribute the tickets to everyone who will be selling, and to establish a bookkeeping system to monitor the process." There were many 'tos' in his sentence but the only two he was concerned about were himself and Fanny. "It will give us an idea where we really stand." Stanley was desperate to know where he stood. "You should keep a record and I should keep a record and we can get together every so often and put them together, if you see what I mean."

Whether Fanny saw what he meant remained unknown, although her reply did give him cause for hope.

"When were you thinking of?" asked Fanny thoughtfully on the other end of the line. "I mean for a first get-together?"

"Well," replied Stanley, "we shouldn't wait too long."

"Next week?" asked Fanny.

He could not wait that long. "Not it we want to have everything ready to start to sell next Sunday after the service," he said. "I was thinking you and I could meet while the others were rehearsing for the cabaret on Thursday." He paused, and added in what he hoped was an artfully casual manner, "That way we wouldn't be disturbed." And, suddenly afraid he had gone too far, he blurted, "And we'd be able to get everything done."

Stanley could hardly believe his ears when he heard Fanny's reply. "Your place or mine," she said, murmuring low into the telephone.

Hector Hums Along

Hector's summer was the complete opposite of Stanley's. He was in his element. With the exception of one or two things that needed to be sorted out, everything seemed to be going well. He knew that when it was all over no one would be up for a Tony Award, or even a Dora, but, overall, things were turning out better than expected. The set for the play was almost complete, the lighting — still more on the drawing board than on the actual stage — would be professional, a date had been given for when the curtains would be hung and ticket sales were as brisk as everyone hoped they would be. It was true that the cast of the play had not yet learned their lines and it annoyed Hector to see the players stumble about the stage with their scripts in their hands but it was, as he declared to Fanny at the end of one disjointed rehearsal, ever thus until the last week when they would panic and get their act together. Mabel, of course, had temporarily disappeared after Bruce's demise and Faun had had to stand in for her for two weeks. Faun was the exception to the not learning rule. With Stanley's nightly assistance, she soon knew her own part and everybody else's too, but she began to enjoy poking at Hector's worries by expressing a sighing concern every time she met him by declaring that surely the other players should have been able to dispense with their scripts by now.

    When Mabel returned to the fold, she arrived hefting in her ample armpit a minute canine, by the looks of it a cross between a more than usually puny chihuahua and a starving rabbit. The unfortunate creature did not last. Two nights later, Mabel sat down on it when getting ready to watch Coronation Street on the television. Pup, as she had called it, suffered a collapsed rib cage and a broken neck and when Mabel appeared at the next rehearsal but one it was with a young schnauzer that barked so much that Hector banned it from the room before the evening was out. If he had any hope that Mabel's doggie tragedies might cause her to back away from her commitment to the play and/or her recitation, he was to be disappointed, however. Mabel soldiered on in her usual manner and, as usual, she left casualties, other than those of the canine variety, in her wake.

Always willing to provide feedback on her fellow actors' performances, Roger St. John Mountjoy became a particular focus for her criticism. She started a running commentary on his line readings and when finally taken aside and asked by Hector to desist, replaced it with a series of grunts that soon reduced Roger to tears. A weepy fifty-five year old did not fit in with Archibald's vision of a young detective taking on the first case of his career but, as Fanny pointed out, Mabel controlled the kitchen while Roger could hardly control himself, so they should not push too hard. More importantly than her relationship with Roger, it had become apparent to everyone that Mabel had taken a sharp dislike to Stanley and was refusing to have anything to do with him. This effectively meant that all things Mabel had to go through Hector and it was necessary for his performance as an avuncular problem-solver to go into overdrive.

Fanny's view of the month was more realistic than her husband's. In addition to everything else, she was becoming more and more worried about Hector's health. She was annoyed with Mabel for the pressures that she was putting on her husband, and even more annoyed with Stanley for not being able to take the weight off Hector's shoulders as befitted his role of producer. It was Stanley who should have fine-tuned the Ladies of the Church for the refreshments but it was Hector who had to do it in the end. Not that Hector seemed to mind: he would have organized every last detail of the evening if Fanny had let him and if he was worn out at the end of each day, he always managed to bounce back in time for the next rehearsal. The theatre, as he often declared, was in his blood. It was left to Fanny to worry about the cholesterol in it.

When it came to the cabaret, Hector had every reason to be content. The little Chinese girl had fractured a foot playing T ball and had dropped out. Hector was all commiseration. He immediately extended his own part in the event from three to four songs and moved on. The singers from the choir were excellent, knew what they were doing and, like he himself, loved doing it. On the other hand, Hector became a little jealous when he spied Vera draping herself all over Laddie. Laddie was his accompanist and should be at his beck and call, not giggling off in some corner with Stanley's secretary. Vera's recitation, on the other hand, had turned up trumps and bid fair to being a high point of the evening, so he did not want to rock that particular boat too violently. Laddie, as he well knew, could be temperamental.

The dark side, once again, was Mabel. Unlike Vera's, Mabel's recitation was turning out to be quite dreadful. Hector tried to put this down to the number of dead animals in her life, but the situation did not improve with the arrival of the schnauzer and Hector was becoming desperate. Then the Vicar came up with a brilliant idea. Having sat — twice — through Mabel's reading, he too knew that desperate measures were required. There was in the church a teenager who was deaf and who signed. The Vicar was well aware that having a teenager in church and a deaf one at that was anomalous, and not a situation likely to last, but he decided they could put the signing to use. The young man could sit on stage to the right of and slightly behind Mabel and sign what she was saying. With a bit of luck the entire audience would be so intrigued by what the young fellow was doing that they wouldn't listen to what Mabel was saying. Hector embraced the Vicar's idea wholeheartedly and would have embraced the Vicar too, but he was afraid that the man might be a little sticky. He compromised by shaking hands. Unfortunately, they were sticky too. Hector was able to sell the idea to Mabel by pointing out that the signing would make her recitation more accessible to the deaf people in the audience, of whom, had Mabel considered the matter for a moment, there were likely to be none. In the end, the Vicar's idea fell apart when the anomalous young man received a cochlea implant and moved away to a more noisome and youth-oriented church. Mabel would have to be dealt with otherwise.

The other continuing thorn in Hector's flesh was his inability to get Stanley to sing. It was difficult to order his co-producer to do anything, even in his position as Artistic Director, and in all other respects Stanley had done well. There was a nice list of patrons, both corporate and individual, all of which or whom had been persuaded to cough up enough ducats that even if no one showed up on the night they would still be in profit. The actual tickets themselves were made of Bristol board so that they felt like something worth having, and the programme, though still in the design stage with the bios of all the performers having to be added, looked set fair to wow all who saw it. Stanley had recruited a couple of front-of-house personnel and also people to transport the elderly to the performance, organized a postal walk to get the word out more widely than anything the church had ever attempted before, and he had introduced a set of financial books the like of which Hector had never set eyes on during his lifetime in the theatre.

But he could not get Stanley to sing. Not a note. After Stanley had been presented with the sheet music, he had, he said, a developed a painful case of swollen glands. Then, oops, he forgot the music at home. Next, he reported that the key didn't work for him and could it perhaps be transcribed a tone lower. Hector suspected that Stanley didn't know what he was talking about, and Laddie suggested with just a modicum of scorn that he could, on the spot, provide any key or any tone that might come into Stanley's head, but here Hector had had to balk. He liked Stanley and, as he said to Fanny more than once, they were both on the same team. Fanny, who could read Stanley like the proverbial book, had long since figured out what was going on. She knew too that until the final programme went to press — when Stanley's name either would or would not appear alongside the name of George Formby — she could enjoy his discomfort even if it meant having to jolly her Hector along with the idea that he should not worry about it and that it would all be all right on the night.

Hector, however, preferred to set a trap for Stanley. He baited it by asking him if he could come to the rehearsal for the play a half an hour earlier than usual so that they could discuss whether to put out a press release for the show, and then he brought along Laddie, who did not usually attend play rehearsals, as his heavy ammunition. Stanley showed up, Faun in tow, both of them unsuspecting, and found a new version of Mr. Formby's song thrust into his hand. Before he could protest, he was hustled to stand next to the piano and Laddie began to thump out an introduction.

And so Stanley began to sing.

To the surprise of everyone there, not least himself, he did very well. It was true that some of the words had the echo of a recently operated on castrati in their reediness, but, he gathered momentum as he went and by the end of the last verse he was — this is a relative term — soaring.

"By Jove, Stan," said Hector, clapping him on the back, "You are the man! Outstanding. Outstanding!"

Fanny raised herself to her tiptoes and planted a big wet kiss on Stanley's forehead. Vera, there in her new role as Laddie's page turner, oohed and aahed, and said that she never would have suspected that Mr. P. had it in him, which was a sentiment with which Stanley himself would have agreed had he been asked. Faun, full of fluster when Stanley began, was thrilled by the song, but, gathering grist for her vendetta against Hector, was furious that he had put her husband through it. She smiled and laughed and the wheels turned. Stanley himself was secretly thrilled. He began, as perhaps all performers do, to envision the hearty applause and the calls of 'Encore' that surely would be his on the actual night when the audience rose to its feet and urged him forth. Hector, who knew better what can happen on any given night, made him sing it again to enunciate the words more clearly and to project properly so that he could be heard in the very last row of a non-existent balcony.

An Amity Of Opposites

Although neither Hector nor Stanley had the time or inclination to think about it, it was also in that month of August that their friendship began to blossom. Cut from completely different cloth, both men were, in their separate ways, determined to produce a garment in the September Soiree that would be both attractive and wearable. It was true that Stanley wanted something serviceable and utilitarian, while, in his heart of hearts, Hector aimed for an end result that more resembled 'Joseph And His Technicolour Dreamcoat,' but with each of them concentrating on his specific duties, they found that they were able to amble along, side by side, with a surprising degree of equanimity.

It helped that neither man knew men like the other. Hector quickly came to fascinate Stanley. Here was a bird of very different plumage and while, occasionally, Stanley wondered whether he hadn't got himself involved with some kind of a cuckoo bird, Hector brought so much that was new, not to mention strange, into Stanley's life, that he would have been a poor specimen indeed had he not been intrigued by his co-producer. Hector loved to reminisce. He had a wealth of stories about the theatre and theatre people — names that Stanley actually recognized — that part of Stanley perhaps even began to regret his more staid and conventional life as a banker. Hector, at the same time, was drawn to the earnestness of Stanley and a man less theatrical it would have been hard to imagine. In Stanley, Hector saw a man of serious intent with what appeared to be an uncomplicated straightforwardness that he rarely saw in his own chosen profession. Stanley was a man who would not have uttered the word 'dahling' to save his life.

Both men discovered that they rubbed along together very well. Oh, there were annoyances and misunderstandings to be sure. Stanley's continued refusal to rehearse bid fair to drive Hector mad; Hector's need always to be adding — to the programme, to the refreshments, to the very expense of the enterprise — remained inexplicable to Stanley. The banker in him demanded finite planning, supported by bullet points and with a beginning, a middle and an end. Hector, as far as Stanley could see, saw no end in sight.

Yet, in their own ways, they amused each other and something like affection grew. They began to meet for Saturday afternoon tea to be able to chat without interruption from either their wives or the other members of what Hector still insisted on calling 'the team.' Stanley would pick Hector up in the foyer of his condo and off they would toddle to a nearby coffee shop where they could spread out their papers to their hearts content or rather Hector would spread out his papers — dozens of unruly, often illegible, papers — and Stanley would open his black binder, its different sections colour-coded and everything written neatly in his fine copper-plated handwriting. In ink.

The conversation invariably began with an inquiry about the other's wife and, if Stanley hung rather more on Hector's response in this regard, it was not enough to be noticeable. The talk would then move on to a word or two about their health before taking a slight detour to comment on the health — physical and, in some cases, mental — of the other participants in the September Soiree. Like many men, although both of them would have denied it vehemently, they liked a little gossip and since there is not a church under heaven that does not have something to gossip about, this usually managed to take up quite a bit of time and occasionally the tea grew cold. In the end, however, the conversation would get down to the task or tasks at hand, each man inquiring of the other how things were going and being genuinely interested in the response.

The fact was that at their age and given the kind of lives both men led, neither Stanley nor Hector was likely to have the opportunity to develop new friends or acquaintances, and they began to look forward to the camaraderie these Saturday afternoons provided. They began to anticipate getting together, just the two of them. A second cup of tea would follow the first and occasionally a second scone, before they would reluctantly pack up their notes. Invariably, Stanley would have to help Hector collect the several of his sheets that had wafted under the table and then the two men would squabble about the bill, never quite having the sense to say that they would take turns, before beginning to wend their way slowly back along St. Clair. Stanley would deposit

Hector on his doorstep and, after punctiliously shaking hands as though they had just been introduced, the two would go separately on their merry way refreshed and even enlightened by the very different life and personality of the other.

As far as their respective wives were concerned, both Fanny and Faun were very glad that Hector and Stanley met on those lazy summer Saturday afternoons.

It got them out of their hair.

Marriage and Maternity

And so August came to an end, although it was not to end quietly. At the cabaret rehearsal on its last Thursday, Vera asked Hector if it would be all right if she made an announcement while they were having refreshments. She asked this rather coyly and over the course of the summer Vera had got "coy" down pat. The secretary had flowered and was now in full bloom. Stanley did not like this at all, but since she had printed the tickets — even slicing them to size on her guillotine — as well as having designed a programme that was as professional as any playbill he had seen put out by Mirvish or The Canadian Stage, he was in no position to complain, particularly as it had all been done in company time and on the QT. In addition, she and Faun seemed to have developed a friendship that seemed only slightly less close than the one she apparently had with Laddie.

"If I could have everybody's attention, please," Vera announced in due course. She was standing with her back to Laddie, who was seated at the piano. He pounded out a triumphant series of chords and the room hushed into interested silence. "I would like," she continued, "or, rather, Laddie and I would like," a fluttering of eyelashes followed, "to invite you all to my apartment for a party on Saturday evening." More chords rattled the piano and Vera played the coquette. "I should tell you that it's an engagement party. Laddie and I," she took an even deeper breath and beamed, "are getting married." The chords rose to a crescendo and Vera turned to kiss the top of Laddie's head.

Stanley could not believe his ears.

He believed them even less when Saturday evening came around. Not having the vaguest idea about navigating the melee of downtown condominiums in which Vera lived, he and Faun arrived late to find the party in full swing. Vera's apartment was a tiny loft with an acreage rather less than Stanley's garden shed and many of the dozen and a half guests had to sit flank to flank on the floor. The Vicar was perched on the edge of an office chair on rollers. Had he sat on the floor, he might never have been able to get up. The rollers, threatening to buckle, squealed under his bulk whenever he moved, but he managed to stay firm. Mabel, who was not expected to attend, had arrived first and occupied the three legged stool that served as Vera's vanity chair which, while it did not squeak, certainly looked as though it might collapse at any moment. Mabel's dog du jour was not in attendance. Fanny, on arrival, had taken to the single bed and lay sprawled across the back of it, her short skirt allowing her to bring one leg comfortably up towards her midriff. The other leg was exposed in all its considerable glory. No one seemed to object to the amount of space she was taking. Stanley made a beeline for her but was unable to find a spot close enough to properly take in the view. Fanny had kicked off her shoes and, as soon as he could, he surreptitiously held on to one, its heel in the palm of his hand. Vera swanned around the room offering what she called nibbles, and Laddie, who was as in his element at a bar as he was at a piano, served the drinks. Stanley could see that Vera had spared no expense on the evening and found himself being offered a single malt much better than anything he would have been able to offer a guest in his own home.

With everyone settled and drinks in hand, Hector took over as Master of Ceremonies and called for quiet. In his booming stage voice, a voice used to being heard up in the gods, he welcomed the guests, made a joke about his Cleopatra lying on the divan and then asked Stanley to stand up next to him. Stanley, who had no wish to be there and even less to be singled out in any way, rose from where he had been squatting on his haunches, looking perplexed.

"Well, I guess, Stan, old bean, it all comes down to thee and me!" Hector looked around the room, milking the silence that had fallen upon it. "It was Stan here who brought Vera into our little group, and it was I who brought Laddie along to play for us. And I guess it was love at first sight. Yes, sir, you lovebirds have Stan and me to thank for it, eh?!" He clapped Stanley on the back while hearty applause reverberated around the small space. Stanley felt acutely uncomfortable. He was shortly to be made more so. Hector continued, "Vera was telling me the other evening that she and Stan have worked together for the past fifteen years and she regards him as both a father figure and a friend, and I know she is kind of hoping, Stan, that, when the day comes, you will be the one to give her away." A chorus of affirmation flowed through the room like the wave at a ballpark. Stanley, who at that point would rather have thrown the woman away, held a strained smile on his face. The guests put it down to the fact that a man his age who had been squatting in one position for so long had a right to look a bit peeved, and clapped loudly. "Meanwhile, I, of course," continued Hector, with ebullient geniality, "have every intention of being my friend Laddie's best man, when he gets round to asking me, that is!"

The room erupted again when they heard this — with the single exception of Mabel Green who was clearly confused at the turn of events and who, in any case, had not really been paying attention as she peered round the tiny apartment trying to discover why anybody would want to live there.

Hector continued. "I am reminded of the Bard's immortal lines... The History Plays... Henry VI, I think it was, — mmm." He paused as if trying to remember words which, in fact, he had researched that very afternoon and written down on a piece of paper currently secreted in his trouser-pocket.

"I'm sure you know them well."

Hector cleared his throat and, bowing low to Vera, began to declaim in what Fanny privately (and fondly) referred to as his imperial voice, "'She is beautiful and therefore to be wooed.'"

Vera's guests cheered. Even the Vicar got into the act as he mimed fanning himself, saying to everyone's delight, "Be still my heart!"

The quotation, however, — as you will have realized — was, as yet, incomplete and, in any case, Hector was not one to appreciate an interruption mid-performance. He held up a stern hand and waited for silence. It took time coming.

"And," he began again, that dulcet baritone in full flight, "'She is woman, and therefore,'" a beat and a pause, "'to be won.'" Bowing now to all and sundry, Hector looked around and drew to a close, "It is our brave Laddie who has won her."

Hector spoke better than he knew, however, for had anyone in the room been monitoring irony, the probity of his quotation was to be verified post haste. Vera, delighted at being the centre of attention after a lifetime of secretarial anonymity, flung herself into her beloved's arms and posed the following question, "Oh Laddie, we shouldn't tell them, should we? Should we?"

Laddie, sober, was a diminutive but presentable fellow, but he tended to unravel under the influence. He had been drinking steadily since his arrival two hours before anyone else, and his appearance was most definitely frayed. He shrugged a pair of sloping shoulders and replied, "And why not, eh? Sure!" It came out as 'Shuerr.' He stumbled as he moved to stand up and put his arm around his beloved's waist.

Stanley felt as though he had wandered into some kind of parallel universe. The sight of the somewhat decrepit pianist fondling his giggling middle-aged secretary was more than he could take in. He closed his eyes and kept them closed for a long moment in the hope that, when he opened them again, normalcy might have returned. It had not. He was, moreover, suddenly aware of the size of Vera's breasts. He had not realized that Vera even had breasts, but now they seemed to be on display, staring him in the face, and he looked quickly away. Fanny, catching his eye at that precise moment, realized what he had been looking at and wagged a finger at him, mouthing the words 'naughty boy' as she did so. He blushed furiously and, again without realizing what he was doing, lowered his eyes to look at her breasts instead. Fanny put her head back and began to laugh. Stanley's face became crimson. Fortunately, no one was looking at him.

Vera had claimed the stage.

"Well," she said archly, bending her knees and essaying a little jump. "What we have to tell you is that Laddie is going to be a daddy!"

The room did not know quite what to do with this announcement and it took a beat for the expected applause to come forth. Certainly, the guests had a variety of fortunately silent responses. "Oh, my dear Lord!" prayed the Vicar. "I would have said she was past child bearing," was Mabel's disapproving thought. "Well, if the act of procreation didn't kill you, Laddie, my friend, the kid probably will," mused Hector to himself. "Better you than me!" thought Fanny and she looked back at Stanley again. He was frowning and seemed to be having difficulty understanding what Vera had said. Fanny saw Faun lean towards him and whisper something in his ear. At first he didn't react and Faun had to whisper again, this time prodding him with her elbow.

Stanley cleared his throat. The vacant expression on his face matched a mind that was absent of words and hadn't a clue how to proceed.

"Stanley, you should say something," were the words first spoken to him by Faun. They had been followed by a more urgent "Say something, Stanley!" and the nudge.

Stanley had never liked being called on to make off-the-cuff remarks and here was a situation so extraordinary that he simply didn't know what to say. Everything was made worse by the fact that what he really wanted to do was to explain to Fanny that he hadn't intended to look at Vera's frontage but it had just, so to speak, swung into his line of sight. He could not say this, of course, but a stream of unrelated ideas began to pop into his head unaided. These began with the undeniable: Fanny's bosom is better. From there, they spasmed through his brain willy nilly. Vera better not wear that outfit to work on Monday. I thought she was forty-eight. Will she still be able to print the programmes if she's pregnant? Surely she won't breast-feed at the office. She is forty-eight! We had a cake for her birthday. Will HR blame me? I had nothing to do with it. Surely it couldn't have been Laddie. He doesn't look capable. Yes, indeed, Fanny's bosom is far more grand.

Fortunately, none of this stream of consciousness, germane as some of the thoughts undoubtedly were, emerged from Stanley's mouth.

"Well," he began, aiming for jocularity and achieving something more like subdued delirium, "congratulations are, um, certainly the order of the day or should I, um, say evening." Still rattled, he struggled on, "Vera has worked for me for fifteen years and I, um, think that this, this is the first time something, um, something like this has, um, come up." Stanley looked over to Vera for verification of the truth of his statement and did not at all connect the befuddled expression on her face with what he was saying. "We will, I think, have to take it day by day and work towards an equitable solution of her..." At this point Stanley began to realize that he hadn't the slightest notion of where he was going with this or how he might continue. He was saved by Faun who was, again, whispering words off to his side. "News! Yes, her wonderful news." Clinging to these words like a life raft, Stanley repeated them. "Her wonderful news! Yes, indeed! It will be one maternity leave that the whole bank will look forward to." Having finally heard something that sounded as though it could possibly have made sense and may even have been a joke, the group chuckled uneasily. Stanley took this as encouragement and something inside him told him to provoke a little more of that, oh, so welcome laughter. "And Laddie, you'd better get lots of rest. I can tell you from personal experience — not, ahem, with Vera of course — that, being a father, fatherhood," he paused and beamed fatuously at the couple, "is a challenge, and given how old you are already..." The words turned to ashes in Stanley's mouth, "and and and so I think everyone here will wish you both the best of luck in your new endeavour."

He sounded like the Queen about to lob a bottle of champagne against the side of a ship and it was left to Hector to put the situation on a more even keel.

"Well," said Hector, an uncertain grin plastered on his face, "What can I add after that, Stan, old man?" He paused to gather his thoughts. They were strewn all over the place. "Except to say that I have known Laddie for many many years and have known how much he has wanted a Vera to come into his life." Laddie had, in fact, been married before to a prestidigitator who had tried for many many years to make him disappear. "And Vera, my beautiful..." Here Hector ground to a stop. His thoughts were not gathering quickly enough. In what way, could Vera be described as beautiful? He ransacked the scripts of every play he had ever appeared in and a vocabulary honed by a lifetime of theatrical exaggeration for a suitable noun and decided to throw verisimilitude as well as caution to the wind. "My, oh so beautiful flower of the evening, what a jewel Laddie has found in you. A lotus flower on a lily pond. A twenty-two carat pearl hidden tucked away in the small little oyster of our endeavours." Hector too had lost what little train of thought he had had and turned towards the Vicar who did not know whether to laugh or weep at everything that was going on around him and who had developed a severe cramp in his left leg from trying to keep the rolling chair in the same spot.

"Reverend!" hallooed Hector, "I am sure that in the fullness of time you will be called upon to bring our dear friends here to the sticking post whence they shall be bound together in the bonds of holy matrimony."

The room, which had only the slightest idea of what Hector was trying to say — although the delivery of it was so much better than Stanley's mangled prose — burst again into cheers before moving to pour itself another drink. Laddie poured himself two.

Oh God, Not Atheism!

That was Saturday evening. The following Monday morning, a Ms. Mary MacDonald Macdonagh stepped off a sidewalk in the Beaches and moved on to her great reward. The repercussions for the September Soiree of this apparently unconnected event will best be understood when it is explained that Mary MacDonald Macdonagh was not only the relic of her late husband but also the mother of the Vicar. The Vicar was distraught when he heard the news. Her passing would throw his schedule out considerably and it was apparent that a mother who had been an inconvenience in life was about to become an embarrassment in death. In the first place, hardly anyone at the church knew of her existence and, in the second, he was unhappily aware that other unknown relatives might shortly be wending their way towards Toronto for her funeral, itself an event likely to try a man with far more patience than the Vicar. Mary MacDonald Macdonagh was the founder and current president of the Society of Canadian Atheists.

Both Stanley and Hector were saddened when the Vicar telephoned them with his news, although neither had ever met the woman and both of them had to struggle to understand who she was. Who knew the Vicar had a mother? He had not spoken of her in any of his sermons, and preferring not to mention her alliterative and well-known name while passing on his sad news, the fact that she, whoever she was, was his mother, had been hard to grasp. Both of them, separately, offered an apparently hearty Vicar their condolences but otherwise their reactions were markedly different.

Hector's reaction to the news of Mary MacDonald Macdonagh's passing was typical of a man who had spent his life in the theatre. The show must go on! It was inconvenient but perhaps the evening could, in some sense, become a celebration of the woman's life. This thought he immediately passed on to the Vicar, still on the line and sweating slightly having had, yet again, to explain that, no, his mother had not been a parishioner, and, no, they had not carried the same surname which, yes, would have made identification a little easier, but she had always been a free spirit who had gone her own way in life, and, so it seemed, from the manner of her demise, in death too.

"Hector, my friend," he said, "you must, of course, do as you think fit with our evening of entertainment, but I, of course, would not feel it proper to participate. Indeed, my presence would be a blight on the jollity of the occasion." The Vicar had been looking forward enormously to the September Soiree and had invited several of the local clergy for a little light refreshment at the manse beforehand, and it was just like his mother to cast a shadow on the festivities.

"Well, if you think so, I will, of course, understand," replied Hector gravely, in a voice appropriate to the occasion. "Perhaps we can put an insert into the programme as a recognition of her passing."

The Vicar shuddered at the thought. "No, dear friend, I hardly think it necessary. My mother would not have wished such attention to be drawn to herself." The Vicar closed his eyes and crossed himself as he said these words. They were an arrant lie. His mother's aim in life, the one after her desire to embarrass him any way possible, was to be the centre of attention wherever she found herself.

It was left to Fanny, when she was able to unravel the tale Hector had to tell, to suggest that it might, in fact, be inappropriate to continue with the Soiree given the circumstances.

"She was the Vicar's mother, his Mom, Hector!" she admonished her frowning spouse. "His nearest and dearest."

"But we have everything arranged, Fan. Everything! Couldn't we just have the lights go dim before the performance? Or wear black armbands? The performers, I mean. Or even a little prayer during the intermission. Something like that?" Hector was only too aware that Fanny was shaking her head. He all but stamped his foot as he continued. "Blast the woman anyway. I didn't know the Vicar had a mother. It's not fair."

It took Fanny the best part of the evening to bring her husband to a better frame of mind. Stanley did not help. It had been immediately apparent to Stanley that the event would have to be postponed, if not actually cancelled, as soon as he was able to decipher the Vicar's somewhat airy explanation of who Mary MacDonald Macdonagh had been. He had heard about the accident at work since several members of his department had arrived late as a result of the transit confusion she caused when she went under the wheels of the Queen streetcar, but the news reports did not mention the offspring of the lady in question.

"But, of course, Vicar, we must cancel," he had said immediately.

"No, no, I think not, my dear Stanley. Just, perhaps, a small postponement."

"If that is what you think..." Stanley hesitated.

He was ambivalent. Part of him still continued to hope that the entire event might somehow disappear. If it took the Vicar's parent — whoever she was — going under the front end of a tram to do it, then, so be it. On the other hand, he would not get to do his number if they cancelled completely and part of him, the part that did not break out into a sweat when he thought about it, was looking forward to singing his song and seeing the surprised faces on the whole lot of them when they heard how good he was. Plus, of course, the event was meant to bring the congregation together in fellowship and all that kind of thing.

"Indeed, yes, Stanley." The Vicar was reassurance itself. "A small postponement. A week, perhaps. Two at the very most! We will all have to look at our calendars and see which will be best. I am so sorry. My mother was... Well, she was..." The Vicar's voice trailed off. It was left to Vera, after he had hung up and Stanley retailed the news to her, to say exactly what she thought the Vicar's mother was.

"I'm sure," she began, hands on her hips, eyes wide open, "I'm sure the Vicar's mother was a very nice person, but she evidently didn't realize what it involves. Everything has been printed. It's most inconvenient, it is. Inconsiderate. Expensive as well. The silly woman."

Whatever their private opinions, those present expressed only sympathy to an oddly jocular Vicar at a hastily convened breakfast meeting the following morning. In addition to those usually in attendance, Fanny and Faun had each accompanied their spouse. A morose and possibly hungover Laddie turned up half an hour after everyone else.

"The first item of business is to decide if we are going to cancel," said Hector, looking as though he was ready to fight anyone willing to vote in the affirmative.

"No, my dear Hector, we are not going to cancel." The Vicar spoke mellifluously, trying to pour balm on a troubled soul. "But," he continued, "for myself I ask that we might delay our performance, if we can, for just one week. My mother's funeral cannot, it seems, be held before Friday and, although I shall not be officiating at the ceremony, I shall of course be in attendance and several members of the congregation have asked whether they might accompany me." Over my dead body, he added silently.

To read this speech on paper without the strangulated stumbling, the clearings of his throat and the unholy embarrassment that the Vicar felt giving it, is to fail to do it justice. It was a short speech but it took a long time to give and his relief at coming to its end was palpable.

Feeling that he had missed something, the janitor spoke. "Haven't been told, Vicar." The janitor was a punctilious man who liked to be kept informed and who annoyed the Vicar and everyone else by never speaking in complete sentences.

"No, indeed, Clarence," replied the Vicar. "The funeral will not take place in the church." He waved an imprecise hand above his shoulder. "It will be on the Danforth." He had no intention of defining the location more closely than that, but he did feel the need to add, "It will be a nondenominational event."

In any other gathering, the Vicar's embarrassment would have been obvious and the strangeness of his message might have been discerned, but his listeners, with one exception, had other things on their minds. Only Faun recognized the depth of the Vicar's emotion but she put it down to his loss. Tears welled up in her eyes as she thought how best she might comfort him.

"I would be honoured if I might accompany you, Vicar," she said, laying a hand on his arm. "I could drive, if you like." The Vicar, who did not drive, had had three similar offers and refused each one of them. He had no intention of allowing any of his acquaintance and certainly none of his congregation to get anywhere near his mother's last rites, but at this point all he could think to say was, "Thank you so much. We shall see, we shall see." Faun would not see a single thing, he would make sure of that.

"Well," continued Hector, determined to get back on track and get the show on the road, both physically and metaphorically as it were. "So we will have the show the following Saturday." He rubbed his hands together. "Wonderful!"

"Can't." Clarence the janitor spoke the single word.

Hector looked at him hard, "Why not?" he demanded.

"Square dance group. Every month. Pay too."

Hector turned a gimlet eye on Clarence. "The following week, then," he said.

"Nope." Clarence shook his head.

Hector looked as though he would like to throttle him.

Stanley hurriedly intervened. "Oh, ah, Hector, I'm afraid not, The last Saturday in September is the rummage sale."

Hector half rose from his seat. "Can't you postpone it?" he asked in the same tones he had used when he played Shylock at the Banff School For The Performing Arts in his youth. His audience began to cower from him, and Fanny said in a warning voice, "Now, Hector, now."

With the exception of Vera and Laddie who knew nothing about this particular church, or any other if it came to that, the people sitting around the table were shocked at Hector's suggestion. The rummage sale was sacrosanct. Christmas had more chance of being moved than such a major event in the church's life.

It was left to Stanley to bring Hector back to reality. "Hector, you'd never convince the Ladies of the Church to change their date. We've had enough trouble with the refreshments for the September Soiree. Mabel Green would never agree, even if she is in it." Stanley blanched at the thought of having to speak to Mabel on such a cataclysmic subject. "Vicar? What do you think?" The Vicar, pale with foreboding alongside him, did not speak. He shook his head sadly.

"So we have to wait for four whole weeks?" Hector exclaimed. He made it sound as though his firstborn was about to be circumcised with gardening shears.

"Hector, love, it's the best they can do." Fanny commiserated with her spouse. "You can use the time. Some of them hardly know their lines yet."

"What if they have other commitments?" Hector's petulance was a side of him that the others had not seen before. "What if they don't want to wait?"

The Vicar, not liking where the meeting was headed, spoke to the janitor. "Clarence, can we have the first Saturday in October? Is the auditorium available?"

Clarence thumbed through a notebook. "Free. Not the next one though. Thanksgiving."

"Well," said Stanley hastily, "there you have it then. It has to be that Saturday."

He had hardly got the words out of his mouth when Vera erupted.

"But it doesn't make sense. You can't have a September Soiree in October. And what about the tickets! The dates will be wrong. And what about the people who have bought tickets already. How will they know you've changed the dates? And the posters! You've put posters all over the place already. With next Saturday's date on them! People will still turn up. How can we tell them different?"

There was a nudge of malice in his voice when Stanley answered her, "You'll have to make new posters, Vera. And change the tickets, too. At least, we'll have more time to sell them."

Vera was not about to be stopped. "And the programmes. I printed two hundred programmes yesterday afternoon with all the bios and everything, and now we can't even be certain that the same people will be in the play or in the cabaret." She groaned. "I'll have to do it all over again."

Faun patted her on the arm. "I'm sure that everybody will still want to be there, my dear. The only thing you will probably end up having to change will be the name on the cover."

"And, yes, the date on the tickets," added the Vicar, thinking it through.

"Posters no good either," Clarence pointed out.

"Suffering sainthood!" Hector threw up his arms.

"Do them over. Everything," Clarence nodded sagely at the group.

"I feel sick." Vera gave a little moan and lowered her head onto the table top.

"Don't fret, Vera," said Fanny, sympathetically. "I'm sure that Stanley will give you time to get everything done." She looked over at Stanley, smiling conspiratorially at him. "Eh, Stanley?"

Stanley, already appalled at the amount of time Vera had spent on the Soiree was not pleased, and had anybody but Fanny spoken about it, he would have had something of his own to say, but Fanny's smile had its usual effect. "Of course, of course. But we must be positive this is going to be the day. We can't go changing it again."

He looked around the table to ensure everyone's agreement. It was Clarence who voiced their thoughts. "Only if somebody else dies off."

"I feel sick!" Vera lifted her head and repeated her previous words.

"It won't be that bad, Vera," said Faun, smiling encouragement across the table. "I'll pop in one day and help collate everything, if you like."

"No," replied Vera, shaking her head, "I mean I really feel sick!"

She pushed her chair back and ran towards the restroom.

Laddie's Lament

What began as a breakfast meeting had almost become lunch as lists were made about what would have to be done to manage the change in dates. In the end only Hector, Stanley, Faun, Clarence and a very silent Laddie remained at the table. The Vicar had arranged to meet an ancient aunt flying in from New Brunswick. Vera had been sent home: the onset of her sickness did not augur well for the completion of the changes she would have to make. Fanny had felt unable to miss an appointment with her chiropractor but in a whispered conversation with Hector before leaving, she had encouraged him to see the bright side in that, given the extra time, everyone would be so much more polished on the night.

It was agreed that all the performers should be contacted immediately to ascertain whether they would be available on the new date and Faun was awarded this task. Stanley, once more, was delegated to approach Mabel Clark to bring her onside with the Ladies' participation on the new date while Clarence was to examine its implications for the custodians' duty schedule. Hector, in the meantime, had had an idea he refused to tell the group about until he was able to think it through in more detail and he became eager to leave so he could begin that very process. His sudden enthusiasm made Stanley nervous: Hector, as this whole endeavour had shown, was most dangerous at his most energetic.

They all began to go their separate ways but Hector, the most eager to leave, was waylaid by Laddie who insisted on leading him over to a corner booth for a private word. Hector, in the full flight of his new idea, practically had to be dragged there. They were seated and had yet another cup of coffee in front of them, when Hector, eager to get going, raised his eyebrows as high as he had raised them when he played the Mikado at the Markham Music Theatre, and inquired, "Well?"

Laddie began to fidget. He stirred his coffee. He licked the spoon and then stirred it again. At length, he sighed.

"I can't do it," he said. "I just can't, Hector,"

The statement sent Hector to the edge of panic. If Laddie were to refuse to accompany the singers in the cabaret, it would be a disaster. He was the best piano player around.

"Sure you can!" answered Hector bracingly. "Is it another engagement? Cancel it! We booked you first!"

Laddie was shaking his head dejectedly. He moaned.

Hector peered at him. "Are you ill? Have you seen a doctor? See a doctor! You'll be as right as rain on the night. Chin up!"

Laddie continued to shake his head. Then he began to sob.

Hector was alarmed. "Old friend," he said, "what is it? Tell me. We have been friends for forty years. You can tell me." He reached across the table and took hold of Laddie's elbow. "Is it," he paused, feeling the drama of the moment, "the Big C?"

Laddie wiped the tears from his eyes and frowned.

"The big...?" He laughed ruefully. "Almost as bad! It's her! The big 'V!' What am I going to do about her? She's got a bun in the oven and what am I going to do about that! Hector! I can't marry her at my time of life and what would I do with a flaming kid anyway? You've got to help me. Vera's driving me nuts."

Hector did not know what to say. He had, in fact, said plenty about Laddie's situation earlier but he had said it to Fanny. Laddie, whichever way you looked at it, was an idiot. "What does he want to get married for? At his age? He has one foot in the grave already and now he's going to have a wee bairn to look after," he had said scornfully to his spouse. "It must be dementia coming on." And gathering steam, he had added, "And he wants me to be his best man! He's crazy as a loon, Fan. Raving!"

Fanny had laughed. "Calm down, Hector. And if I remember right, it was you who suggested being his best man. Just like you — always jumping in headfirst and then having to think about it afterwards. But, at the end of the day, it is none of your concern. Let the two of them sort it out. It is none of your business."

"Ah, but it is, love." Hector disagreed with her assessment of the situation. "That's exactly what it is. My business! They met on my show. That's where they met and when it all goes sideways, who'll get the blame? Yours truly, that's who!"

It seemed that everything had, indeed, gone sideways, and if Hector wasn't getting the blame quite yet, he was being asked for advice and God only knows what all else would be next. Seated there with Laddie, he had another, even more disturbing, thought: if Laddie and Vera broke up before the show, what would happen to his accompanist? What would happen to his programmes and the tickets and the posters? What would happen to the cabaret?

"Laddie," he said, "you know what you've got? You've got first night jitters, that's what you've got. Take a breath. You've got..." Hector paused to think what it was exactly that Laddie had, "you've got a lovely lady, someone to take care of you in your old age. Someone to be with." He heard Laddie groan. "You've got the next generation. Comin' right along."

Laddie groaned again. "I'll be almost flaming eighty before it's a teenager, for Christ sake."

Hector tried to keep going although he had said the exact same words to Fanny less than two days before. "Someone to love you and take care of you when the time comes." From the stricken look on Laddie's face, that time wasn't likely to be far away. "A wee bairn." Hector was aware that a wee bairn was unlikely to be able to look after anyone. He was also aware, having been told by Fanny on numerous past occasions, that whenever babies were mentioned he invariably turned all Scots and referred to them in this manner, even if it did not make the slightest sense. Nevertheless, something made him repeat the phrase for emphasis. "A wee bairn!"

To which Laddie thumped hard on the table and groaned, "I hate kids."

Hector was fond of Laddie in his own way, and while he would never have said that he himself hated children, he had never found them particularly endearing either, so he had a degree of sympathy with his friend's predicament. Child rearing and matrimony were, however, far from being anything like a subject of his interest at this point in time and he sloughed Laddie off with vague generalities and reassurances. All the while his brain was working overtime on the idea he had been playing with as soon as it became obvious that a postponement was unavoidable. What he wanted was to get home to discuss it with Fanny to see what she thought. Finally managing to distract Laddie by suggesting to him that, at the very least, living with Vera would be better than his current one room flat in Etobicoke and since the baby was still, some six months away from fruition or whatever they called it much might happen before it made its debut in person.

Only when Hector was safely home, was he finally able to broach his idea to Fanny.

"I've been thinking," he said thoughtfully when they had finished a rehash of the events of the morning, "that we could really use the extra practice for the play and for the cabaret."

"Well, it will certainly give the cast more time to learn their parts. I have visions of Roger St. John Mountjoy having to use his shirt sleeve as a crib sheet. And a couple of the others too. And however much Mabel Green tries to boss everyone around at rehearsal, I'm not convinced that she won't have stage fright on the night and end up standing there like a deer in the headlights."

"So this will give us more time to whip them into shape," he concurred.

Fanny laughed, "'Whip' may be the operative word, my love."

"Yes, but the cabaret is just about ready to go, don't you think?"

"Hmm, yes, the people in the choir definitely, and Vera should be fine as long as she gets over this morning sickness business. You, of course, could walk on stage tomorrow and be just lovely." Fanny lent over and kissed Hector on the cheek. Then she frowned. "Stanley might be another freezer though."

Hector nodded. "That's what I was thinking. But don't you think that everyone might enjoy a live rehearsal? A little first run, so to speak."

Hector was up to something, and Fanny knew her husband. What he meant was that if there were to be two performances — whatever the first of them might be called — part of him was thinking that he would get to perform twice.

She sat back, folded her arms and smiled. "What are you thinking, Hector Hammond? Come on, I know you!"

"Well no, but yes," he replied. There was no point in dissembling in front of Fanny: she knew him too well. "What I was thinking was we could also do a performance somewhere else. Like a charity benefit." He added, gathering speed, "We could do it this very Saturday night. After all, everyone will be free because they think this is when we are having the September Soiree. And it would give us a chance to iron out the kinks."

Fanny sat back and nodded. He had it all figured out, of that she was quite sure.

"Perhaps," he continued as though the thought was coming to him on the fly, "perhaps at a retirement residence. They are always looking for entertainment, aren't they? And it would be in a good cause."

Fanny opened her eyes wide and pretended amazement.

"What a good idea!" she said, "But where, oh where, Hector, could we go at this late date?" She furrowed her brow and shook her head, a picture of puzzlement. "It's pretty late. It's only five days away."

Hector, getting into the spirit of the thing, rested his chin on his hand and appeared to be deep in thought. "Hmm," he said, "I guess it'd be too late for Christie Gardens. Belmont House?" He shook his head, paused a beat and then sprang to his feet. "By, Jove," he continued, wonder and excitement in his voice. "Beacham Hall Place. The very place, love! Suitable for our kind of programme, not too far away, and," he added in a voice that knew it was delivering the coup de grace, "Noni Figueroa lives there!"

"And isn't she in charge of entertainment?" Fanny asked her question in childlike innocence.

"I do believe she is, my love." Hector replied. "I do believe she is!"

Noni Figueroa, a well known relic of the Toronto theatrical scene from the hippy sixties when she had played the dimpled ingenue both on and off the stage, was an old chum of Hector. Fanny suspected that the two of them had been more than ships that passed in the night way back when. Noni had docked with many a vessel in those days. Today, however, she was more of an old barge than a seaworthy frigate. In any case, she was a character and it would be fun to see her.

"I haven't seen Noni in a dog's age," she said. "A bit before my time really. Did you know her well?"

"What, me?" She could hear bluster in Hector's voice.

Fanny could not resist. "I mean you played with her often enough, if I remember right."

Hector cleared his throat. "Once or twice," he allowed, "And we've seen her at parties. You know her just as well as I do, Fan."

Fanny couldn't help herself and laughed out loud at her husband's embarrassment. "I'm not sure about that, Hector Hammond, but give her a tinkle, my love, and let's see what she has to say for herself," she said.

The Blithe And Bonny Noni

Thus it came to pass that the cabaret was engaged to perform at Beacham Hall Place on the evening previously designated for the September Soiree. Hector informed everyone about the new arrangement at the rehearsal that evening and if there is one thing an entertainer likes to do more than once, it is his act. Mabel Green, in particular, was pleased with the idea of performing at Beacham Hall Place since several of her acquaintance were housed there and she had, herself, considered putting her name down for a place until she was told that animals were not permitted. Bruce had been in fine middle age at the time, and there was no way she was going to be separated from him.

It was Noni Figueroa's idea that Hector and his wife — Noni could not remember her name — be invited for dinner before the performance. Hector, wisely thinking that there might be safety in numbers, asked if he might bring his co-producer and his spouse along, suggesting that Noni might find a kindred spirit in him since she had functioned, more than once, as an impresario and had been, he said, a producer of note. Noni heard very little of the latter part of this sentence. The thought of dining with not one but two of the male species was enough to get her hot and somewhat bothered. She answered in the affirmative, booked the private dining room, and got down to the more serious business of what she would wear. Men were in short supply at Beacham Hall Place. What a coup to have two of them! The women would go mad! Hurrah!

Faun Parkinson did not like places like Beacham Hall Place. It did not matter whether they were called retirement residences or old folks' homes or senior-care facilities. Faun and her sister had put their mother in one of them and their mother had never forgiven them. She was there for eight years and would turn her face to the wall whenever they came to visit. When Faun heard that she and Stanley were invited for dinner, she told him, flatly, that she was not going to go. She was not in the cabaret and while she really wanted to hear him sing, she was just going to have to wait until the real performance. Stanley was surprised at Faun's vehemence but every effort to change her mind failed. She would not budge. Consequently, Fanny arrived at the facility with two men on her arm, a state of affairs that did not endear her to the multitude of females who were buzzing around outside the dining room waiting to go in. Noni Figueroa did not endear herself to them either when she let out a bellow and advanced on her guests with a halloo at the top of her considerable lungs.

Stanley had noted a preponderance of blue-rinsed women in front of him when he went through the front door, but he was totally unprepared for the vision that came bearing down on him. Noni Figueroa had never been what would be called beautiful and her career had been based more on the power of her personality than her looks. She had vivacity. In spades. Once small and slender, the years had added nothing to her height, but her width had expanded exponentially. Noni now bore an astonishing similarity to a fire-hydrant. The fact that she wore a yellow caftan added a considerable degree of verisimilitude to this resemblance. Yellow was her favourite colour.

"Hector, dahling," she shouted across the room, sailing forward to greet them, arms outstretched high above her head. Since Noni had smoked every available brand of cigarette for a period of over fifty years her voice sounded like someone scraping a pot-spoon around a rusty barrel. "So good to see you. And who," she asked suddenly breathless, turning one shoulder coquettishly towards Stanley, "is this lovely man?"

Stanley had seen Noni coming towards them — everybody had — and he was alarmed. Closer examination, once he got past the blinding sun of her approach, indicated that the woman appeared to be under several, some probably permanent, layers of make-up. At first, she held a hand out to be shaken or possibly kissed, but before he could take hold of it she had somehow managed to bump into his front and they were standing breast to pelvis: her breast, his pelvis. It was not a situation with which Stanley had experience. Noni did not come up to his Adam's apple and she leaned away so that she could better see his face. She beamed up at him and she was, he was terrified to realize, what could only be described as wizened. Stanley's fascination with Noni's visage was, however, short lived. He was becoming aware that his groin seemed to be being manipulated in some fashion by the woman's stomach.

"Noni, love," said Hector, oblivious to these goings-on, "You remember Fanny. And this is Stanley Parkinson, my co-producer. Stanley is a banker."

Noni moaned orgasmically. Second only to things theatrical, she liked men who had money, and bankers had money. She had none. "Hello, Stanley," she cooed. The flutter of false eyelashes created a slight draught between them. She turned to stand leg to leg with him, managing to secrete her hand underneath his jacket as she did so. Stanley's momentary relief at having his front freed, faded when he felt this hand slowly descend and begin to caress his bottom. He almost yelped.

"Hello, Miss Figueroa!" he said, sounding like a boy soprano. "It's good to meet you."

"Stanley!" growled the redoubtable Miss Figueroa. "Stanley! One of my favourite names. I shall call you Stan. Stan is the man, eh, Fanny?"

Stanley cast supplicant looks in Fanny's direction, but as long as Noni kept her claws off Hector, Fanny wasn't about to stop them from going in any other direction.

"Stan is quite a man," she replied playfully, and winked at him.

Before anything else could be said, a bell rang. The doors to the dining room opened and the mass of hungry lady pensioners began to surge forward.

"Let us through! Out of the way!" Noni called out in her gravelly contralto, "We're in the private dining room." Such was the force of her personality or, at least, the clarity of her diction, that the four of them were allowed through the throng. Hector led the way holding hands with Fanny. Noni wound up the rear, shepherding Stanley along, her fingers still clasping his buttock. It took no urging for him to move forward.

Hector wanted to get through the crowd as quickly as possible. Usually, he liked being looked at, but his experience with retirement residences was that they contained a preponderance of older females, many of whom were possessed of predatory stares that went beyond merely admiring his talent to amuse. It had been Fanny who first explained this phenomenon to him.

"Hector, look around you," she had said. "These places have far more women than men. Their menfolk died years ago. They haven't seen a handsome man — hell, they've hardly seen any man — for God knows how long. Then you come along. Catnip is what you are, my love. What do you expect them to do? Just be kind to them."

Hector was a kind man, but he could not get over the fact that he felt threatened by so many blue rinses and so much osteoporosis. The number of walkers and walking sticks did not help. They unnerved him and they made him wonder how he would survive if something happened to Fanny and he ended up in one of these places. It did not bear thinking about. Just then the handles of two walkers ahead of them snarled and any movement forward ground to a halt.

"We'll have to wait a mo'," said Hector over his shoulder nervously. "It seems as though there is a traffic jam ahead." And raising his voice so that Stanley could hear him over the general din, he shouted, "We should have a good crowd out, Stanley. A great crowd."

Stanley was unable to respond. Noni's fingers were touching places only his physician had touched before and he was sweating profusely. In any other situation he would have told Noni to stop what she was doing, but what she was doing was so beyond anything he had experienced that he was at a loss for words. He could not tell her to desist because he simply did not have the vocabulary to do so, so he began a series of pelvic contortions that pushed him forward on his toes, his shoulders writhing as he went. When at last he was able to turn round and face Noni he was out of breath. She was grinning up at him and her tongue was slowing licking her upper lip. He was speechless.

Dinner did not improve matters. Noni, seated on his left, kept reaching over to take samples of his food with her left hand. Her right hand played chords up and down his thigh. Fanny eventually took mercy on him.

"Noni, how come you don't perform these days?" she asked sweetly. The answer was a diatribe about professional standards, casting aspersions on the legitimacy of several of the producers around town. "I auditioned for the innkeeper's wife in Les Miz but those bastards said I was too old to play Éponine's mother." She drew herself to her full height. Her bosom was still below the level of the table. "Me!" she cried, dramatically. "I would have aced the part." The act of pulling herself upwards brought on a coughing fit that caused concern among her guests, but it allowed Stanley a few minutes of relief since her hand was needed elsewhere as she pressed it against her chest trying to draw air into her rattling lungs.

Fanny decided to have some fun: payback for a dalliance forty years past.

"Hector, why didn't you ask Noni to be in the cabaret? Noni, you would have been great."

Hector looked at his wife malevolently. Working with Noni was not something anyone looked forward to. She could have upstaged Olivier in his prime if she put her mind to it, and Hector had no intention of sharing the spotlight with such an inveterate scene-stealer. She would change the script and insert a fandango if it got her applause. She had been known to strip naked to get a standing ovation. That had worked fine in the original production of Hair, but what people remembered was when she did it in Shakespeare's 'Shrew'.

"Yes, Hector, darling, why didn't you?" Noni asked the question imperiously."Why not?"

Hector blustered. "Noni, my dear! It's just amateur night. A few people from the church and Stanley here doing one song."

Fanny, enjoying herself thoroughly, remonstrated with him. "But Hector, my love, you are doing three numbers. At least, I think it's three."

Noni shouted. "Three songs? Darling, you don't have the voice for three songs. You'll sound like an old toad before you finish! You had a sweet voice, but it was small and it never carried by the time you got to the third act. God knows, you were always best before the second intermission."

Hector swelled. "I was always good, my dear. Better than good." He struck a pose and looked at her down his nose. "Great, in fact. While you, my dear, always lacked that inner spark that would have taken you to the next level. Fine for the Factory but lacking something for the Alex."

Then, to Stanley's surprise, both Hector and Noni began to laugh.

"You devil, you!" cried Noni.

"Vixen!" responded Hector.

Even Fanny joined in. Only Stanley sat there, slack-jawed, thinking to himself that he'd never understand theatre people and that he didn't want to and if that woman was to touch him again he'd have to a coronary.

The concert did not go off without a hitch. Everyone arrived on time but Noni's introductions of the performers tended invariably to come back to some anecdote about her own career in the theatre. In the end, Hector had to wrest the microphone from her. The tussle between them did not bode well and his dulcet tones, as he stood there dapper in his tuxedo when he finally got hold of it, only partially placated the audience.

Of the performers, some were better than others. The young soprano from the choir had difficultly getting started when a woman in the audience shouted out that the singer was her granddaughter and she had not been to see her for months and how her mother was a cow and it was no wonder. The soprano's grandma was, in fact, safely at home watching the Jays, but the woman in the audience managed to convince several of the people around her otherwise, before she was led away by her nurse.

An angel-faced young tenor, also from the choir, had no better luck. Many of the ladies present fell in love with him. Unfortunately, they expressed this emotion by beginning to clap every time he took a breath. This completely threw him for a loop, particularly since he was having difficulty hearing Laddie on the piano at the back of the room. Laddie, tipsy but entirely professional, scanned the women in the audience and, on the whole, found Vera to be preferable. Decisions would have to be made, but not quite yet, he decided. Vera herself was pale but competent. More so, it should be said, than Mabel Green. When it came to her turn, Mabel clambered onto the small stage and viewed her audience as though she were standing in front of a firing squad.

Hector leaned over to Fanny and whispered, "Oh my lord, she's going to freeze."

And freeze Mabel did. Nothing came out of her mouth. The audience stared at her and she stared back at them. Then, through the silence, a small voice was heard.

"Oh my," it said, "Isn't that Mabel Green?" A pause. "I thought she was dead."

The words revived Mabel. She clamped her eyebrows together and surveyed the throng.

"No, Moira Livingstone, I'm not dead. Shut up and listen."

Thus restored to life, Mabel monotoned her way through her recitation without, it seemed, once taking a breath. When she was finished, she turned and walked off the stage without waiting for any applause and without hearing it when it came. Not that much did.

Stanley, next after Mabel, his mind still busy parsing Noni's ministrations, did not have time to be nervous and finished his piece before he knew it. He was rewarded with considerable applause from the many ancient Brits in the audience and a big kiss from Fanny. She held his face between her two hands and said, "Bravo, Stanley, bravo!" He was in heaven. He didn't mind where Fanny put her hands.

It was left to Hector to round out the evening. His performance was exemplary. Given a standing ovation at the end, he bowed and beamed before finally calling the other performers back onto the stage to take a bow.

"You have been," he began, "a wonderful audience. Just wonderful." He sounded a bit like Lawrence Welk. "So much love here!" he said, sweeping his arm across the room to encompass every person there. "Thank you for having us. Thank you so much." And, prearranged with Laddie, he began to sing the old Vera Lynn song, "We'll meet again..."

For Hector, at least, the evening was a triumph, but Noni had her own triumph too. She had persuaded Hector to let her sing one of Eartha Kitt's songs at the newly named Fall Follies.

Scripts And Superstitions

The applause at Beacham Hall Place allowed Hector to climb into bed that evening a happy man. Fanny was not at all surprised, however, to wake early next morning and see him sitting up against his pillow, notepad on his lap, nibbling the side of his thumb.

She sighed. "Oh, Hector. What now! Everything went well last night and you've got, what is it, four more weeks to pull the play together. Relax." She reached across to place a hand on his arm. "I don't want you stressing yourself and making yourself sick."

Hector pulled away and waved his notepad in her face.

"Fanny, there's so much to do. The play is a mess. Look at this list. They were supposed to bring in suitable clothes but no one has. Clarence has just — finally! — begun to do the actual work on the lighting. We need to dress the set. I spoke to them about dressing the set and they didn't know what I was talking about! And more than everything else, they don't know their bloody lines, Fan, they don't know their lines." The tragic tone in which Hector declaimed this last statement made his wife smile, but it did not make it any the less true, as she realized.

"You should take their scripts away from them at the next rehearsal. Scare them. That will teach them."

It was Hector's turn to sigh. "If I took their scripts away it would be like watching a silent movie for crying out loud. Only Faun would be speaking — and she could do the whole thing as a monologue."

"Well, tell them next time that this is their last time with a script and that there'll only be a prompter after that."

"I don't know, Fan. I just have a feeling that something is going to go desperately wrong." Hector shook his head and slid down into the bed and, the showman in him temporarily winning out over the worrier, pulled the sheet over his head.

Fanny punched his chest, "Well, you won't know until it does, so get up and get ready for church."

It looked for a while as though Hector might be wrong. At the Tuesday rehearsal, he issued an ultimatum about the script and told his cast that they would not be allowed on stage the following week if they were still using it. This caused a great deal of mumbling but the wisdom of what he was saying was obvious and everyone promised to set to and be prepared at the next run through. Hector also declared that everyone was going to be measured for costumes. The play was set in the not too distant past and, initially, Hector had seen no reason why they should have to use the services of a theatrical costumer when most of the people in the church dressed as though they were still living in the past anyway, but if he didn't decide one way or the other, the lot of them were likely to be wandering round with no clothes on at all. Fanny spent almost an hour taking measurements, measurements that the actors invariably chose to dispute. Roger St. John Mountjoy, for instance, stated unilaterally that that could not possibly be his waist measurement and he refused to let her anywhere near his inseam.

Apart from his actors, and perhaps above everything else, Hector wanted to see how the production would look. This led to him delivering a lecture on dressing the stage. "We need to make the set look lived in," he began. "It can't just be a bare drawing room. Look around at home and see if you have anything suitable for a drawing room in the 1930s." Privately, Hector was of the opinion that if Mabel Green were to transport her entire living room to the church, they would have everything they could possibly need. "Let's see what we can come up with for next week."

"I have an old black and white television, I can bring in," offered Roger, raising his hand, "if someone can help me lift it."

Stanley, bored silly sitting up front in his role of co-producer, heard Hector mutter under his breath, "Christ Almighty, I'll kill him yet," but what Hector said aloud was, "That's wonderful, Roger old boy, but we're thinking the thirties here, not the fifties."

"Ah," replied Roger, as though the wisdom of the ages was being imparted to him. "Um. What about an old ice box then?"

"I might be wrong, Roger, but I don't think that bed and breakfasts kept their iceboxes in their drawing rooms. Not generally." Hector spat out the words. "Let's see what we can come up with, eh, folks."

It was at the next rehearsal that Hector's fears about things going wrong came true. He had been held up by a late appointment at the dentist and arrived to find his cast already on stage. No longer allowed to have their scripts in hand, they were uncertain and skittish. Hector had already opened his mouth to offer words of encouragement when he noticed that a large mirror had been hung on the back wall of the set above the sideboard on which breakfast crockery and cutlery for the guests at the B and B was to be laid out. The mirror was some five feet tall and almost two feet wide. It faced the audience and it dominated the set. Hector could see himself in it from the third row.

"Lord love us!" he croaked, "Who put that up there?"

Stanley had been waiting for Hector's approbation. He and Faun had taken the mirror from their guest bedroom and manhandled it into the car to bring it to the church. Clarence, abetted by monosyllabic grunts, had hung it at their direction.

"I brought it," Stanley said, "It was Faun's grandmother's, so it fits the period."

"Take the damn thing down!" Hector was practically shouting and Fanny, just now coming into the hall from the kitchen, ran forward to hush him. "Oh, God, Fanny," he wailed to her despairingly, "We're sunk!"

This was not the response Stanley had hoped for. The cast, taken aback by Hector's outburst, shuffled sideways on the stage and surveyed the mirror cautiously. Faun, standing next to her husband, was about to give Hector a piece of her mind when Fanny, elbowing her agitated spouse aside, spoke up.

"I'm sorry to say," she explained, smilingly trying to diffuse the tension that had enveloped the room, "that a mirror on stage is regarded as bad luck. Very bad luck." With a nervous laugh, she added, "Hector gets quite upset about these things."

"Never mind bad luck," Hector blustered, pointing at the mirror. "The audience would be able to see itself watching the play — not to mention that the footlights would be shining in the thing." He turned to Stanley. "Stanley, old chum, it'll never do, I'm afraid. I'll have Clarence take it down."

Seeing that Stanley was upset, Fanny went over to him. She whispered ruefully into his ear, "There's another reason no one ever has a mirror on stage: actors tend to get distracted and forget their lines when they see themselves in them. Heaven knows our lot are having enough difficulty as it is. Can you imagine what would happen if Roger caught sight of himself half way through his big scene?" She gave a conspiratorial giggle and squeezed Stanley's bicep.

Fanny's words mollified Stanley, but he would have been less than human if part of him had not enjoyed the disastrous rehearsal that followed. Hardly anyone knew their lines although everyone tried to take a stab at them. Awkward pauses occurred while people waited to be spoken to and, on more than one occasion, wrong lines elicited wrong responses so that the play would have lurched forward with whole speeches missing had not Hector, standing on a wobbly chair in the second row, and, acting as prompter, bellowed the correct words at the top of his voice. Fanny was concerned that he would have a heart attack. Faun who knew every one of her lines and everyone else's too, did not help. Hoping to assist her fellow players, she took to hissing their lines at them like a ventriloquist. This had the effect of annoying everyone around her and it was left to Mabel Green who couldn't, it seemed, recall a single sentence in her script, to deal with her. "Will you shut up!" said Mabel turning on Faun when, for the third time, she tried to help her out, "You're upsetting my concentration." And peering out to the auditorium, Mabel called out to Hector, "Mr. Hammond, will you tell this woman to stop it. She's treading on my lines."

Hector had no idea where Mabel had picked up this theatrical expression — which she was using incorrectly — but he had had enough and called for a break. Clarence had arrived to remove the dread mirror and Hector wanted it gone as soon as possible.

"All right everyone," he said. "Break time. Fifteen minutes. Have a wee look at your part while you're at it." He added, half to himself, with considerable understatement. "It won't do any harm."

Stepping down off his chair, Hector was raising his eyes heavenward with an expression of absolute exasperation on his face when Clarence came onto the stage. The janitor had been told to remove the mirror but no one had given him a reason why it was to be done. "Looks good!" he exclaimed in a loud voice, as taciturn as ever, "Fine mirror." Laying down the tools of his trade on the sideboard, Clarence began to whistle while he worked. Hector, hearing him only too well, congealed with apprehension. Clarence had just called up another theatrical superstition: if someone whistles on stage, someone will be fired.

Of Pregnancies And Prompters

The consequences of Clarence's whistling were to remain in abeyance for the time being. Bad luck was, indeed, about to strike the Fall Follies, but its origins were not from something as mundane as mere janitorial whistling. Disasters of a medical nature were about to strike several of the performers and they would bowl a couple of them almost completely over. Stanley's mirror may not have been the cause of them, but, in his heart of hearts, it was there that Hector placed the blame, and it was there that he would direct his numerous "I told you so's" to his wife in the coming days. If Fanny did not quite believe with the same fervour as her husband, she was to come close to cursing Stanley and Faun's mirror before the Fall Follies finally took to the stage.

It all began when Vera telephoned Stanley one morning to tell him that she would not be in to work on time because she was suffering from Hyperemesis Gravidarum. Stanley had no idea what this was but said that when she did come in, he would be at a meeting. He said she should go ahead collating the reports for the coming financial year end. As a mere male, possessed of his sex's typically vague knowledge of women's uterine complexities, it took a while before Vera was able to get her point across and have him understand that she was suffering from an almost constant nausea, was vomiting hourly, and that the doctors were worried about her becoming dehydrated if she did not look after herself. To Stanley's horror, Vera informed him that it might be weeks before she would be able to return to work full time, and that she wasn't sure whether she would be able to perform in the Follies. He was not amused. Vera, with all her faults, was a competent secretary and about the only person on his floor who knew how to work the Xerox machine without jamming it. The reports were vital, of course, but Stanley also knew that she had not yet completed the revised flyers for the Follies. Plus, they were still waiting for Noni Figueroa's bio for the playbill, before it could be reformatted and go to print. Stanley hesitated to think how many reams of paper had been wasted on the programme already. About the only good piece of news was Vera's possible absence from the Follies themselves. It would serve her right.

Another person who thought it served Vera right, when he heard the news, was Laddie. Still unable to cope with the idea of incipient fatherhood, Laddie now found himself in the position of having to hold his beloved's head while she vomited noisily every time he went to see her. The role of caregiver was not likely to ease his disenchantment. If he did not show up at Vera's, she called him. If he did show up, she threw up. It was enough to drive a man to drink, and, even at the best of times, Laddie did not require a chauffeur.

So it was that a second medical disaster occurred.

Laddie, sitting in the mess of Vera's bedroom, having finally managed to get her to sleep one evening, took stock of his situation and found it wanting. Vera, without benefit of make-up, was snoring lightly across from him, a slight eddy of drool about to run down her cheek. Laddie was not a happy man. Finishing off the rye he had brought with him that evening, he looked around for someone other than himself to blame for the slough of despond in which he found himself. It was, even for Laddie, too easy to blame Vera. Through the haze of alcohol, he recognized that if the blasted woman had not gone and got herself up the duff, he would have been enjoying a nice bit of slap and tickle and, let's face it, at his age, it wasn't often he got the opportunity.

Laddie searched his marinated memory for someone else to blame. It could hardly be his Dad because he couldn't remember him. His mother had been a chorus girl in Glasgow and the belle of several balls: always good for a laugh but she never did anybody any harm. There was the old sow who had had him thrown out of his retirement home but she had gone on to her reward. Just over a little how's-your-father that wouldn't have harmed anyone. He shouldn't have taken Hector's advice and just up and left: he should have fought it. Hector had said to let it drop and move on, but moving on had taken him to a piss poor flat in the boonies and to Vera as well if, it came to that. So there he had it: it was Hector who was to blame. It was Hector who had introduced him to Vera. Well, he'd just have to have it out with him, that's all, and right away. Just as soon as he'd had another little swig to whet his whistle.

Hector and Fanny had spent the evening with Stanley and Faun — not that any of the four had particularly enjoyed it.

"I think Stanley is not exactly a happy camper these days, my love," Fanny had said on their way home after the Thursday practice. "He's finding it difficult to cope with Vera being away from work as well as having to chase Clarence all over the church to get anything done."

Clarence had a reputation for disappearing into the bowels of the building whenever his labour was required. Stanley, in charge of hanging the old curtains and making sure that any rips in them were invisible, did not understand the technical aspects of the task and needed Clarence's supposed expertise, not to mention his brawn. Stanley's frustration with not being able to get the job finished was evidenced by an increasing testiness. The need to finalize refreshments with Mabel — a second time — had put an extra burden on him as well. We won't even mention the mirror. When he began to snap at Fanny, she knew that some tender love and care was required.

"Let's have them out for Thai tomorrow night, eh?"

Hector's mind was otherwise occupied. The play continued to go badly. His actors hiccuped their dialogue along and at least one of them seemed to have developed Tourette's. The awkward pauses in what were meant to be sophisticated conversations were giving him heartburn.

"Hector! Are you listening to me, love?" Fanny shook Hector's shoulder. "Is it okay to invite them out for dinner?"

Hector roused himself. "Okay, sure," he replied. "It will do us good to have an evening away from it all."

Fanny had another reason for wanting the four of them to get together. As much as she wanted to keep her husband content, with things percolating nicely along, part of her was feeling neglected. All of Hector's energies were going into preparations for the big night. Well, if he wasn't going to pay her the attention she deserved, there was always Stanley. A little harmless flirtation would be fun.

"I'll phone Stanley and fix a time then, shall I?" she said, smiling. "Just leave it to me."

Stanley's enthusiasm when he told Faun about the dinner surprised her. He didn't like Thai food and she couldn't remember when they had had it last. Sitting down to eat with Hector was not something to which she looked forward, but the more she knew about the upcoming Follies the better. Still undecided about the exact spoke she intended to put in Hector's wheel, every detail she could find out about the evening would help. Stanley moaned on to her about Vera and the programme and how ticket sales were going, but that wasn't the kind of detail she was after.

The evening provided information aplenty and Faun sat quietly, absorbing it like a sponge. She couldn't see that the Laddie situation would be of use. She was pretty certain that Hector would be able to find a substitute from among his acquaintance if Laddie didn't turn up. On the Vera side, Faun knew quite well that even if Vera were to spontaneously combust, Stanley would get everything done. He always did. As for the Follies themselves, the cabaret seemed to be out as an avenue of revenge since, again, Hector would be able to bring in substitutes from the outside. Stanley had told her all about the dreadful Noni — well, an abridged version anyway. The time for refreshments was also out. Stanley was so frazzled by having to deal with Mabel Green that Faun hadn't the heart for anything to go wrong there. No, she decided, it would have to be the play and you didn't have to be a theatrical critic to know that there was plenty that could go wrong with that. Faun gave a small gurgle of merriment at the thought that it probably wouldn't even need her assistance for the play to be a dreadful mess. It already was.

Hector made this exact point while they were picking lemon grass out of their teeth after the soup.

"It will be the first play in my career," he moaned, "in which the prompter should get top billing."

Fanny laughed.

"You can laugh all you want, my love, but with two weeks to go, I'm practically hoarse bawling my head off by the end of the first run through and I can see that blighter Roger reading his part off his shirt cuff. I am still having to feed every line to Mabel and to just about everyone else as well." He turned to Faun adding hastily, "Present company excepted of course, my dear."

Faun smiled shyly, but to throw a little fuel on the fire of Hector's ire, said gently, "I don't see what the problem is, really I don't. It's not as though anyone has a long part and it's only a one-act play." Here she paused thoughtfully, took a breath and continued, "It's not really for me to say but..." she paused, "well, I think the core of the problem is Mabel. If you didn't have Mabel, the others would do so much better. Don't you think?"

If Faun did not want the redoubtable Ms. Green to be vexed with Stanley, there was no reason at all why she should not be vexed with Hector, and the more vexed the better.

Hector sighed. "Easier said than done, my dear. I'd get her out if I could, but it would be easier to shift Stonehenge than to get that woman to budge."

"What about offering her something else?" suggested Stanley. "I mean move her off the stage completely. It's not that big a part and she'd still be doing her recitation. Appeal to her vanity, you know. Make her think we can't do without her."

"What a great idea, Stanley," said Fanny, giving his hand a squeeze.

Stanley blossomed. "Something that would make her feel more important. Something that would sound good, but wouldn't be visible on the night.

The four sat masticating their mango salad for several moments before Faun came up with a solution. She wasn't certain that Hector would go for it, but she could try.

"What about," she began tentatively, "what about making her prompter? After all Hector, you can't be prompter at the actual performance. You are the director. You will have far too much to think about to be the prompter as well." She added judiciously, "And with her gone from the play, the others would be able to learn their parts and she would have nothing to do on the night."

If there was much that did not hold water in Faun's suggestion, we must remember that her audience was residing in the middle of a desert.

Fanny slowly began to nod agreement. "You could sell her on it by saying how important it is for someone with a good clear voice, who knows the play, to be the prompter."

"How it has to be someone who can follow the script and be decisive and able to jump in at a moment's notice when necessary," added Faun thoughtfully.

"Yes, but would it work?" Stanley expressed his doubt cautiously. "If she had to speak, to really prompt someone, the whole audience would hear her right to the back row."

Faun could have kicked him. "Ah yes, Stanley," she said, "but with Mabel gone, they'll all know their parts and there will be no need for her at all." She beamed at Hector. "You'd see to that, wouldn't you, Hector? That they'd all know their lines. Wouldn't they?"

"By Jove, it might work!" A deluded Hector nodded. "It might just work."

A Diva Disinterred

It wasn't until he was safe in bed that night that Hector began to have second thoughts — not about whether he could whip his cast into shape, but rather whether he would be able to persuade Mabel that the work-a-day job of prompter could be more consequential than her being seen, in all her finery, on stage. He was just about to voice his concerns to Fanny when Laddie called and announced he was on his way over.

"For Heaven's sake, what does he want?" Fanny asked when he told her who it was. "You go see him, I need my beauty sleep."

"You will never need beauty sleep, my love," said Hector, patting her on her rump. "I think he wants to talk about Vera."

"Again?" Fanny moaned into her pillow.

"Still!" replied Hector, putting on his dressing gown. "I'll call you if I need help."

"Don't you dare!" The reply was muffled and sleepy.

Hector had poured Laddie a double scotch even before he opened the door and he handed it to him with trepidation. Evidently, it would not be the first Laddie had had that evening. Hector was surprised, however, to learn that he was the target of Laddie's ire.

"Why did you have to get me involved in these damn Follies in the first place?" Laddie asked the question and remained standing. "Couldn't you have found someone else?"

Hector appealed to his vanity. "Come on, Laddie, old boy. You're the best there is. Who else would I get?"

"You didn't need the best for this lot." Laddie shot a bitter glance back at Hector as he downed the scotch and held out the glass for a refill. "They're not exactly top draw, are they?"

It was not wise to impugn Hector Hammond's ability to choose talent. "They're a good, amateur group, Laddie. Some of them could be professional."

Laddie downed the refill. He was beginning to sway ominously. "Yeah!" he said, "And some of them couldn't carry a tune in a handbag. And that Stanley Parkinson. He has as much stage presence as the ruddy lamppost he's on about. Stands there as though someone shoved a broom up his arse."

There was a certain truth to Laddie's comment, but Hector was not about to condone an attack on his friend. "They're not supposed to be professional. It's a church do. A fun evening."

It was at this point that Laddie, who, in part, had gone to see Hector to enlist his support in finding a solution to his problems, made a strategic mistake. He handed the empty glass back to his host, saying as he did so, "And you, you've seen better days. You're supposed to follow the beat not beat it to death."

Now it was true that Hector had a tendency to go his own way during a performance, sometimes using the accompaniment as a mere placeholder for his showmanship, but it would have been a brave director who dared point this out to him. And Laddie wasn't a director at all. He was the bloody pianist. Hector stared at Laddie and shoved the replenished glass back at him.

Laddie emptied it in one and warmed to his theme. "Couldn't work out where you were supposed to be the other night. All over the place, you were. About as much musical finesse as Florence Foster blooming Jenkins."

We must digress momentarily. The Ms. Jenkins to whom Laddie referred was a woman of means in the 1930s and 40s who hired venues across America to entertain the populous with what she called her singing and what everyone else referred to as caterwauling. Laddie's was a low blow and it was, quite simply, untrue. It was, however, a fuse to Hector's fury. He pulled himself up to his full height and his bosom swelled.

"Why you little...," he began. The noun he intended to bestow on Laddie was destined to remain unsaid. Even as Hector took a breath to spit the word at the former friend standing unsteadily in front of him, he was aware of a sensation of tightness across his chest and the sound of a pulse beating thunderously in his ears. Suddenly he was hot and he could not speak. His body began to sway in counterpoint to Laddie's. The bottle of single malt slipped from his hand and he began to sink slowly to his knees. The pain in his chest was sharp, but Hector had had worse in the past and the professional part of him managed to make sure that the sinking was played to effect. He clutched Laddie's arm on the way down and essayed a look of resigned acceptance as he did so. It was a pity he had so small an audience.

His audience, however, although it had imbibed enough to flatten many another individual, was still standing, and it was, moreover, blearily aware that it may have gone too far. One did not, under any circumstances, liken anyone, and certainly not one's chum of many years' standing, to Florence Foster Jenkins. No wonder, he managed to think, that Hector had gone into a faint; he would have done the same thing himself.

"Jesus, Hector," he said, slurring the words and covering Hector's head with a fine spray of saliva, "I didn't mean it. You know I didn't mean it." This apology, if it was one, having no effect whatsoever since Hector now lay semi-comatose at his feet, Laddie did the only thing he could think to do next, and cried out, "Fanny! Hector is dead!"

Fortunately for all concerned Hector was not dead, although Fanny herself nearly collapsed on seeing him when she emerged half asleep from the bedroom. It wasn't the first time that something like this had happened and she had the presence of mind to call for an ambulance before she turned to slap a blubbering Laddie who kept repeating that he hadn't meant it.

In the event, it was decided at Sunnybrook that Hector had not suffered a full blown heart attack but what he had had was a warning that he should take very seriously. He was allowed to return home the following afternoon. Fanny waged an almighty battle to persuade him to give up the Follies but she waged it in vain. If nothing else, Hector was determined to perform and to make Laddie eat his words. As far as he was concerned, if Vera had triplets it would serve Laddie right. He would, he vowed, never have another word to say to him and he would rather stick his hand into the fires of hell than be his best man and he would be delighted to tell him so. Just as soon as the Follies were over. Whichever way you sliced it, Laddie was still the best accompanist around.

The one thing that Fanny did manage to accomplish was that Hector agreed, after threats that she would leave him, not to attend the next practice of the play or the cabaret. She herself would be perfectly able to represent his views. Indeed, the absence of their leader turned out to have a beneficial effect on all concerned. Everyone — the players, the singers and the dancers — all of them determined to do better. Fanny spoke privately to Stanley, describing what had happened to Hector as an 'episode' and stating that the two of them — she and Stanley — would have to bear the weight of the Follies between them. Simultaneously managing to infer that Hector would be all right in the long run and that she and Stanley soon might somehow be together in perpetuity, Fanny jockeyed her husband's partner along to the degree that Stanley also found himself agreeing to be the one who would speak to Mabel Green about the role of prompter as well as about the refreshments, which, he had to admit, he hadn't gotten around to doing quite yet anyway.

Mirror, Mirror On The Wall

Obtaining Mabel's agreement to be prompter proved less fraught than anyone could have imagined. Stanley arrived at her house in a state of trembling only to find that it was Mabel's schnauzer's turn to have a medical emergency. The unfortunate pooch, Prussian to its side whiskers, had long determined that no other animal — of any species — was to be allowed onto Mabel's property. When, therefore, a meter reader appeared, as was his wont, and passed through the garden gate, little Bitzie, previously semi-somnambulant on the driveway, launched an attack that would not have disgraced Field Marshal Rommel and his Africa Corps. In the meter reader, however, the teutonic canine found that it had met its match. Reaching back to high school days as a field goal kicker at Northern Secondary, the meter reader connected with the approaching jaw of the highly strung animal and lobbed it across the lawn into Mabel's open garage door. Stanley obtained Mabel's considerably abstracted agreement to both items on his agenda while driving a whimpering Bitzie and its distraught mistress to the vet.

 The amiable Bitzie was not, however, the only being associated with the Fall Follies to be found mewling in the presence of the medical profession in these last days leading up to the performance. Noni Figueroa had been mightily pleased with herself when she persuaded Hector to allow her to appear in the cabaret. True, she thought, it was only for one song, but who knew where it might lead. The chances that a director in dire need of a headliner might be in the audience seemed remote, but stranger things have happened in the theatre and one had to be prepared. Noni's mirror, when she came to stand in front of it to see how she was looking these days, proved less than reassuring, however. She could, and would, increase her stature with stiletto heels and a bouffant hairdo. She could, and definitely would, try for an illusion of sveltness with corsetry and strict adherence to the crash diet she intended to begin the next evening as soon as she had finished dinner. But, and it was a big 'but,' a 'but' she could see right there staring back at her, the face left something to be desired. Noni would have been less than the trooper she was if she did not admit it. Truth be told, Noni's face was a roadmap of her life and her life had been full of highways as well as byways, not to mention boulevards, avenues, crescents and more than a few cul de sacs. She could, she thought as she peered at her reflection, see an autobahn or two running across her forehead as well.

Sighing heavily, Noni pressed the palms of her hands to her cheeks and pulled them aside. It took some doing, but eventually the skin on her face became taut — even if, by the time she was satisfied, her ears were almost touching each other at the back of her head. A rather oriental creature stared back at her. Noni put her tongue out at it and attempted to raise her eyebrows. This proving impossible, she tried a smile instead. The result was not happy. For a while now, Noni had what, in the quiet of her boudoir, she admitted to herself were 'old lady lips'. She had not realized, however, that these too were a thing of the past. What she had now was no lips at all. Pursing them did not help and when she made a moue, the gesture was so unappetizing that she had to turn away.

There was nothing else for it. She would have to take the plunge. She had been thinking about it for several years, and although she really could not afford it, it would have to be done nevertheless. If half of Hollywood could do it these days, why couldn't she? It was probably what had been keeping her on the sidelines for so long. She needn't go to Yorkville and those expensive salons and spas to get it done; there must be cheaper places. Out a bit down on Queen, perhaps, or off along Dundas. Noni took a deep breath. Collagen injections. That's what she'd get. That would do the trick! And, come to think of it, why not go the whole hog and go for the Botox too? Get rid of a few of those wrinkles. A real tune-up, you might say. She'd be the belle of the ball. Just wait until Hector Hammond saw her. He'd come running then.

It took a week of due diligence before Noni fixed on the place to which she would entrust her precious features. She had been shocked by the prices until she came across an ad on the back of a free newspaper that seemed to have been written just for her. A discreet little ad, nothing fancy, but it had called out to her and she felt constrained to answer: 'For a limited time only! Two for the price of one. Botox and Collagen together. Call for an appointment today and change your life.'

Noni returned to Beacham Hall Place by taxi after the two procedures, coming in through a side door looking like a Muslim woman committed to permanent purdah. She was swathed in layers of cloth and heavily veiled. She went straight to bed and, even when stumbling out of it to go to the lavatory during the night, she did not turn on the light. That she felt woozy, she put down to the pain-killers she had demanded from the lady at the Golden Spa Clinic, but it was unclear why her head seemed so much larger than she remembered it. Only in the cold light of morning did Noni dare look into a mirror. She could hardly credit it. She had expected swelling, but her whole lower face seemed elevated too. Its focal point was what could only be described as two volcanic lips that she found impossible to join together. Two smaller volcanoes of a livid red were positioned where her cheeks should have been and they threatened to reduce her eyes to mere slits. Noni Figueroa's eyes were not large to start with. Above them lay a vast expanse of virgin forehead that, when touched, felt more plaster than skin and which, for some reason, was a yellow colour that further set off the vermillion hue of her cheeks. Noni adored things flaxen or daffodil but this was ridiculous. The overall effect of her face was of a roasting turkey, glazed and in desperate need of basting. She let out a shriek that resounded through Beacham Hall Place more chillingly than Florence Foster Jenkins singing 'The Queen of the Night' at Carnegie Hall.

It took Noni some time to recover from the shock of seeing herself and longer again to stop the weeping that made her eyes disappear completely rather like a shar pei puppy. Burkahed once more in scarves and now honestly frightened, she left her residence by the side door and took herself off to the Emergency Wing at Sunnybrook. Ironically, she lay on the same gurney that Hector would lie on just a day later. She stayed there for several hours drawing the attention of staff and patients alike with a horizontal performance of dramatic moaning that in other circumstances might have merited an award. Reassured, eventually, that everything should return to normal in a few days, Noni was sent home in an ambulance that she insisted drop her off several blocks from her residence.

Noni did not leave her room for a week. She claimed, through closed doors, to be infectious. Her face did gradually improve but at seven days to the Fall Follies she still looked like someone in the second row of the chorus of 'Turandot.' Determined, however, to appear, Noni began to experiment. Make up might, she hoped, both enhance her natural vivacity and, at the same time, tone down some of the seemingly permanent alterations to her features. In the end, she was forced to admit that vivacity was out: her face was incapable of movement even when she pushed the skin around with the heel of her hand. She was marginally more successful with her eyes. They could be enlarged when circled about with copious amounts of mascara. False eyelashes were useless: they had the effect of hiding the actual eye behind a shrubbery of spiky vegetation. In the end though, it was the lips that gave her most pause. There was no sign that they were beginning to deflate and lipstick only served to advertise their prominence. Her mouth continued to resemble an extremely angry carbuncle.

Needless to say, Ms. Figueroa refused to show up at rehearsals. She did not need to rehearse, she said. She was a professional. She said this over the telephone and if Hector thought her words sounded rather pouty he did not say so. Tired and apprehensive that an argument with Noni might bring on another episode like the one with Laddie, Hector tried to remain calm. On the surface, he had made up with Laddie, although he would never forgive him. He had ceased to worry about whether the cast of his play knew their lines. Popping another pill helped. Mabel Green had not come to rehearsals given Bitzie's condition, but he sought comfort in the fact that she would be there as prompter on the night. Moreover, her replacement in the play had proved to be a member of the congregation who could actually speak and move at the same time. Between hope springing eternal and the increasing doses of artificial placidity that he was ladling into himself unbeknownst to Fanny, Hector was cautiously optimistic that everything might, indeed, turn out all right on the night.

A Weighty Dress Rehearsal

Hector was to be disabused of his optimism at the dress rehearsal. It did not help that Fanny had caught him in the bathroom chomping on his little white pills as though he were feasting on Smarties. She confiscated them forthwith and gave him a lecture on keeping his body pure and holy. Since it was many years since his body had been 'pure' and there was not much about Hector that could loosely be termed 'holy,' he put on a fine act of contrition and began to plot obtaining replacements. In this he was unsuccessful and, in the next two days, his nerves grew more taut than the skin on Noni's face. All of this, however, was minor compared to the nightmare that the dress rehearsal provided for his increasingly perfervid mind.

It is axiomatic in the theatre that a bad dress rehearsal augurs a good opening night. The Fall Follies dress for Mr. Archibald's play must rank high among the annals of the disastrous events that have occurred in the whole history of Canadian theatre. Only one aspect of it concerns us here, however. It was during the performance — if the running time for a rather jaunty one-act play that somehow stretched to three and a quarter hours can be called a 'performance' — that Stanley joined the ranks of the physically and pharmaceutically unfit. He, too, was to find himself laid up on a gurney at Sunnybrook and if his moaning did not quite reach the crescendos that Noni achieved, he came in a close second.

Things began ominously with several members of the cast arriving late. Tardiness was not something that Hector either understood or tolerated and the fact that there had been an accident on the subway he regarded as an excuse rather than a reason. Nor did he appreciate the fact that his cast, when finally assembled on stage in costume for the first time, behaved as though they were at a fancy dress ball with all the concomitant swanning about and raucous laughter. He had finally decided that the play should have a forties feel and the women, particularly, felt old fashioned, shrieking at the outlandishness of boxy shoulders and calf-length skirts. For Hector, putting on the clothes of a character was the last step in becoming him. For the actors in the Fall Follies it was an excuse for hilarity. Even Faun could not get over how odd she felt. She resembled her grandma. Roger St. John Mountjoy, in funereal black, strutted around the stage puffing out his cheeks and flexing his knees.

Since Mabel had announced that she would only be available for the actual performance, Hector again stood in as prompter and it was immediately apparent that the role might not be unimportant. They were hardly three sentences into the play when Roger, who should have essayed the following words, "I say, it's chilly out, what!" said, after a long pause, "Line, please!" rather like someone calling for a taxi in front of the Royal York. This drove Hector to the brink of apoplexy and stopped the play in its tracks. He spent the next five minutes explaining to Roger just how the role of prompter was supposed to work — on the rare occasion it was to be used at all, as he added with heavy emphasis — before saying that they would start over. Unfortunately, one of the other actors had decided to use the stoppage to go to the lavatory and it took several minutes for him to return. He looked rather wan. "Sorry. Nerves," was what he said when he finally took his place on stage.

In the interim, Clarence had decided to practice opening and closing the curtains. It was a sensible use of his time. They were old and the system of pulleys that accomplished the task was not working well. Enormous tugs tended to make the curtains jerk unhappily along and to assist in the task Clarence had appended to one end of the rope a large and extremely heavy weight. The weight had no real function, and it swayed back and forth at the end of the rope occasionally banging against the scenery at that end of the stage causing it to ripple as though the walls of the bed and breakfast were being buffeted by a gale force wind.

"Places, please, everyone!" Hector called out, "And close the curtain, Clarence, if you will. Stanley, would you mind dimming the auditorium lights?"

Stanley had been having a bad day. Vera had returned to work full time but she still found it necessary to walk about nursing a tureen in case of emergency. She looked as miserable as she felt and had also taken to wearing a grey wooly cardigan that had seen better days. When Stanley told her that she would need to make yet another adjustment to the programme to include a bio on Mabel's replacement in the play, she had erupted.

"Stanley," she said, hugely upset. "I can't do it. I still have the year-end reports to print and collate and then send out." She glared at him and added sarcastically, "You are aware that the bank year-end is October 31st. and that I am, in fact, employed by the bank!"

Vera had several more things she wanted to say but found it necessary to leave Stanley's office precipitously at this juncture. Stanley, recognizing the justice of her statement, had opened the document file on his computer and set to work to insert the short but necessary bio of the new player. By the time Vera returned, looking as grey as her cardigan, he had managed to ruin her carefully placed columns and delete two other bios, one of which was the extremely long one on Hector. In the end, after heavy breathing from both parties, it was decided that Stanley would collate the reports and Vera would attempt to resurrect the programme. By then Stanley was late for a meeting at which he was expected to explain why his department had not met its financial targets for the year and what he intended to do about it.

It was true that Stanley had had an unexpected success with Mabel but he was finding that the other women in his life were leaving much to be desired. In the weeks leading up to the Fall Follies, Faun had begun to take a far larger than usual interest in his welfare and this had begun to manifest itself in what he considered to be unscheduled amorous advances. He and Faun were in the habit of engaging in sexual congress twice a month on the first and third Friday, social obligations permitting. Friday was a slow night on television and it gave Stanley a chance to unwind after the stresses of the work week. What it gave Faun is not precisely known. Now, however, Stanley could hardly climb into bed without a hand feeling its way towards him and sweet nothings being whispered into the darkness. Stanley loved his wife, but he did like routine and the physical toll of the Fall Follies, not to mention worries about his song that grew exponentially as the day loomed nearer and nearer, plus the enormous workload at the bank were just about all he could handle.

On top of all that, there was Fanny. As stated, Stanley loved Faun and was having to prove it quite often, but he was in something approaching lust with Hector's. He had, so far, managed to balance the two quite nicely but he was aware that when the curtains closed on the Follies, they were also likely to close on his window of opportunity with Fanny. Hector had hinted to Stanley that the two of them might consider a January Japes or possibly a 'Sing Into Spring,' but Stanley shuddered at the thought. Were Fanny to offer herself stark naked on a bed of roses, there was no way he intended to be involved in another theatrical endeavour in any way, shape or form. Ever. However, if he could get Fanny stark naked on that bed of roses before the end of the Fall Follies, it would be another thing entirely. What was more, Stanley still had hopes that this might occur. Since Hector's coronary episode, Fanny had become more friendly than ever. You might almost even say cuddly, in fact. It was true, as Stanley dimly perceived, that she was at her most come hither when she wanted something from him, but the strength of her perfume invariably had the effect of pushing any more healthy realization into the further recesses of his brain. Stanley was not thinking with his brain.

By the time he arrived in the auditorium on the evening of the dress rehearsal, Stanley was tired, on edge and generally fed up with the world. As Hector requested, he strode silently to the back of the hall and flipped off the lights. Sitting down at the back, next to the Vicar, to watch the play, he was still able to admire the set and how well everything looked while he waited for the curtains to close.

"Curtain, Clarence, please!" Hector called out the words again, a little louder this time.

The curtains remained obstinately open.

"Curtain!" Hector barked the one word.

"By God!" the Vicar muttered under his breath, "He's in his office playing solitaire on his computer."

It was one of the congregation's little jokes, that if you could not find Clarence he had taken his laptop somewhere and was playing a card game on it. The Vicar's suspicion was almost, but not quite, correct. Clarence had determined that he could safely leave the stage. Nothing was going on. The curtains were open and ready for the play to begin. He had recently purchased an interactive game of Scrabble on which he could play against the computer and he was fast becoming addicted to it. Clarence had, in his usual monosyllabic manner, announced to one of the actors standing in the wings that he was "Off" and taken both himself and his computer 'off' to the nethermost region of the church where he thought he would be left alone for the next hour or so.

He did not, therefore, hear Hector yell the word, "Curtain!" a third time. Nor did he hear the hollow voice of Roger St. John Mountjoy call out from the wings, "He's not here."

"Streuth!" said the Vicar to Stanley, "This is beyond enough. The man will have to go."

For those keeping count, it should be stated, parenthetically, that Clarence did, in fact, lose his job shortly after this, thus proving verisimilitude to the second theatrical superstition.

The Vicar stood and shouted down to Hector, "My dear fellow, heaven alone knows where he is. Would you like me to work the curtains?"

Hector was beginning to feel a tightness in his chest and the thought of having to watch the hulk of the Vicar trundle slowly from one end of the auditorium to the other before arriving in the wings several minutes later was already giving him palpitations.

"No Vicar, you stay where you are," he said. "Stanley, could you work the curtains." It wasn't quite a question. Nor was it exactly a command. Whatever it was, it infuriated Stanley. He stood, stomped through the auditorium, stamped up the backstage stairs and marched into the wings. Faun, waiting there for her entrance could see how angry he was and reached out to pat him on the arm. Pushing past her, Stanley strode forward until he was standing in the centre of the stage. He was blinded by the footlights but he knew exactly where Hector was and he stared in that direction.

"Just what, exactly, would you like me to do?" he asked. His teeth were clenched and he stood more stiffly than a guardsman at Buckingham Palace.

Hector, oblivious to all the world, except the necessity of getting the show on the proverbial road, called out with an airy wave of his hand, "Ah, Stanley, there you are. Just close the curtains and then open them again, there's a good chap."

Stanley, devoid of words, flounced to the side of the stage. The rope that kept the curtains open was tied to a bracket on the proscenium arch. At its end, the weight swayed awkwardly. The assembled players, waiting to go on, moved aside to allow Stanley to untie the rope and when he found difficulty in doing so, they began to proffer advice on the matter. Faun, furious with Hector all over again for the way he was treating her Stanley, put a hand over her mouth and dared not say a word.

Roger did not exactly offer advice, but he did make a comment. "You might do better," he said as though addressing an immigrant with zero knowledge of the English language, "if you loosen the weight. It's holding you back."

Stanley was in a fury but he was not irrational. He could see a certain sense in what Roger was saying. He hefted the rope so that the weight came to rest on the slight protuberance of his belly. Then he pushed forward so that the heavy object was trapped between him and the wall of the proscenium. Stanley was not able to see what he was doing, but, feeling his way, he began to untie the weight, preparatory to easing it onto the floor. The players clustered around as he tried next to reach underneath the weight with his right hand the better to control its descent.

It was at this point that Hector spoke again.

"Stanley," he called out, "ready when you are, old boy."

Stanley had had enough. He took a deep breath, pulled in his stomach, and began to turn, the better to give Hector what would have been a totally incoherent piece of his mind. The weight, of course, had its own agenda. Free at last from the constraints of the rope, it determined to escape Stanley's decamping belly and decided to drop as hard and as fast as it possibly could to the security of the floor.

In this, however, it was not entirely successful. Stanley's leg was in the way. The weight hit his knee, bounced off his shin and landed on his foot.

Rude Awakenings

"Great Caesar's ghost!" Hector shot upright in bed and shook Fanny by the shoulder. "We forgot to order the flowers." It was seven o'clock on the morning of the Fall Follies and Hector had been awake for two hours worrying away at a list of things that possibly could go wrong that evening. It was a long list. He shook Fanny again. "Bouquets for the artistes! We forgot them."

Fanny moaned into her pillow. "What time is it?" she asked without any hope that it would be anywhere near ten, an hour with which she felt reasonably comfortable. "For heaven's sake, Hector, don't go and get yourself all hot and bothered. You know what the doctor said." Fanny knew what the doctor had said too. She also knew her husband and she had been dreading the day. Hector would be worrying about everything, trying to do it all, and by the middle of the afternoon he would be so tightly wound up that nothing would be able to calm him. She had seen it all too often — including the time he hyperventilated and had to breathe into a paper bag for five minutes before he could catch himself. It scared her silly then and it scared her silly now.

She turned and sat up. Hector had pieces of paper scattered all over the bed. His glasses, which he never wore in public, were perched on the end of his nose. He looked at her despairingly. Fanny shook her head. "Oh, Hector Hammond," she said with a snort of laughter, "you'll be the death of me yet. And you'll be the death of yourself first."

"But, Fan," said Hector, waving her away, "how could we forget the flowers?!" His tone was somewhere between a pout and a plea and Fanny laughed again. "Tell me, Hector, what exactly do you need flowers for? No female has a part so much bigger than any other that she should be given a bouquet, so who are you going to give them to?"

Hector was not about to give up. "But you have to have flowers. To present a bouquet. It's tradition."

Fanny looked at him shrewdly and said archly. "Of course, we could always give you a bouquet, couldn't we, my pet?"

Hector looked down his nose at her and answered airily. "Well, I was thinking that Stanley would get one too."

Fanny lay back on the pillow and frowned. "Stanley will be lucky if he is able to be there, Hector. We should phone them."

Hector was triumphant. "You see! That's why he should get a bouquet. He's been injured and he's my co-producer. You'll have to order two bouquets."

Fanny moaned again. "Is it all right if I wait until the shops open?" She glanced at her watch. "God, it's only seven fifteen. Leave me to sleep, please. Wake me when it's over." And to herself she added, "It's going to be a long day."

An upset Fanny in the morning was not a pretty sight and Hector thought better than to disturb her further, but it was not long before he crept out of the bed and made his way to the kitchen. There he made coffee and, his mind accelerating through an ever expanding index of things to do, sat down, pen in hand, notebook open in front of him. The kitchen clock seemed to have stopped and his watch, even after he shook it, was not much of an improvement, but finally they both showed that it was eight o'clock and he could wait not a minute longer to call Stanley.

It was Faun who heard the telephone. She also was in the kitchen, being as silent as possible the better not to disturb what was, she hoped, a sleeping Stanley in the guest room upstairs. The ringing was annoyance enough. The disembodied voice announcing who it was merely added fuel to her fire. The last person Faun wished to speak to was Hector Hammond. Faun had enjoyed the idea of plotting revenge on Hector but, truth be told, enjoyment of the plotting probably outweighed her thirst for revenge. Faun was not a vindictive woman. "Nasty" was never an adjective that would have sprung to the lips of anyone attempting to describe her. "Devious" even less so. Faun had always been a Christian lady who sought to live by the golden rule, willing to see the best in her fellow man.

Until two night ago.

The howl of pain that had emanated from Stanley when the weight came crashing down on his foot, and the childlike whimpering that followed, energized Faun. It was several hours before she had time to think, but a night in the emergency department at Sunnybrook, holding his hand and wiping the sweat from his forehead, convinced her that the person responsible for what had happened to Stanley was, without any shadow of a doubt, Hector Hammond. Oh, Clarence should have been there and, yes, he was a fool to have tied the weight to the rope in the first place, but Clarence was a known idiot and couldn't have been expected to do better. Hector, the great impresario, the man who demanded obedience from all, the martinet who issued commands as though he were a second Moses, he was the one responsible. The elements of enjoyment and day dreaming in Faun's plotting evaporated. They were squeezed out by a burgeoning thirst for a revenge that, so far from being served cold, would be as sizzling hot as the skillet on the stove in front of her.

When the telephone rang, Faun was brooding about how this revenge might be accomplished. She had spent a sleepless night alone in the double bed upstairs deliberating similarly and she knew that she would also spend her day in the same manner until she settled on a plan of action and possibly even until that plan, whatever it might be, moved from being a plan to being action itself.

Breathing in through pinched nostrils — not the easiest of tasks at the best of times — Faun picked up the telephone.

"Yes," she said. Her voice was like glass, hard and brittle.

"Faun, my love, is that you?" asked Hector, never having heard in her voice what he was hearing now, but attempting his trademark affability nevertheless. "How is the patient this morning?"

Faun's nostrils flared. "He's about as well as can be expected," Her voice was almost without inflection, each word bitten off before the next was uttered.

"Ah, um, yes!" Hector was a trained actor and, in any case, a man not without the ability to read the emotions of his fellows, but this morning he had a great many things on his mind and having learnt that Stanley had not gone on to his reward, that mind jumped, flea-like, onto other things. Part of him gathered that something was amiss but his initial question asked and answered and with Stanley's demise off the table, the rest of him hurried on to his tick-sheet of things that had to be brought to heel to ensure the successful outcome of the Follies.

"Will he be able to collect the programmes from his office or should he ask Vera to bring them, do you think?"

Concern about the programmes was reasonable enough. They were ready and waiting in Stanley's office downtown. There could hardly be a Follies without a programme and they would have to be brought to the church. The phrasing of the question left a little to be desired, however. Faun, to coin a cliche, could not believe her ears. Would a non-ambulatory Stanley be able to collect the programmes? Hardly! Would Vera? Vera's morning sickness was continuing unabated and she would be lucky if she were able to drag herself to the actual performance without having to taxi around Toronto at Hector Hammond's behest.

Faun took a deep breath. "Now, Hector," she said, with as much sweetness and light as she could muster, "don't you worry yourself. I'll make sure you get the programmes. What would we do without a programme, after all!" It was certainly a thought to conjure with. "Oh my," she added, "I think Stanley is calling me. I better go and see what he wants. You take care now. I'm sure everything will go all right. 'Bye."

Faun hung up before Hector could reply, but, as she did so, she essayed a little cough, almost tubercular in shape and sound. It was the merest beginning of a revenge plotted as well as any one act play by A. J. Archibald.

The Day Goes Slowly By

Hector was not the only person who remembered the programme. Upstairs in the guest room, Stanley had had the same thought but it was only one of many, and not one as all-consuming as the one concerning the pain that enveloped his entire right leg. This leg was swathed in a protective bandage, preparatory — he had been told — to being mummified in plaster of Paris when the swelling went down, and it throbbed. It throbbed when he moved and it throbbed when he lay still. God knew it throbbed if he tried to get more comfortable by shifting about in the bed and it throbbed with a pain that he had not believed possible when the cat jumped onto the bed to see just what was going on with Stanley who shouldn't, according to its lights, have been in this room anyway.

Stanley was not what one might call a brave man and while he might, on occasion, have been willing to pretend stoutheartedness, he was also one of those unfortunates who are completely incapable of swallowing pills. When the nurse at Sunnybrook had — finally — thrust into his outstretched hand a bunch of pain killers he had momentarily forgotten this and shovelled them into his mouth like so many breathmints. It was not until his gag reflex told him otherwise that he was reminded of his bother with pills. It had taken time to explain the situation, but liquid pain medication eventually appeared and a frightening degree of torment was replaced by a dull ache.

When he returned home, having been manhandled like a sack of potatoes en route, Stanley had overindulged the medication the hospital sent with him and a bottle, now empty of the calming elixir, stood on the night stand next to the bed. Faun had promised to go to the pharmacy to have it replenished as soon as she was dressed and he wondered what was holding her up.

"Faun!" Stanley hollered the single word as loudly as he dared. If he shouted too loudly it made the pain worse. "Have you gone yet?"

Stanley listened for an answer, but heard nothing. "Ooooooh," he moaned, rather enjoying the effect it had in the empty room. He tried it again, "Ooooooh."

The cat, ensconced now on a straight back chair against the far wall, looked on curiously but remained silent.

"Is anybody there?" Stanley essayed the question plaintively and waited for an answer.

The cat, not the brightest of felines at the best of times and morbidly obese, meowed in response, jumped off the chair and leapt again onto the end of the bed. Stanley, lying prone and only able to see the ceiling, felt it land and panicked.

"No, no, no, no, no!" he pleaded. "Keep away!" Uncertain of where the animal intended to go, Stanley could feel it moving stealthily up the bed towards him and he lifted both knees to keep out of its way. One knee moved easily; the attempt with the other made his whole being shudder.

"Help me!" he yelped. It was a plaintive call and Faun would not have heard it had she not been tiptoeing past the bedroom door getting ready to leave. She did not want to go in to see Stanley. He was not a good patient and, frankly, he could be a big baby whenever he was sick. The whole business of him not being able to swallow a pill had annoyed her ever since he had had a headache on their honeymoon and she was quite convinced that he had exaggerated every symptom he had ever had. It was, in Faun's opinion, one of Stanley's few weaknesses. She could allow that her Stanley was not a hypochondriac but she did wonder sometimes about Munchausen's Syndrome. She sighed.

"Yes, dear?" she said, putting her head round the bedroom door.

"Take this damn cat away. It's going to kill me."

Faun frowned. Tigger wouldn't hurt a fly.

"Can I get you something before I go, dear?"

"Haven't you gone yet?" Stanley moaned. "I'm in pain."

Faun came forward to plump up his pillow.

"Hector kept me back. He phoned. He was asking about the programmes."

"The programmes? The programmes!" Stanley could not believe that anyone would be asking about anything other than himself. "Didn't he ask about me?" he asked petulantly.

Faun had to smile. Her spouse was loveable even when he was being extremely childish, she thought, smoothing the hair off his forehead. "Yes, dear, of course he did, but he wanted to know who would bring the programmes to the church."

"Well, I can't do it," replied Stanley, with a thrust of his lower lip.

"No, you certainly can't." Faun patted Stanley's clenched fist.

"Do I have to think of everything?" he demanded. The sigh that followed was the stuff of martyrdom. "I'll phone security and have the programmes put in a taxi, for heaven's sake. Watch out for my leg!"

Faun had perched herself on the side of the bed, hoisting the corpulent Tigger onto her lap as she did so. She coughed.

"You know, Stanley, I think I am getting a sore throat. I'm a little hoarse. Do you think I should gargle? It seems to be getting worse."

Part of Stanley wanted to point out that Faun couldn't compare her throat to his leg, but he knew that this would be unkind.

"Well, you can't get sick now," he said. "I'm not going to be able to sing, so you'll have to be the one to represent the Parkinson name tonight."

"I suppose I will." Faun smiled wanly at her spouse. "But, you know, it hurt a little when I was eating my toast at breakfast." To illustrate her point, she held a hand across the front of her throat and swallowed.

Stanley frowned. It wasn't like Faun to be sick. She was never sick and she could not get sick now. If he were laid up, she would have to be his eyes and ears at the Follies. There were all kinds of things he had to look after and she was the only person he could rely on to get them done. Fanny would be busy with Hector and her plate would be pretty full with that, plus she had her own duties with the tickets and everything. If nothing else, Faun really had to go to the pharmacy to get some more medicine for him. His leg was throbbing fit to beat the band and her sitting around nursing the dratted cat wasn't doing it much good either.

"When are you going to the drugstore?" he asked, adding unnecessarily, given the tone of his voice and the feverish twitchings of his body, "I'm in pain."

Faun, who during the course of the conversation had decided on a definite plan of action, put her hand in front of her mouth and coughed harshly into it. "I'll go as soon as I get dressed. And I'll see what they have for my throat, too. It wouldn't do for me to end up with laryngitis, would it?"

It was an hour and a half before Faun put her head round the guest room door again. During this time several things had occurred. For one, she had parked the car in a supermarket parking lot en route to the pharmacy, and, making sure that the windows were tightly closed, coughed and spluttered and even screamed in an attempt to add verisimilitude to the story of a sore throat. Finding this ineffective, for reasons best known only to herself, she had entered the supermarket, bought a can of salted peanuts and returned to the car to eat as many of them as she could. The logic behind this, Faun said to herself, was that so many peanuts, without water, would parch her throat. Her stomach was beginning to feel rather uncomfortable when one of the peanuts went down the wrong way. Faun found herself so desperately gasping for breath, any kind of breath, that it made her previous performance of hawking and spluttering appear as amateur hour. By the time her breathing returned to any kind of normalcy, her face was wet with tears and her throat so raw that the sounds she tentatively uttered into the silence of her automobile were the merest of husky croaks.

Stanley, meanwhile, had lain in his bed in a state of ambivalence. It had finally dawned on him that, whether Faun was going to be able to perform at the Follies or not, he, in all probability, was not. All previous thoughts notwithstanding, this, now that the day was here, did not seem fair. His singing had been praised and, even if everyone seemed more surprised than anything else, he had liked the applause. The Vicar had shaken his hand and said, "Stanley, old chap, I never thought you had it in you." In his heart of hearts, Stanley hadn't either and now it seemed that all would be for naught. Stanley, who was human after all, had been conjuring with a standing ovation and now there wouldn't even be a smattering of polite applause.

There was something else, too. Stanley had only the haziest of memories of what happened immediately after the weight fell on his leg, but there was one thing he did remember and he recalled it very well. In the crush of people standing around him, he remembered that Hector had stood, for once speechless, above him, while Faun, as tenderly as possible, tried to remove his shoe — even in his pain, he had balked at the removal of his trousers — and it was left to Fanny to cradle him in her arms. Well, not so much, as it happened, in her arms as in her bosoms. One of the baubles on her necklace had tried to poke his eye out, but he had been able to dislodge it and, in doing so, he had managed to wedge his nose ever more comfortably in her décolletage. Had Faun not, at that precise moment introduced torment into his being by tugging on the heel of his shoe to ease it off, Stanley might have been in paradise.

Or perhaps not.

Unfortunately, even apart from the grim reality of what was going on with his nether portions, the feeling did not last. So wrapped up in the emotion of the event was Fanny, that she began to hug Stanley as tightly as she could. This had the unlooked for effect of pushing her luscious breasts towards each other, squeezing their pillowy selves together as it were, with Stanley's probing proboscis firmly trapped between them.

In the present, lying on a bed in that rarely used and rather empty guest room, Stanley was ambivalent. For the first time, he began to wonder whether too much of a good thing, might not be just that. Too much. To be surrounded by pulchritude was entrancing: to be trapped in it was something else. And then there was her perfume! He had, it seemed, inhaled so much of it — and Fanny had daubed it about in a very generous fashion that evening — that he could still smell it. It had impregnated his nostrils; his very sinuses had inhaled it. And, again for the first time, Stanley began to weigh the modesty of his Faun against the fecundity of Fanny — and find Fanny wanting. Reality might not yet have returned to reign in Stanley's brain, but perhaps — just perhaps — that organ was not quite as addled, as besotted, as before.

How his brain made the jump from these thoughts to the specific one that he should, somehow, perform in the Fall Follies will never be clear, but it was not long before, lying there still unable to move, that it did and Stanley, a practical man when roused, began to consider the how of it. It would be difficult, he knew, and it would hurt like hell, but, yes, with enough medication he could manage it. He nodded to himself and, thrusting out his unfortunately concave chest, said the following words aloud into the silence of the empty room, "Tonight, it's my turn."

For both our heroes, the day was interminable. Hector worried himself into a frazzle about every possible thing that came to mind from whether Fanny had a big enough float on hand to give change to people who wanted to buy their tickets at the door, to whether Roger would remember not to wear his usual brown shoes since his suit, rented for the occasion from Malabar's, was black. Stanley, on the other hand, began to worry about one thing only: how to levitate his prone self from the second floor of his semi and take it in an upright position to a stage that could only be accessed by a flight of uneven stairs. Neither man had time to speak to the other, although they would both have wished the other well for, in their own ways, they did acknowledge that the Follies were a joint venture. Hector allowed to Stanley all the accolades due to the man who organized and managed things back stage, although, truth be told, he had meddled in pretty well all of them and his wife had had a major input in several. Stanley had seen both the play and the cabaret slowly come together over the summer and was in awe of Hector's knowledge in all things theatrical, although he was well aware that his own wife was by far the best actor in the former and he himself — even if it killed him, and it might — was going to knock the socks off the audience in the cabaret. Laddie had used this phrase when he first heard Stanley sing and although Stanley thought it a little vulgar, he relished the sentiment.

Hector proved incapable of staying away from the church after three o'clock in the afternoon, arriving only slightly later than Mabel Green and the ladies who were to prepare the refreshments in the Wycliffe Room next to the auditorium. It was all he could do to refrain from issuing instructions to them but an army cannot have two commanders and as soon as he saw Mabel standing, hands on hips, by the kitchen door he knew better than to say a word, particularly as the words she barked in his direction, "Can I help you?" made him feel like an errant schoolboy who had wandered into the principal's office. The appearance of her dog, wearing a protective cone, made him want to laugh, but he knew better than dare to do it.

Hector had more success in the auditorium. There, he examined the stage, made sure that the furniture was correctly placed and moved the occasional prop to his satisfaction. He was loath to play with the curtains and shuddered once again as he remembered the fiasco of the dress rehearsal, but, in things theatrical, Hector was a perfectionist and he opened and closed them twice to see that the pulleys were working correctly and then he did it once again for good luck. When he was finished, he went back into the auditorium to see how everything looked and whether the curtains were hanging properly. Sitting in the fifth row, he sighed. It felt good to be there. Back in the theatre. It was where he belonged and if this wasn't exactly The Royal Alex it was still going to be good. Hector could feel the excitement in the air, and he had that anticipatory feeling he always had in the hours before a curtain went up. Soon, he would begin to feel ever so slightly nauseous. He rubbed his hands together and grinned. By the time the lights went down, he would be sweating. It was a longtime practice to use his Old Spice as a deodorant before a performance. He must remember to do it. It was a ritual, and, like many performers, Hector believed in his rituals.

He would have stayed longer: he felt as at home in a theatre as he did in his own apartment, but he had promised to pick Fanny up from the hairdresser and he did not want to be late. He walked up the slight incline to the back of the auditorium, his footsteps echoing in the empty stillness. At the door, he turned and surveyed the empty room. Well, he thought, I've done everything I can. It's up to them now. Gently sucking on his lower lip, he blew out his cheeks and, silently, said a little prayer. "Lordy, Lordy, Lordy, see what you can do to get them through the night," he prayed, laughing ruefully to himself. "Some more than others. Strange things happen when the lights go down, even to the best of us, so keep watch over my flock, eh? Your eye is on the sparrow and we've got, you and I, pigeons to see to tonight."

Hector turned out the lights and let the door close on the empty auditorium. Perhaps it would have been better if he had shouted his prayer into the empty space, but he didn't and there might be some who would say that God didn't hear him.

On the other hand, one might argue that God has His own wonderful sense of humour.

Hector did not believe in cell phones. Had he, he might have heard from Faun who had been trying to get in touch with him since she woke after a short nap on the settee in the living room. What woke her was a great thump above her head coming from the guest room, but when she endeavoured to call out to see if Stanley was all right, a significant degree of discomfort was apparent. Agony almost. The back of her throat was raw. Swallowing gingerly to lubricate it didn't seem to help and a quick trip for water from the refrigerator was no better. Stanley's earlier ambivalence was catching. Part of her was delighted. Faun would be able to discard a plan to merely feign laryngitis and to state, instead, with absolute honesty, that she would be unable to take the stage that evening because she really could not speak. She had wanted a simple and straightforward way to put a spoke in Hector's well-oiled wheel but this was a stroke of genius. She would not have to do anything. She wouldn't even have to speak! She couldn't! Well aware that she was by far the best actor in a very nondescript bunch, Faun also knew that she would be irreplaceable. There were no understudies. The play would have to be abandoned. It would serve Hector right!

Even as part of Faun relished this thought, however, another part of her felt the guilt of ruining the Follies. It would mean, alas, that all of Stanley's work on the evening was for naught. Nevertheless, it had to be done. She was determined. What was it that Lady Macbeth had said when they saw the play at Stratford? Something about screwing your courage to the sticking post and not failing, wasn't it? Well, she was not going to fail. She'd feel badly later, but now she had her Stanley to worry about and he, poor fellow, wasn't even going to be there so what would he care? Oh yes, it would serve Hector right all right! Faun had hardly processed this thought when a louder thump above her head drew her back to more immediate considerations. Had she not known that Stanley was incapable of movement, she would have said that he had fallen out of bed. The remote possibility of this drove all thought of telephoning Hector out of her head and she fled upstairs to see what was going on.

A How-To Guide To Popping Pills

Faun had returned from the pharmacy with the unpalatable news that Stanley's prescription for liquid pain medication was out of stock and a little paper bag containing the only available version which was in the form of the more traditional pill. Stanley's shouting at his spouse that she knew he was not able to swallow pills did nothing to ease a rather fraught situation and before long both of them were on the verge of tears: Faun from being yelled at; Stanley both from the pain in his leg and from a growing fear that there wasn't anything he would be able to do about it.

"I told the pharmacist that you couldn't take pills, Stanley," Faun's throat had developed an aversion to speech and the words wheezed from it gratingly. She also took umbrage at being yelled at, particularly when she had done her level best to get what Stanley wanted, and in other circumstances she would have told him so. Instead, she offered the pharmacist's solution. "He said we should mash them up and then dissolve them in water."

"Mash them up! And how do you intend to do that?" Stanley raised himself so that he was leaning on his elbows, the better to reproach Faun. Red in the face, he managed to be furious and peevish at the same time.

"Well...," replied Faun, thinking about it, "Perhaps we could start by trying to cut them in two and see if that helps."

"Helps with what, Faun?" Stanley realized he was yelling and took a deep breath. He continued as though speaking to a child. "If I can't take a whole pill, what makes you think I will be able to take a half with all kinds of little jagged edges to it? Umm?"

Faun saw the logic of his statement, but she was losing patience.

"I suppose I could grind them down for you, if you like. If you're absolutely sure you couldn't swallow them this once. Couldn't you just try?"

Stanley did not notice the crepitatious rasp in his wife's speech. He was beginning to sweat and before answering one of the most asinine questions anyone had ever put to him, he tried to wipe his brow with the sleeve of his pyjamas. This meant, however, that he had to prop himself up on just one elbow and he lost his balance. Falling over to the right, he howled as more weight was put on his injured limb and, for a moment, he too — perhaps fortuitously — became incapable of speech. Faun's attempts to assist him helped neither his physical nor his emotional equilibrium and it was several minutes before a semblance of order was restored. The result of it all, however, was that Faun adjourned to the kitchen taking the pills with her to see whether it really was possible to pulverize them into a powder that Stanley would be able to ingest.

It was a good idea, but the pills did not cooperate. The first refused to sit still and accept its fate. When hit with the blunt end of knife, it skittered across the room and hid. Faun found it a week later while mopping the kitchen floor. A second pill proved as flighty as the first and managed to move sideways at the last moment when Faun tried to cut it in two. Instead of two halves of a pill she ended up with two halves of a plate when her handiwork caused it to shatter. The third pill enjoyed a momentary respite when Faun decided to use the meat tenderizer on it and managed to miss it completely. It was less fortunate when a second blow splintered into about twenty pieces.

Two pills later, Faun returned to Stanley, carrying the pieces on a napkin. When, however, he attempted to swallow them with a large glass of ginger ale, he was still unable to curb his gag reflex and the end result was a soiled and soggy sheet. He fell back against his pillow with a moan that would not have disgraced Hector at his theatrical best, begging Faun to leave him alone, and, stressed out herself, she was quite willing to do so.

Left alone, however, Stanley continued to fret. He hurt, it was true, but it was more than that. They were going to have a fine old time without him. He would be stuck here in this bare room while everyone else garnered applause that should, in a better world, have included him. It was as he gazed around the room that his eye came to rest once more on Tigger, again sitting buddha-like on the straight back chair, as calmly arrogant as only a well-upholstered house-cat can be. Their eyes met and for a long second neither human nor feline had a thought of any kind. Then it came to Stanley that Tigger did not like to take pills either and that when the vet said it was necessary, he and Faun had the devil of a time with the job. And how did they manage it in the end? They held the animal in a death grip, threw the damn pill to the back of its gullet, clamped its mouth closed and rubbed its neck until it bloody well swallowed the thing. That's what they did. And this is what Stanley determined should happen with him.

Thus it was that Faun heard the great thump on the floor as Stanley tried to get her attention. And thus it is that a second throat enters our story so soon after the story of Faun's. Life is a haven for coincidence and truth truly is often stranger than fiction.

"I've got an idea," said Stanley, when Faun reappeared apprehensively at the bedroom door. "Come in."

Stanley had to explain what he wanted to happen, and her part in it, several times before Faun understood what was expected of her. Had she been able to speak, she might have remonstrated with him, but her own throat was now closed for business and she was having problems swallowing. She nodded more than she spoke and Stanley took this as acquiescence.

"Okay," he said finally, "let's do it."

Stanley pulled himself higher up the bed, grimacing as he did so, until he was almost in a seated position. He handed her the little vial of pills and asked her, sternly, "Are you ready?"

"Yes," she rasped, "I'll try."

Stanley looked at his wife for a long moment before closing his eyes. He then whet his lips with his tongue and opened his mouth. Tigger, still on the straight back chair, was reminded of a time when it was young and svelte and had climbed a tree, stalking a baby bird in its nest waiting to be fed by its mother. Reflexively, the cat licked its lips in anticipation.

"Now!" commanded Stanley.

Faun tossed the pill with some little force towards his mouth. It bounced off his chin.

Stanley opened his eyes, scowled at Faun and said, "Try again."

Faun's second attempt found its target satisfactorily but her accuracy surprised him and the pill bounced out of his mouth before he could close it.

"Damnation!" he said.

Practice makes perfect, however, and several pills later, Faun's aim had improved. Thrown underarm, one of the minuscule white monsters went right in, bounced off Stanley's uvula just as he clamped his mouth well and truly shut and there was no need to massage his throat. The pill went down. Both Stanley and Faun were jubilant: it was a bit like shying at coconuts, croaked Faun between husky giggles. Even Tigger was impressed. Stanley, all business, was not satisfied with one and did not stop until he had consumed three of the deceptively small Demerol pills. Suddenly, he was feeling so little pain that he could have danced a jig. Perhaps.

It was almost six o'clock by the time Faun was able to dress Stanley satisfactorily. Getting his trousers up and over the soft bandage was a challenge, even when his head seemed to be floating and his body was more than a little relaxed. Faun noticed that his speech was slightly slurred, but since hers was essentially non-existent, she didn't mention it. It was only then that she remembered that she had never got around to telephoning Hector with the news that although the show might go on, she would not go on with it. She felt a twinge of guilt but her throat was sore and her shoulders were aching from the effort of maneuvering Stanley's backside into his trousers, the belt of which had adamantly refused to go through the loops in the pants.

Few entrances have been more effective than that of Mr. and Mrs. Stanley Parkinson when the doors of the auditorium swung open for them an hour before the curtain was due to rise on the Fall Follies. Stanley was still feeling no pain and would have stomped on through to the stage entrance had Faun let him. She, coming ever more quickly to the realization that Hector could not be kept in the dark about her situation much longer, looked around the auditorium warily to see who was there. Not seeing Hector, she was quite willing to bob along in Stanley's wake. The assembled performers came up to him to ooh and aah about the fact that he was actually there. Had Faun not taken a shard of one of Stanley's smashed up pills — just to try it, you know — she might have been even more nervous, but, as it was, she flinched when Hector appeared through the stage door and advanced towards Stanley, arms outstretched, hallooing with delight.

"Stanley, old boy! Hello! What a trooper! A fellow after my own heart! I knew you would be here!" he shouted. Actually, he knew nothing of the sort and had spent the last hour thinking about just how he might revamp the cabaret programme to fill the hole that Stanley's absence would leave in it. "Come. Let's get you backstage before the audience arrives. You'll be the surprise of the night, my friend." He rubbed his hands together. "What a hit we'll have! A hit. A palpable hit!" To emphasize his point, Hector pounded Stanley between the shoulder blades and enveloped him in a bear hug.

In the end, it was Stanley who told Hector about Faun's voice. Maudlin now about his spouse and the help she had provided him that afternoon, Stanley first regaled those present with the story of his taking the pills — though for some reason he persisted in calling Faun "Tigger" which confused everyone — and then sobbed briefly before declaring that, alas, she, Faun, would not be able to go on that evening since she had a bad case of laryngitis. Hector spun round and looked piercingly at her.

"Speak!" he commanded. "Let me hear your voice!"

Faun stood before him, a silent mixture of triumph and shame, but the squark that emerged from her mouth convinced Hector that Stanley was telling the truth. He was livid, but he knew well enough that this was not the moment to either box her ears or to play Hamlet and rail against the slings and arrows of outrageous fortune that were being hurled in his direction. Hardly thinking either to commiserate or to inquire why he was only being given the news at this extremely late date, Hector took a deep breath, closed his eyes and bellowed the immortal line "The show must go on!" It was left to Fanny to sympathize with her two friends about their separate situations while he departed for the quiet of the empty stage to consider some very limited options.

Clarence, A Corpse Becomes You!

The auditorium was packed well before the show was to begin. Ticket sales had been reasonable but people were turning up who hadn't been at the church in a dog's age. Fanny, who was Front of House, sent a note to Hector to say that he should hold the show for at least five minutes because the audience needed to settle down. Latecomers were left having to look for single seats. Fanny had had an argument with the woman who Mabel left in charge of the Wycliffe Room when she, Fanny, began to move chairs into the auditorium to seat the overflow.

"You can't move our chairs," the woman declared in a panic. "Mabel Green will kill me if you move her chairs!"

"They're not her chairs. They're the church's chairs," replied Fanny with a calm she did not feel. "And I won't let her kill you," she added reassuringly, although she suspected that if Mabel Green decided to kill someone, it would take more than herself to stop her. "We'll move the chairs back in the intermission. She'll never know."

"Mabel Green knows everything," bleated the woman, wringing her hands.

"Ain't that the truth!" murmured Fanny to herself. To the woman, she said as positively as possible, "You just make sure that you have enough food to feed the five thousand."

Fanny might have said more but voices were being raised in the auditorium as ticket holders objected to having to sit at the back on folding seats.

Behind the curtains, Hector and the cast of the play heard only the sound of a packed house and felt thrilled and more than slightly frightened. Hector, perspiring freely and liberally basted with the pungent aroma of his aftershave, beamed and did a little jig.

"Is everybody ready? It's time. Fanny wants me to hold the curtain. She wants people to settle down, but I want you all here in your places and ready to go," he said.

"Hector, old man, you shouldn't have to hold the curtain," said Roger St. John Mountjoy in his usual lugubrious way, "you've got enough on your plate. I'll help you. Which end would you like me to take?"

"Jesus wept!" muttered Hector to himself. By the time he had explained to Roger the meaning of the phrase — someone had once described Roger as being preternaturally thick — Hector was feeling more tense than ever. He took a deep breath and looked around. He needed to calm down. The Faun situation hadn't helped. Neither had the corpse.

It had been about a quarter past six when the corpse, looking very pale and apparently in full makeup, sidled up to Hector and told him that he was very sorry but he didn't think he could go through with it. The corpse, you will recall if you have seen Mr. Archibald's play, is central to the plot.

"What do you mean you can't go through with it?" Hector demanded, the back of his throat tightening alarmingly as he tried to sound reasonable when what he wanted to do was to scream in the man's face.

"I don't think I can do it," came the nervous reply.

Hector just about lost his temper. His perspiration went into overdrive. He steeled himself to appear calm.

"You don't have to *do* anything," he said. "You're dead. You just lie there. That's it. Dead."

"Yes, but what if I forget."

"Forget!? What can you forget?"

Hector reached out to take the corpse by the shoulder. It — or rather, he — more aware with each passing second that his director seemed about to have apoplexy and fearing that Hector might strangle him as well, retreated.

"I might move," he explained. Realizing that he should perhaps enlarge on this desperate thought, he continued, "I mean, I might forget I was dead."

Hector could not believe his ears.

"We have people here," he began, waving an arm wildly at the rest of the cast who were looking on fascinated, "who have had to learn their lines — some of them have to say whole paragraphs, for crying out loud — and you, you are afraid that you won't be able to remember that you are supposed to be DEAD..."

He could say no more. He couldn't believe it. He bent his head, closed his eyes and clutched his chest with his left hand. He was wringing wet. Everyone was looking at him and, yes, it was a good pose, and he might be forgiven if he milked the moment just a little. Slowly, Hector raised his good right hand and pointed into the wings.

"Go!" He declaimed the word. It vibrated in his best baritone as he scanned a repertoire of exit lines from across his theatrical career, and continued, "Away! Get thee hence!" Running out of both steam and sense, he shook his head, "Out, damned spot!"

Lady Macbeth would have been proud.

Back in the present, the curtain still being held, Hector called out, "Where's Clarence?" Given Clarence's well known tendency to disappear, Hector was wise to ask, especially since the janitor, though now under two week's notice of dismissal, had been persuaded by Hector, at the very last moment, to appear as the replacement corpse.

Clarence had not accepted the role without some hesitation. Upon being approached to take the part, he had pointed out that his name did not appear in the programme as the corpse, and he did not think this was fair. The name of the previous corpse was in the playbill and his was not.

"But you're only a bloody corpse, man," Hector had never met such a bunch of lunatics in his life. He could hardly wait to tell Fanny.

Clarence, a man of so few words that, had Hector considered the matter earlier, he might have realized that Clarence was born to play a corpse, managed to articulate two. "Important though," he said.

In this, of course, Clarence was entirely correct. In Mr. Archibald's original version of the play, the corpse, hidden behind a sofa, is invisible until the end of the second scene. Hector, however, always liked to bring his own directorial flourishes to a production, and he had changed this by positioning the sofa at an angle, its back to the audience. The deceased, behind the sofa, was, therefore, to be visible throughout, although, as in the original, he remained hidden from the actors on stage.

"God's streuth!" Hector did not know whether to laugh or cry.

Clarence proved intractable and the first words heard from the stage that evening were to be those of Hector coming out in front of the curtains to announce in a strangulated voice, "Ladies and gentlemen, the role of the corpse, Fred Critendon will be played this evening by your own Mr. Clarence Moran." The announcement, since almost everyone present knew Clarence and very few were yet aware that he had been fired, was received with hearty applause.

The Vicar, seated in the front row and unaware of the casting change, was mystified by the announcement but, as it happened, he had other things on his mind and a short detour is necessary to explain why. To put it as succinctly as possible, the Vicar had brought a date to the Follies. The lady in question, one Miss Lilith Payne, was seated on his right hand and the entire audience had been staring at the two of them since their arrival several minutes earlier. They were worth staring at. We have met both the Vicar and his girth already, but there wasn't a person present that evening who had set eyes on his lady before.

The Vicar and Lilith had met at his mother's funeral. Any attraction that he might have felt for her would have been neutralized had Lilith shared his mother's theological bent, but, as it happened, all the two women had ever shared was an elevator, since they lived on the same floor of their apartment building. Lilith, as she had explained to the Vicar over coffee after the cremation, held no religious views either way, and the Vicar took this as a good sign. It was something he could build on. Lilith, however, did like weighty men and she had confessed to him somewhat coyly that it did not matter if most of that poundage was located around the midriff, as long as a significant portion of it was also to be found between his ears. Currently working on a doctoral thesis in post-Jungian psychology, Lilith seemed an entirely sensible individual.

This alone would not have been enough to lure the Vicar into a Starbucks' at that stage in his life, but Lilith was also blessed with what he had long considered that most feminine of all physical attractions: a slight overbite. Ever since reading the works of Beatrix Potter in his nursery days, the Vicar had fixated on this portion of the female anatomy. If it did not exactly constitute a fetish, it certainly could be counted on to light a small fire in his libido. Moreover, in Lilith's case the slight toothiness was enhanced by an equally slight but absolutely enchanting chin that receded just a tad and which, oh so delightfully, highlighted her dental divinity even farther. The Vicar had tossed caution aside and asked her out on a date more meaningful than one that merely offered Starbucks' best.

It had not been the Vicar's intention to invite Lilith to accompany him to the Fall Follies, where he was fully aware the two of them would be scrutinized to a forensic degree by his entire congregation, but having mentioned the event in passing, he had kindled her interest in it and she had more or less invited herself. Sadly, by the time she did so, the Vicar had also discovered a flaw in her rabbity perfection, and it was a flaw more serious than a large fissure discovered in an otherwise perfect diamond. They had been eating a green salad one evening when Lilith started to laugh.

"You've got a piece of lettuce between your teeth," she announced. "It looks so funny! Haw. Haw. Haw." This 'Haw Haw Haw' was uttered in a kind of soprano monotone, and was followed by a short downward arpeggio of chromatic snorts. It took the Vicar some moments to grasp what he had heard and, initially, he assumed it was some kind of aberration, but when, later that same evening, Lilith found something else amusing, she did it again. And then again. The petrified preacher had determined that the Follies would be their last evening together. He and his buck-toothed babe would go their separate ways.

Embarrassed at being whispered about by members of his congregation, the Vicar was looking forward to both the end of the evening and the end of his relationship with Miss Payne when she leaned over and whispered into his ear, "Isn't that the same guy you just fired?" To say that the Vicar was one who liked a little gossip would be to understate the case considerably and Lilith had been kept abreast of church business almost daily.

Hector's announcement had been a surprise and the Vicar did not quite know what to make of it. Lilith caught the look of puzzlement on his face and was amused. Laughter ensued.

"Losing control of your flock, I guess, eh? Haw. Haw. Haw."

Snorts naturally followed.

The Vicar was about to reply when Hector called for silence.

"Also, Ladies and Gentlemen, I am very sorry to have to tell you that Faun Parkinson is unfortunately indisposed," he said.

A ripple of concern went through the audience. It was bad enough that Stanley Parkinson had been injured, but what could have happened to Faun? Hector moved quickly to address the ripple. "Unfortunately, Faun has come down with a bad case of laryngitis. She is unable to speak." Having been given something more substantial to chew on, the ripple seemed set fair to become a wave and Hector was forced to speak over it. "As you may know, um, er, Ladies and Gentlemen, we have a saying in the theatre that 'the show must go on.'"

Here Hector stopped and looked slowly about the dimmed auditorium, valiantly surveying the audience. Then he added the kicker, "I shall play the part of Dulcie Broadfoot in Faun Parkinson's absence."

This announcement was met with a momentary and complete silence. Many of those present knew both Faun and Hector and it did not seem likely that Miss Dulcie Broadfoot, whomsoever she might turn out to be, could be interpreted by two so very different persons.

One individual in the audience, however, knowing neither of the principals, was immediately enchanted at the prospect of seeing a man replacing a woman playing a woman. The Jungian possibilities were not to be sneezed at.

"Haw. Haw. Haw." Lilith's signature laughter, followed by its concomitant snort shattered the quiet and the auditorium became engulfed by a hubbub of speculation and frivolity.

How would it be done?

Could Hector pull it off?

Poor Faun, was she sick?

Who on earth was that with the awful laugh? It sounded like the woman sitting next to the Vicar.

And who is she anyway?

On the stage, Hector looked at the audience, considered what else he might say, thought better of it, and bolted behind the curtain.

The Play's The Thing, Of Course

Perhaps it was Lilith's laugh, a laugh that was to continue undiminished throughout the entire play, that convinced the audience that Mr. A. J. Archibald had written a comedy. Such was not his intent, of course. His was a one-act whodunnit to be played out in three scenes. Neither Hector nor his fellow actors had ever rehearsed a comedy, but nothing that was to happen on the stage that evening after the curtains slowly opened to reveal the drawing room of a Bournemouth Bed and Breakfast would disabuse the audience of that idea.

The set warranted the applause given to it and Hector had instructed his actors to let the stage remain empty for several seconds so that the audience could take it in. Of course, the stage was not quite empty. Clarence, invisible to anyone who might enter the drawing room, was entirely visible to everyone watching it. The deceased, according to Mr. Archibald, was to be dressed formally in business suit. The gentleman for whom Clarence was the replacement had had such a suit. Clarence did not. No one had ever seen Clarence in a suit and he was not wearing one now.

The corpse, prone on the stage, its back to the audience, was in its shirt sleeves. Had it not been jacket-less, it would still have been identifiable: Clarence wore his trousers high up to the ridge of his ribcage, usually managing to look as though he were in the process of giving himself a wedgie. Immediately recognized by the majority of the people there, he too was given a spontaneous round of applause and, in case there were any doubt about the matter, Old Mr. Simms, seated next but one to the Vicar in the front row, called out, "Good job, Clarence!" This led to renewed and quite prolonged clapping, particularly from those who had not immediately put a name to his posterior.

Thus it was that the three actors who were to enter the drawing room, arrived there to the accompaniment of hearty applause that was not, alas, for them and they did not quite know what to do with it. Chloe Loftus, whose role had been transgendered because of the lack of male volunteers, chose to curtsey towards the footlights. This led her to being elbowed for her trouble by her non-transed partner, Millie Pratt. Chloe ricocheted to one side and bounced against the sofa. The sofa, in turn, found itself being thrust backwards as a result. The movement alarmed Clarence, who had been on the verge of taking a nap (Clarence could sleep anywhere) and the audience was treated to the sight of the corpse raising its head to see what was going on.

"Haw. Haw. Haw."

Lilith's guffaw was loud and clear in the front row, and it promised to be catching.

When the audience finally returned its attention to the persons on the stage, they surveyed a sight that was not immediately understandable. Hector, a male, and in trousers, was — as they had recently been told — playing a woman, who, as far as they knew, had no reason to be dressed as man. The two women with him, on the other hand, who, as we have seen, were meant to be a young heterosexual married couple according to the playwright, were now two women, although Chloe Loftus, a maiden lady who cut her hair rather like K. D. Lang and wore about as much make-up, had always tended to look like a male in drag. This visual confusion was underscored when the audience began to consult its programme. Stanley, with all the changes that had had to be made to that important document, had forgotten to change the names of the couple in the original play and Millie and Chloe were identified there as Priscilla and Cecil.

"Haw. Haw. Haw."

Lilith repeated her refrain, this time adding a significant snort to the proceedings.

Dulcie Broadfoot (now being played by Hector) was to speak the first words of the play, but, for only the second time in a long theatrical career, Hector had trouble remembering his line. Or, to be strictly accurate, her line. He knew every last word in the play, which was why he felt comfortable appearing as Faun's replacement, but it was one thing to know Dulcie's opening salvo seated in the fifth row at rehearsals, and another thing entirely to remember it amid what he considered inexplicable laughter in the glare of the footlights. A professional to the core, he bought time by inventing a bit of business in which he righted the tottering Chloe and straightened the skewed sofa. This had the effect of again reviving the corpse behind it. Hector searched his memory for his line but could not find it. Long ago in his youth, he had forgotten what he was supposed to say during a rehearsal at the Banff School of Fine Arts, but it had never happened again. He immediately became drenched in perspiration. Old Spice began to waft its way towards the front row seats.

Hector was, however, a professional and he knew what he needs must do. There was a prompter and it was her job to feed him his cue. It went through his head that she should have fed it to him already but he waited another beat, bending over to plump up a cushion on the sofa in yet another bit of stage business.

"Haw. Haw. Haw."

Hector could hear someone hooting in the audience but he could not see who it was. It appeared to be a woman and he would throttle her in the intermission, but first he had to get through the play. This unfriendly thought was replaced by another: Where the hell was Mabel Green? He peered into the wings. There she was, sitting on the stool she had insisted on having provided for her, and she appeared to be flipping through the pages of the script. The damned dog was seated next to her, wearing its stupid cone, and it was staring at him. He would kill it too.

"Line, please!" Hector hissed the words through clenched lips, his head turned away from the audience.

The words that came back to him were heard throughout the auditorium. They sparked the beginning of a joyful wave of hysteria that was not to fully ebb until the very end of the play. Mabel Green never liked to be hurried. Her response to Hector's quietly desperate plea came booming back at him, loud enough to the heard even by the ladies steeping the tea in the kitchen. "Just you wait a minute! Now where is the page? Drat!"

There is no need to follow the course of the play in detail. If you have seen it, you will know the plot. If you have not, it is worth the effort of tracking down a copy and having a read. You should be warned, however, that the version performed at the Fall Follies was far removed from the playwright's intent. And just as far from the director's, if it comes to that! Hector, of course, realized this early on and, ham that he was, began quite quickly to have fun with it. He played Dulcie Broadfoot like one of the dames in a British pantomime — broad, arch and knowing. He may not have changed into a dress for the role but everyone soon knew that he was a woman. Hector belonged to an earlier generation, however, a more naive one perhaps, but a more innocent one certainly, and there was nothing at all in his performance that could offend his audience.

Fanny and Faun watched it all from the back row of the auditorium. Fanny smiled benevolently, with more than a smidgeon of pride at how her husband handled himself. Faun, not wanting Hector to do well, was initially pleased with how he looked on stage, but she soon saw that he was winning the audience over and, knowing the part as well as she did, it was hard not to admire how he played with it, and, through the playing, played also with the audience. It was not how she would have acted the part, she thought ruefully, but it worked. Faun also had to admit to herself that her absence had not ruined the play: in a strange sense it had saved it. She knew that at the final curtain, she, like everyone else, would be applauding wildly.

The reality, however, was that Mr. Archibald's play was still in desperate need of saving. Hector had forgotten the first of his lines, but he recovered. Roger St. John Mountjoy managed to remember every one of his lines, but proved totally incapable of moving about on the stage. At his entrance, having been thrust through the door by someone backstage, he came to a sudden stop two feet from the footlights, and he might have stood there for all eternity had he not been shunted about like an errant skittle by the rest of the cast whenever it was appropriate to move him. Like many a first time actor, Roger was mesmerized by the thought that right there, just beyond the footlights, people were staring at him. He could not see them but they were, he knew, examining his every movement. Therefore, he thought, the sensible thing to do was *not* to move.

Then there were his shoes. Despite Hector's admonition, Roger had arrived for the performance in brown shoes and he had had to stand there while Hector barked at him that it was not good enough, that he should have known better and that such a sartorial solecism would spoil the look of the production. Roger, he said, should find another pair of shoes. This was easier said than done. Roger wore a size twelve wide and a search quickly proved that his feet were unique. He lived too far away from church to go home to change and, since the show had to begin, he was pushed onto the stage in a pair of very visible brown clodhoppers that squeaked whenever his handlers thrust him hither and yon.

The unfortunate casting of Millie and Chloe did not help matters. A certain section of any church congregation always seems to regard itself as the guardian of public morality and this section was present at the Fall Follies. Managing somehow to locate certain lesbian overtones in Mr. Archibald's completely innocent and rather dated dialogue — dialogue, remember, that had been written for a man and a woman rather than two women — its censorious instincts went into overdrive. Golf terminology as well as innocent sweet nothings between a young married couple sounded very different from the lips of two persons of seemingly indeterminate sex who were, nevertheless, kitted out as women. The Vicar, much to his date's amusement, was to fight a losing battle during the intermission trying to calm down one old biddy who complained vigorously that she never thought to hear the word "bogey" in her church and that it was shocking that he had allowed it. The majority of the audience, of course, thought the idea of two women — both of whom they knew very well — playing parts obviously written for newlyweds to be hilarious and joined in the fun.

Then there was Clarence. In the second scene, Clarence made a name for himself by becoming possibly the most mobile corpse in the history of theatre. When the curtains closed at the end of the first scene, Clarence stood up to stretch and moved off-stage. This would have been acceptable during rehearsals, since Hector invariably held a little post mortem between scenes. At the actual performance, on the other hand, what was wanted was continuity and momentum. The curtains were to open again almost immediately and the play continue. The result, as the audience saw it, was that the still undiscovered corpse was no longer there. Or at least it was not there initially. Instead, they were treated to the unusual sight of the late Fred Critendon backing crablike, feet first, onto the stage, and settling himself into a comfortable position from whence he was to be discovered just before the end of the scene.

The audience enjoyed the moveable corpse immensely, although, during refreshments afterwards, there was to be much discussion about whether it might not have been better to have had Roger play the role since he seemed to have a natural aversion to movement, whereas Clarence, plainly, could not keep still. Absolute proof of this had been provided when the same dead Mr. Critendon reached round to his posterior and began to pick at his trouser bottom, the better to make himself more comfortable. The sight of Clarence adjusting himself reduced several in the audience to paroxysms and no one more so than Lilith whose laughter rose in a crescendo from "Haw" to "HAW." This encouraged many in the audience to burst into even greater laughter themselves.

Long before the end of what was, in theory, a very short play, the Vicar had decided that his relationship with Lilith surely must cease and that there was no point in putting off telling the woman. No, indeed, he should not hem and haw about it! The Vicar's self admonition was silent, the guffaw that followed was not. She was even invading his thought processes! Vowing silently never to look another overbite in the mouth again, the Vicar settled down to enjoy the show, ignoring, as much as it was humanly possible, the aural onslaught in his ear.

We should turn our attention back to the stage. The actors were doing their best despite the waves of unexpected laughter that kept pouring over them. Most of them had eventually learned their lines quite well. True, Hector had dragooned them into it. True, Chloe tended to shout a bit and Millie did have an unfortunate way of adding 'eh?' at the end of her sentences, but, as Hector said afterwards, "By Jove, they weren't bad!"

This assessment did not address the matter of the voluble prompter, however.

Inexplicably, having given Hector his line at the very beginning of the first scene, Mabel Green began to read the play along with the actors. They spoke on stage, of course, and, to give them their due, all of them followed Hector's dictum that they speak out so that they could be heard in the back row of the auditorium. Unfortunately, Mabel, on her perch in the wings, had heard the same dictum and she had learned it equally well. She became a veritable echo of everyone's words and since she was incapable of modulating her voice, she too could be heard in the back row. More than anything else, it was this that reduced both Faun and Fanny to something approaching delirium by the end of the first scene.

On stage, the reaction was a little different. Hector was fit to be tied. As soon as the curtain closed, totally enraged, he did something that he would never otherwise have dared to do. He marched over to the wings where she sat nursing her script and took hold of Mabel by the shoulders.

"Woman!" he hissed, "Don't you ever shut up?!"

Everyone backstage recoiled, even Bitzie, momentarily. No one had ever told Mabel Green to shut up and no one had ever dared lay a finger on her. Had the stage manager not yelled, "Places everyone. Scene Two. Curtain," at that precise juncture, Armageddon might have occurred.

During scene two, Mabel, although stunned by Hector's laying on of hands, continued to replicate the dialogue just as she had before. She would, she decided grimly, deal with Hector Hammond later, and he would find out that no one spoke to her like that and she was not about to be touched either. No man had touched her in almost fifty years and they weren't about to start now. Just wait until she told the Vicar! In the meantime, she had a job to do and do it she would. She was, moreover, thrilled that whenever Hector, as Dulcie, come across the stage in her direction for any reason, her little Bitzie began to growl.

Then the play began to go haywire. Even Hector with all his experience could hardly credit it. Towards the end of the scene, Dulcie had to move towards where Mabel sat in the wings to deliver a fairly long piece of explanatory dialogue. Bitzie, apparently convinced that its mistress was about to be ravished, bounded out from the wings and began to bark. The audience recognized the dog, of course, and, even if it could find no logical reason either for its appearance or why the dog should be wearing a medical cone, they were delighted at the novelty of there being a dog in the play (like Clarence, it too was not listed in the programme!) and interrupted the action with prolonged applause. This confused Bitzie who turned and barked at the audience before scampering off stage, shaking its cone vigorously as it went.

It is at this point in scene two of the play that the sofa is to be moved aside and Mr. Critendon, a.k.a. Clarence, is discovered. The discovery causes consternation and the whole cast stands there looking at one another in dread silence, wondering who the murderer is and how everything will play out. During the silence — not that there was much of it here — Bitzie decided to make another attempt on Dulcie's ankles and came skittering back across the stage barking more ferociously than ever. Hector began something resembling a highland fling, to avoid the animal's eager mouth, as a disembodied voice bawling "Bitzie! Bitzie! Bad dog. Come to Mama! Bitzie!" was heard throughout the auditorium.

In the original version of the play, it is here that a sheet is placed modestly over the corpse by Roger's character. Roger, thrust forward by Cecil (or if you prefer it, Chloe), had begun to move across the stage in a fair imitation of Frankenstein's monster, to do the necessary when, in mid lumber, he changed course. Bending down lugubriously, he hefted the unsuspecting Bitzie from behind and holding the animal high above his head, brown shoes squeaking, Clarence all forgotten, tramped off stage.

The line "Don't you dare hurt my Bitzie," soared throughout the auditorium. It was not in the script but the audience heard it loud and clear as Roger dumped the animal, bodily, onto Mabel's lap.

When the curtain finally drew a polite veil over the existential end of the scene, Hector, determined to rise above it all, turned his back toward both dog and mistress, and called his actors to the centre of the stage. His clothes were wetter than if he had spent half an hour standing in the shower and another thespian might have quit, but Hector's faithfulness to his theatrical muse remained pure.

"Well, my friends, well done!" he said, rubbing his hands together. "We are almost there. One more scene! Let's give it all we've got. And, everyone, don't forget. Puzzlement! And then when each of you says who you think did it, conviction!"

His actors, stunned by everything they had just witnessed, nodded uneasily at one another. Everyone was scared to even glance towards Mabel and one or two were seriously wondering whether they would survive the evening. Chloe was absolutely convinced that she would not be able to remember another line of her dialogue, but, more important than that, she knew that she would have to take sides before the evening was out and although she liked Hector and wanted to be loyal to him, Mabel would have her guts for garters if she did not support her.

It was at this juncture that Fanny appeared. She had been worried about Hector throughout, even when she was roaring with laughter at what was going on on the stage. The appearance of Bitzie was the last straw, however, and Fanny felt an urgent need to comfort and console her husband. She was also terrified at what he might do to the dog if he got his hands on it. Having raced through the auditorium and up the backstage steps, she gave no thought at all to the fact that the time between scenes was to be short. She had hardly been able to embrace her beleaguered spouse when the stage manager announced, almost jocularly, "Places everyone. Scene Three. And curtain!"

The following tableau presented itself.
Hector and his spouse, surrounded by the cast, were found locked in an embrace, a small dog again snarling around their ankles. Roger, lumbering in from the wings seemed to be chasing it in slow motion. Clarence was almost horizontal but was still in the throes of covering himself with a sheet. The audience, fast becoming experts in the finer points of surrealism in contemporary theatre, rose to give everyone a standing ovation. Clarence, not wanting to be left out of anything, threw off his makeshift shroud, leapt to his feet and bowed low into the footlights. Old Mr. Simms in the front row, very much getting into the spirit of the thing, leaned over to the Vicar and shouted, "Like a religious experience, eh, Vicar? By all that's holy, another resurrection! Praise the Lord!"

It was several minutes before any kind of order could be restored. Fanny bowed her way off stage acutely mortified. Bitzie barked fit to be tied and, frightened by the commotion, began to run round in smaller and smaller circles, at which point Mabel appeared and attempted to get hold of the animal. By then the dog was in a frenzy. It avoided her outstretched arms and fled from the stage. Mabel followed, but not before, having noticed the applauding audience, she executed a gargantuan curtsey in its direction. Hector, standing in the middle of the stage and taking his cue from her, also bowed deeply to the audience, and it, in turn, roared its appreciation.

The third scene of Mr. Archibald's play was not performed that evening. Hector, quickly calculating his options as he stood basking in the applause, knew that it would be impossible to top what had already come to pass and, heaven alone knew whether they would be able to shut Mabel's mutt up anyway. Hector, moreover, had seen Clarence rise from the dead and had no great hope that he would be able to persuade him to die again. Most of all, he didn't think he could put his cast through having to recall where they were in the script and having to get back to the discovery of the corpse. So what if the audience never had a chance to guess who the murderer was? He doubted that most of them even remembered the play was a whodunnit anyway, but he had given them a theatrical experience they would never forget and he would never forget it either. Applause is mother's milk to theatre folk and, one way or another, A. J. Archibald's nice little play had provided gallons of it. Hector bowed again, accepted the never-ending accolades of the audience and made a mental note to tell Fanny that he had been right all along about bouquets. He deserved one.

Pandemonium continued, unabated.

Little Eaten In The Entr'acte

The intermission was meant to last no longer than half an hour. Hector thought the momentum of the show would be lost if the play and the cabaret were too far apart, and — he had warned about this interminably — the older members of the congregation might not be able to handle an evening that went on too long. Since almost every member of the congregation was over fifty, he determined to get the whole thing finished by nine-thirty. As it was, when the curtain finally closed on the play, the evening was already running forty minutes late. Not that anybody was complaining. Everyone was delighted with the play and, as people made their way to the Wycliffe Room for refreshments, they were having a high old time.

In the kitchen, the Ladies of the Church had assembled to dole out the usual fare of shortbread, brownies and those minute savoury items the contents of which always defy identification, while others — you should pardon the expression — manned the coffee cylinders and the unwieldy iron teapots out of which they would pour the only liquids available. Mabel Green did not approve of other beverages and had not yet come to accept the concept of bottled water as an acceptable alternative.

It was with Mabel that the ladies in the kitchen were concerned.

"Where is she? Is she coming?"

"Was that Mabel I could hear during the play?" The questioner was notoriously hard of hearing and not the brightest of the sisterhood.

"What was she doing on the stage with that damned dog of hers?"

"Where is she? I thought she would be here by now."

This last was said with a nervousness that all the assembled ladies felt. Mabel ran a tight ship and they did not wish to be found wanting.

"I hope she doesn't see that Fanny Hammond borrowed some of her chairs."

"Poor Fanny if she does!"
"Poor me, for letting her."
"O Lord help us all, here she comes now."

Mabel had been of two minds whether to stay right there, on the stage, and have it out with Hector at the end of the play or go directly to the kitchen to make sure everything was shipshape. She had decided on the latter course because, unless she were there supervising them, she did not trust her crew to rinse out a dishcloth properly, much less have everything ready to go. She would deal with Hector Hammond later and she preferred to do the dealing on her own home ground rather than on his. She would have been there more quickly but it had taken time to round up Bitzie who had gone completely berserk and was in the process of savaging the hem of the curtains.

"What's this I hear about them stealing our chairs?" Mabel deposited the dog on the countertop and surveyed her crew.

The Ladies of the Church eyed their captain uneasily and recoiled.

By the time Mabel had laid waste her Ladies and given final instructions as to the pouring and doling out of refreshments, most everyone was seated and the Vicar was able to call for order so that he could say grace.

"Good evening, everyone," he said, raising his voice against the babble all around him. "What a joyous evening this is! I am sure that everyone will agree that we have been given a wonderful treat. I don't think I have ever seen anything quite like it before." The Vicar said this benevolently and without intended irony but at least one person misunderstood this.

"Haw. Haw. Haw."

Like pebbles thrown into a pool, Lilith's haws had their own effect. A murmur of conversation began as the tables set about inquiring just who on earth the woman was and whether or not she was with the Vicar and, if so, in what capacity.

"May I have your attention, please!" bawled the Vicar, fully aware of what was going on around the room and not at all pleased about it. "Let us bow our heads for grace, so that we can partake in this feast our ladies have prepared for us. And don't forget," he added archly as the room subsided into a quasi silence, "the evening is only half over."

For whatever reason, Lilith thought this hilarious. "Haw. Haw. Haw," she said. "SNORT!"

The Vicar, a man of considerable forbearance and one generally well versed in crowd control, moved quickly to his prayer. Before he could open his mouth, however, laughter began to flood the room. As if this were not enough, in the melee that followed, Old Mr. Simms, seated at the table next to him, called out to his neighbour, "It's the piranha, that's doing it. The Vicar's tootsie! Her sitting next to him. The one with the teeth." Unable to get his mind around any kind of prayer other than a fervent wish to be rid of both the irrepressible Old Mr. Simms and the putative tootsie, the Vicar merely made the sign of the cross over his flock and sagged onto his chair, the better to ponder the cruelty of life.

He was not left to ponder long.

It was a cardinal article of faith in Mabel Green's lexicon that when one wanted something done, one went to the top. In this case, the top was the Vicar and Mabel was on her way to him almost before he was seated.

"Vicar," she announced, "I have been ravished and trampled upon!"

The Vicar had other things on his mind but he was not so far gone that he did not realize that Mabel had to be speaking metaphorically. The idea that Mabel Green might have been molested in any manner whatsoever did not bear imagining and her bulk made it extremely unlikely that she could have been trampled upon.

"Bitzie has been manhandled and is terrified."

The Vicar could hear an animal howling in the kitchen but the sound was more one of fury, he thought, than terror.

"And it was Roger St. John Mountjoy that did it!"

Even as his world seemed to be collapsing around him, the Vicar heard the solecism in Mabel's language. He frowned.

Lilith may have heard it too, but she was delighted by the sight of this squat bullfrog of a woman looming over her evening's companion, clearly intent on some kind of mayhem, while he, more than equal to her in bulk, seemed to shrink before her, apparently incapable of speech.

Lilith dispensed with her haws and went straight to a signature SNORT.

The thought of having to sort out Mabel Green not to mention her bloody dog was too much. It would have been too much without the snort, but with it, the Vicar went over the edge. In a voice usually reserved for the peroration of one of his more spell-binding sermons, he cast his eyes upwards, and hissed through his clamped closed teeth, "In the name of heaven, woman, won't you please shut up!"

If it was not a prayer, it was, at the very least, a cry from the heart.

Prayer or otherwise, Mabel Green heard the words and, for the second time that evening, thought that she was being told to be quiet. Hector's on stage imprecation had been inexplicable to her but it came from a mere human; this second occasion emanated from someone whose very position she had been taught from childhood to esteem. If the Vicar was not quite a voice from Mount Olympus, he at least occupied a niche half way up the side of it. For him to tell her to be quiet was incomprehensible and it made her momentarily speechless.

Lilith, on the other hand, had no doubt to whom the Vicar had been speaking. She was not so self-absorbed that she did not realize that her laughter was unusual, a little odd even, but the Vicar had never said anything about it before and just because the toad woman with the bulging eyes was bawling him out for something or other, there was no reason to turn on her. Her laughter shrivelled in mid-snort and she rounded on the Vicar.

"How dare you, Gilbert Gilchrist!" she shrieked, "How dare you speak to me like that! You nasty man!" Winding to her theme, Lilith took a deep breath, "You're not so perfect yourself, and don't you forget it, you, you big sack of lard!"

These might not have been words expected to emanate from a Ph.D candidate in the throes of writing the last chapter of her thesis — and Jung might well not have approved of the emotionality of her tone (though, to be fair, he would have had difficulty arguing against the accuracy of the physical description), but the Vicar had come out of left field, so to speak, and she was not going to put up with it. She planted herself firmly in her chair and refused to budge. Old Mr. Simms was reminded of Lot's wife, but he did not have the temerity to say so.

No one would have paid closer attention had Mabel, Lilith and the Vicar been standing there in their underwear. The idea of anyone addressing the Vicar as a big sack of lard was almost as extraordinary as him telling someone to shut up. The silence in the room was as complete as it was uneasy. The crowd, willing to hang on words said by any person who might choose to enter the fray, waited with bated breath. Even when Old Mr. Simms, was heard to mutter, "Jesus H. Christ! This is even better than the play!" hardly anybody said a word. A couple of people at the far end of the room were heard to hush him, but they did it so that they would not miss anything rather than in disagreement of his sentiment.

Whatever else anyone might say about Roger St. John Mountjoy, it is undeniable that he had a well developed sense of self-preservation. His action in grabbing hold of Bitzie on stage and depositing the barking animal on Mabel's lap had been a surprise even to himself. Having to defend his actions in front of the Vicar and the congregation made him wish he had never set eyes on the beast.

"I don't know what you mean, Ms. Green," he said tremulously to Mabel. "I never meant to harm your dog. I thought it might bite someone." Since the animal in question was still barking its head off in the kitchen, this seemed reasonable. Mabel was having none of it, however.

"Bitzie would never bite!" she retorted loudly, her bosom swelling mightily at the very idea. She shook her fist in Roger's face, and he, like most everyone who had ever thought to go up against her, retreated from the battle.

Hearing its name bandied about in the next room, and possibly considering its mistress to be in mortal danger, Bitzie leapt off the kitchen table, madly trying to find Mabel and race towards her defence. The animal snarled at any shin, ankle or foot it met en route. Roger fled. Screams of concern accompanied the animal's journey as did a couple of yelps when the occasional walking stick found its target on the little Prussian posterior. What might have happened next is open to conjecture, for it was at this juncture that Hector and his merry band of players entered the room.

After the audience's applause had died down, Hector had repaired briefly to the ladies' downstairs lavatory which he had commandeered for the evening. Neither his prostate nor his deodorant was what it might have been and he also had to change from a 1930s male Dulcie Broadfoot into a tuxedoed sophisticate for the cabaret. His cast, likewise, had wanted to get out of their costumes and they had adjourned to the larger Men's Room where there was a sufficiency of cubicles for members of either sex to do the necessary. Roger, who had an aversion using such public facilities, had gone on ahead. They arranged to meet at the doors of the Wycliffe Room to enter in triumph. It was Hector, arm and arm with Fanny, who led the way, pushing open the doors onto a strangely silent room in which the only immediate sound was the barking of one plainly out of sorts canine, a barking that Hector had heard quite enough of already that evening.

Before he could stop himself, Hector, for reasons best known to himself, the performer in full flight, delivered, in a broad cockney accent, lines that no one there would ever be likely to forget, "Lawd, Gawd Awmighty! Put the little blighter out of its misery, won't you!"

From there, things went swiftly downhill.

Bitzie recovered first and ran pell mell at Hector, jumping so accurately at his groin that, had the dog not been coned, Hector's frilly bits might have been, as he phrased it circumspectly later, considerably abbreviated.

Mabel uttered the one word, "Bitzie!" before shouting at the crouching and frightened figure of Hector, "Don't you dare hurt my Bitzie, you brute!"

The Vicar, avoiding so much as a glance at at Lilith, hauled himself to his feet and called for order. It was an unnecessary call. No one said a word. The room could not have been more transfixed had the twelve disciples arrived there to re-enact the Last Supper. Only Bitzie's yapping broke the silence and this only ceased when Fanny, bristling with rage at the indignity wrought on her beloved, took hold of the animal and tossed it underhand through the doors into the corridor.

The people in the room were in the process of taking sides. Many of the older heads were naturally inclined to support the Vicar. He was the leader of his flock and they were members of it. However, some of these persons were the same ones who had been offended by the sexual overtones of the play, and since the Vicar had clearly failed to put the kibosh on what they had seen on the stage, they began to evince a degree of sympathy for Mabel, who surely should not have been shouted at whatever her poor little doggie was up to. The more perspicacious of the same group pointed out that they didn't think that the Vicar had been shouting at Ms. Green at all and that he had been addressing the woman with the awful laugh. Ah, came the response, but should a man of the cloth have raised his voice at all? That was the question.

Then there was the group who heartily enjoyed the idea of someone — anyone at all really — shouting at Mabel Green and thought that she had it coming. This same group also wanted to congratulate Fanny for forward-passing Mabel's mutt out of the room. Its bark had been a strain on their nerves and why was a dog allowed into the church in the first place? It wasn't as though it was a service dog. Of course, the dog-lovers in the room objected to any of its kind being punted in any circumstances and joined the Mabel alliance.

Hector's actors, and their families and friends, lined up — metaphorically speaking — against Mabel. Apart from their annoyance at her repeating every blessed word of their dialogue, they also objected to her cutting in on their applause when the play was over. Who did Mabel Green think that she was anyway? The Ladies of the Church would — had it been a secret ballot — have voted against Mabel unanimously but they knew better than to voice this opinion openly and generally kept their heads down. Only one or two had the nerve to point out that Mabel had been very wrong to put her dog on the kitchen counter. Heaven alone knew what germs it had left behind.

Clarence, still smarting from the Vicar firing him, had not intended to even appear for refreshments but had changed his mind because of the applause he had been given. He had decided to drop in to quench his thirst before taking a nap. In the event, it provided too good an opportunity to denigrate the Vicar, and Clarence joined in the fray. The point of view which he presented — that a man of the Vicar's weight should be more careful about how he threw it around — did not contribute to either side's argument, however, and Clarence soon found himself elbowed aside as the debate continued. In the end, he was left to the company of Old Mr. Simms who complimented him again on his lively performance as the corpse.

It remained for the Vicar to fix matters as best he could.

Bowing so deeply that the people near him were afraid he would topple over and need some kind of crane to be pulled upright again, the Vicar held out a hand toward Mabel. It was part genuine supplication and part theatrical gesture for everyone to see.

"Come, Mabel," he said, with all the smarm a man of his calling could muster, "I was not speaking to you. Indeed not. I could not."

He took a deep breath and was about to continue when Old Mr. Simms put him completely off his stroke. "Who were you speaking to, then, Vicar? Your lady friend, was it? The toothy tootsie?"

The Vicar ploughed on. "This is an evening of celebration! We must be as one!"

"Aye, but which one?" Old Mr. Simms was not giving up.

"And it is not yet finished! I believe we still have the cabaret!"

The Vicar had spoken so many exclamatory sentences that he was finding himself out of breath. Even more red in the face than usual, he surveyed the room, carefully avoiding having to look at Lilith, and beamed broadly. "And we are to see you again, Mabel! I believe you have a surprise for us! I know I speak for everyone here when I say that I can hardly wait!"

In this, the Vicar was in error, but silence, it seemed, was consent, and he nodded his head several times in benediction.

"Everyone," he continued, "I know that you would want me, even though the evening is not yet over, to give our thanks to our good friend Hector here, for all the work that has gone into these festivities."

The Vicar looked towards Hector and his little band of players waving a second outstretched hand to them. Hardly a lesser showman than Hector himself, he managed to embrace the whole room in his gesture.

Hector was impressed. He knew when he was beaten. He knew that retreat is not necessarily defeat and, plastering a wide grin across his face, he advanced to where Mabel and the Vicar were standing, grabbed both of them by the shoulders and brought their three heads together in a show of amity.

It was not a meeting of the minds, but his gesture did allow everyone to move on to the cabaret.

A Great Reckoning
In A Little Room

Stanley had spent the play alone in the small dressing-room backstage lying on an ancient couch among scenery from long ago. With the painkillers beginning to wear off, his mood vacillated from 'I'm-going-to-do-this' to 'God-get-me-out-of-here' with recurrent pitstops for 'it-hurts-it-hurts' along the way. The roars of laughter and applause he had heard were of little comfort and although he knew it was irrational to think that people had no right to be enjoying themselves while he was in such agony, he had the thought anyway. And where was Faun when he needed her? Part of Stanley was enjoying his self-pity immensely but he would have much preferred an audience, even an audience of one. The rational side of Stanley, and if nothing else Stanley saw himself as 'the rational man,' could not understand too why he seemed to hear Mabel Green speaking throughout the play and why a dog had begun to bark at the end of it.

Faun's arrival explained none of these things since when she sat down on the couch next to her husband, her weight disturbed its straining springs. One of them pushed up against the bandage of Stanley's calf. Stanley yelped and forgot everything he had been going to ask her.

"Get up!" he commanded. "For crying out loud, don't sit on me, Faun!"

Faun would not have sat on Stanley for the world and she leapt to her feet

"Oh, Stanley," she croaked, "I'm so sorry. How are you doing? Does it still hurt?"

"Well, what do you think, Faun? Do you think that the pain has miraculously disappeared?" Stanley could be sarcastic when he wanted to. It was a mandatory skill at the bank.

"I mean, will you be able to go on, Stanley? I don't want you to make it worse."

The rasp in Faun's voice went all unnoticed as Stanley addressed this very issue. He had been wondering much the same thing himself and his response was a rather plaintive, "I don't know, Faun. Do you think I should?"

Where this conversation would have gone is anybody's guess. Faun was ambivalent. She did not want Stanley to perform but she did want him to be a success. She also knew that whatever she said, it would have to be said very carefully or she would end up getting the blame. Fortunately for her, just then Vera arrived at the door dragging a reluctant and very well-oiled Laddie in her wake.

"Oh, Stanley," she said, "we just wanted to see how you are doing. Does it hurt?"

The expression on Vera's face was one of pained sympathy. The sympathy was for Stanley; the pain was all her own. Her brow was furrowed and she was pulling on her lower lip. Laddie, on the other hand, looked as though he could cheerfully commit mayhem on his consort.

"I am as well as can be expected," Stanley replied bitterly, at the same time casting a look towards Faun that clearly said, "get them out of here!!"

Before he could say anything else, Vera clapped her hands and sat down on the couch, missing his leg by centimetres.

"I have some news to cheer you up!" she said, looking coquettishly from Stanley to Faun. "We've decided to move the wedding forward. Haven't we Laddie, my love!"

Laddie looked as though the Governor had just told him a new supply of rope had been delivered and the hanging would take place next morning at sunrise.

"Umm," he said glumly. He brightened somewhat when he added, "Perhaps Stanley won't be well enough to give you away next Saturday, Vera. Can't have him hobbling down the aisle, now can we?"

"There is no aisle, silly," she replied, and turned to Stanley to reassure him, "It will be at City Hall, Stanley, and I'm sure we will take good care of you. Won't we Faun? Won't we take good care of our Stanley?"

Once again, Stanley wondered how his relationship with Vera had gone from, 'Yes, Mr. Parkinson, sir' to 'our Stanley' and once again he resolved to have it out with her. But not here. The woman's capacious thigh was in danger of touching his leg. Abandoning all thought of anything else, he said, his words dripping with ice, "Will you please not touch my leg! Please!"

Faun, wanting to head off trouble, patted his hand. "But Vera, dear," she said, "why move it forward? I thought the date was set."

"Well," replied the increasingly pregnant and coy Vera. "I'm not getting any smaller, now am I? And this way we can all get back to normal so much the quicker."

Faun thought that a woman of Vera's age was going to be in for quite a surprise when she had to look after a baby, but she wasn't about to say so. She was also taken aback when she glanced over at Laddie and saw, written across his face, what she could only describe to Stanley later as a look of murderous intent. Since Laddie seemed to be on the verge of saying something to match his look, she laughed hastily and said with a strained smile, "First of all, we have to get Stanley through the evening, don't we!"

Vera managed to trump this statement with one of her own. "I think I am going to be sick," she said and fled from the room.

The silence that followed Vera's departure was broken when Laddie slowly sank down next to Stanley's couch like a deflating balloon, clutched Stanley's arm and cried, "Help me, Stanley! Oh God, what am I to do! For God's sake, help me!"

Neither Stanley nor — apparently — God quite knew how to respond to this and the tableau remained mute until the arrival moments later of a triumphant Hector with Fanny at his heels.

"There you are! There you are!" declared Stanley's co-producer. "I bring you good tidings. Great tidings, in fact. The first half went well. Not as it should have done perhaps, but well, nevertheless. Didn't it, Fan, my love? Didn't it just go so well?"

Hector was wound up and he was not about to wind down for a while yet.

"And now we have to get you ready, Stanley my friend, for your debut! I was thinking — what do you think of this? — that we will put you on first. The curtain will open and, voila, there you'll be! Of course, I will introduce you, then the curtain and there you'll be!"

Brevity had never been one of Hector's virtues.

"Give Stanley a chance to speak, Hector." Fanny interjected with a laugh. "How are you feeling, Stanley? And what on earth is the matter with you, Laddie? You look most uncomfortable."

Laddie would have been only too happy to tell her what the matter was and was just about to begin the onerous task of pulling himself to his feet when Hector, not about to have anyone interrupt him again, frowned at his wife and continued.

"Everyone is wondering if you are all right, Stanley, and they are waiting to see you. Some of the older folk came just to see your leg." He laughed ruefully. "Ridiculous I know, but you know how people like to chase ambulances. Anyway, let's get you organized. The show must go on!"

Stanley had always had a problem resisting Hector when he was in full flight but this time he looked towards Faun and then Fanny for support. Both of them seemed to be holding their breath waiting for him to make a decision and this was no help at all. Neither was a glance at Laddie whose forehead was resting on the edge of the couch at Stanley's elbow. He seemed to be whimpering.

"Well," said Stanley, hesitantly, "I suppose I could give it a try." He smiled wanly up at Hector, and would have continued further but he was preempted when Hector, Faun and Fanny all spoke at once.

"By Jove, that's the spirit!" said Hector, giving Stanley a punch of encouragement on the arm.

"Are you absolutely sure?" asked Faun, frowning doubtfully.

"Now Hector, behave yourself!" warned Fanny. "Stanley must do what he wants to do."

Laddie said not a word.

"Ah, there you all are!" The voice of the Vicar boomed into the small space of the room. "I just wanted to see how you are doing, Stanley."

This was not entirely true. The Vicar had fled the Wycliffe Room to escape not only the rumblings of Mabel Green's supporters but also the evil eye of Lilith Payne who was to remain stubbornly mute in her seat until she finally left he church just before the cabaret began. Clearly, she was not happy. Her left eye had developed a twitch and when Old Mr. Simms leaned over and said to her, rather too convivially, that it looked as though romance was dead, one large tear had trickled down her cheek. The Vicar was not a man who liked to hurt anybody's feelings, but he thought that, on balance, he had suffered enough and so he had taken himself off to look for Stanley. He would deal with everything else later. Much later, if he had any say in the matter. In the meantime, he did want to check up on Stanley.

The little room at the back of the stage was full to overflowing. The Vicar edged his way in with a quick "Excuse me," to Fanny. His girth forced her to move forward and bang her leg against the side of the couch. Stanley flinched. The Vicar didn't immediately notice Laddie taking up rather more than his share of space on the floor as he stood with his mammoth back to the door, essentially blocking anyone else from entering, even if there had been room for them inside.

"We have decided to go ahead, Vicar," declared Hector with, perhaps, rather too much glee, "and I'm just about off to get everyone ready. Stanley will go on first, so Faun you should get him organized." Hector was in charge and in his element. "Fanny, start rounding up the audience. Get them out of the Wycliffe Room and back to their seats. I want the curtain up in ten minutes. Ten! No more." He was about to tell the Vicar to kindly remove himself when he realized that the Vicar was not listening to him and seemed to be giving all his attention to Laddie who, still slumped on the floor, had withdrawn a bottle from his inside jacket pocket and was upending it directly into his mouth.

"And you, Laddie," continued Hector, "you get on out there. You're on piano. Play some tunes while the audience settles. And remember, Stanley is going on first."

A mickey of scotch had no place in Hector's world that evening and he grabbed hold of Laddie's bottle and yanked it out of his mouth. The amber liquid chugged down the front of Laddie's shirt and to make sure Laddie could not retrieve it, Hector put the bottle behind his back. It was a good idea but Hector did not execute it properly since the bottle was upside down. The remaining content flowed freely down the back of Hector's tuxedo jacket. The reek of a very inexpensive brand of scotch began to seep into the room.

"Oh, my dear good Lord," said the Vicar woefully, looking down at the front of his cassock which had been sprinkled from crotch to hem. Faun, she was not quite sure why, wanted to giggle and when she saw Fanny begin wipe at Hector's backside with her handkerchief she was unable to resist. Stanley, who had also been sprayed, could not resist the thought that he could do with a double himself. He was involved, he was sure, in some kind of apocalypse. Without even thinking, he tossed one of his remaining pills into his mouth and swallowed it whole.

Laddie, with an immense dignity, pulled himself slowly to his feet. He surveyed each person in front of him. "I just have one thing to say," he declaimed with a hiccup, "Hector, I will play at your cabaret," The words were slurred as he paused to consider how he was going to continue, "but you are a nasty chap and after tonight I will never play for you again." He cleared his throat. "Stanley, you, on the other hand, are a nice chap, and I hope it goes well. It probably won't, but I hope it will." He was swaying slightly. "But," he began again, wagging a finger slowly at each of the persons in the little room, "I will not marry that woman!"

Laddie failed to notice that 'that woman' had returned and was standing in the doorway. The Vicar's girth blocked her view and Vera could not see a thing, but she heard every word.

It'll All Be All Right On The Night

It was not often that words failed Hector Hammond, but when he stood in front of the curtains to introduce the cabaret, they did not come easily. Several things had occurred — or, indeed, had not occurred — since he had stepped over Vera's unconscious form in the doorway of the little back room, saying, with an airy wave of his hand, "Someone look after her, will you. I've got to get things going or we'll be here all night." First of all, Noni Figueroa was late. Hector had invited her to watch the play and join the assembled company for refreshments before the cabaret, flattering her with the thought that her public would want to meet her in the flesh as it were.

Noni, however, had no intention of letting anybody see her flesh if she could avoid it. Her face was marginally less swollen than it had been but she still looked like she had been hit several times with a two-by-four. Makeup helped a little and Noni had every intention of going on but, for the life of her, she could not understand why the face that stared back at her from the mirror seemed more than slightly Chinese. She looked, she thought, like something out of 'Chu Chin Chow.' As it happened, she had been in the chorus of a revival of the show in her youth and she hadn't liked how she looked then either. Never without a sense of the ridiculous, however, Noni had put her hands together, bowed to her image, and said, "Ahh, so!" determining that she would forget about refreshments, and go straight to her dressing room. It was a good plan but there were several churches in the neighbourhood and she could not remember the name of the one at which she was to perform. The taxi driver was to find several in darkness before they hit on the right one.

Hector sent Roger St. John Mountjoy to stand outside on the street to look out for Noni but Roger had returned several times to tell him in a strangely plaintive tone that she wasn't there. Hector found this infuriating — although, to be fair, Hector found pretty much everything about Roger infuriating. More to the point, however, if Noni were not to appear, it would leave a rather large hole in the programme, a programme which seemed to be becoming more porous by the minute. Even when Hector had stepped over the prostrate Vera — an ingrained politeness ensured that he said, "Excuse me," — he had been afraid that the chance of her recovering sufficiently to perform was not something he would like to rely on, particularly as she was still in the habit of throwing up at the most inopportune of moments. Fanny had also just whispered to him that, if he listened carefully over the buzz of the audience, he would be able to hear a now screamingly hysterical Vera vowing that she would castrate Laddie when she got hold of him and that he would not be able to locate certain parts of his anatomy when she was finished with them. Hector could only pray that Vera would not get hold of Laddie until the cabaret was over. He did ask Fanny to shut Vera up, however. It would not do if the performers were to be interrupted by the banshee howlings of a mad woman in what appeared to be premature labour.

As if all this were not enough, there was the question of Mabel Green. Hector did not know whether the dreadful creature still intended to perform. He did not care if he never saw the woman again as long as he lived, but if she did not appear, it was undeniable that it would leave yet another cavity in his programme. The metaphor of a sieve struck him rather forcibly. Mabel had last been seen leaving the Wycliffe Room in search of her Bitzie who, or which, had disappeared from the corridor into which it had been thrown by Fanny during the late unpleasantness. Since Roger was otherwise occupied, Hector could not send him to search for Mabel and no one else volunteered. Chloe Loftus, usually most sympathetic to Hector's needs, laughed in his face when he asked her. "Hector," she said, "people around here spend their entire lives trying to avoid that woman, and I'm one of them."

There was one person who knew Mabel's whereabouts and he wasn't talking. This was Clarence. Clarence had been alone in his maintenance room bemoaning his upcoming unemployment, and wondering if there might not be a way round it when Mabel appeared in his doorway and yelled, "Have you seen my dog?" Now, Mabel was not one of Clarence's favourite people at the best of times. He had had to deal with her far too often in her role as the head of the Ladies of the Church. She always acted as though he were her own personal servant. Truth be told, Mabel was one of the main reasons that Clarence had taken to hiding out while on duty.

"Well," yelled Mabel again, "have you seen my dog?" This time the question included an accusation.

The trouble was that he *had* seen her dog. He had found the animal wandering around in the basement, sniffing about and, by the looks of it, getting ready to do its business. Since he would be the one to have to clean up after it, Clarence had grabbed the animal and shoved it out the side door of the church, instructing it, with more words than he was in the habit of using with most humans, to go play in traffic.

"Second basement," he announced. "Think."

Not the sharpest chisel in the toolbox, Clarence had had a thought. If he could get rid of Mabel, everyone would be so grateful that he would be rehired. It was a long thought and there was an 'if' in it, but that was what came to him. Not to kill her or anything as permanent as that, but if he could lock her up for the evening, get her out of everyone's hair as you might say, and particularly out of the Vicar's, he would be the hero of the hour. It would be even better than being a corpse.

"Come," he said.

Clarence led Mabel Green down the stairs into the bowels of the church to the floor below the basement where the gigantic boilers clanged and spluttered, and to that little space in which, long ago, he had placed an ancient armchair and a side-table on which now stood two empty beer bottles.

"Listen," he said. "You sit. I look," he added loquaciously. Mabel, parsing a random thought about Christine in 'The Phantom of the Opera,' sat. Clarence made a pretence of looking underneath one of the boilers before he, even more loquaciously announced, "Back in a mo'" and ran up the stairs. He bolted the big steel door at the top of them.

Hector knew none of this of course and he, himself, might well have left Mabel there for the duration if he had, but her absence left him in a bind. The audience was eager for the show to begin. It had moved en masse from the Wycliffe Room, still deep in its discussions about the play and the goings-on during refreshments, but very ready to be entertained once again. Old ladies were quite happily carrying chairs back into the auditorium. Wheeltrans would be long gone by the time the evening was over, but no one seemed to care. A hilarious play had been followed by an intermission that had engendered enough gossip to satisfy even the most voracious of busybodies, and there were quite a few of them present. No one intended to miss what came next. Even the Ladies of the Church, who should by rights have stayed behind to wash the dishes, had abandoned their posts. Mabel Green was nowhere in sight and the thrill of hearing her — as they thought — being told to shut up had been like a dream come true. Still wearing their aprons, and occasionally glancing over their shoulders in case she should suddenly reappear, they stood at the back of the auditorium. There was not an available seat in the house.

Hector raised a hand. "Ladies and gentlemen," he began. The hubbub in the room continued unabated. Above it all Laddie, at the piano, was hammering out music which, had anyone been listening, might have been thought odd given the occasion. Vicious bits of Frédéric Chopin's Piano Sonata No. 2 in B-flat minor, Op. 35 — more widely better known as 'The Funeral March' — were followed by a very loud version of 'Onward Christian Soldiers' as Laddie obeyed the letter, though not the spirit, of Hector's instruction to entertain the audience before the cabaret began. When Laddie saw Hector come out onto the stage, he stopped in mid-stream and began to thump out the opening chords of Mozart's Requiem. He stopped only when Fanny came up behind him and, exerting a little pressure, put a hand on each side of his neck, as she whispered in his ear, "Now Laddie, just you play nice! I'm right here, okay?" There was something in the way she said it that sobered him considerably.

The lights in the auditorium began to dim and at last the audience was quiet. Hector waited just a moment or two more to let the stragglers clear their throats and settle. He had not reckoned with Old Mr. Simms, back in the front row but how sitting right up next to the Vicar in Lilith's vacant seat. The old gentleman had the voice of a fairground barker but he also had the nose of a bloodhound. He sniffed. And sniffed again. Then, he leaned over to the Vicar and, in a voice that any actor might have envied, asked, "Needed a little snort, did we, Vicar?"

"And so Ladies and Gentlemen, we've had to make a few changes. Some of our performers are, sadly, unable to appear and we have had to change the order of things, so I suggest you leave your programme to be read when you get home and sit back and relax." Hector sounded somewhere between a high-end used car salesman and a TV anchor introducing a segment on the pros and cons of euthanasia. He had hardly got these words out of his mouth when an enormous crash was heard behind the curtain. Hector flinched, and then, eyes wide and looking petrified, he turned it into a bit about being alone in a haunted house. The audience loved it.

"I am guessing, folks," he continued, laughing, "that the corpse has come to life again, but we are going to begin with our own Stanley Parkinson singing George Formby's wonderful old song 'I'm Leaning On A Lamppost' from back in the thirties. Some of you know, I'm sure, about Stanley's recent accident, but what a trouper he has turned out to be! He insists on being here to-night and I am going to ask you to give Stanley a big hand. Stanley, I hope you're ready back there! Ladies and Gentlemen, my good friend, my co-producer this evening and the brain behind the Fall Follies, Mr. Stanley Parkinson!"

Hector raised his hands towards the curtains with a dramatic flourish. The curtains shook slightly but remained firmly closed.

"Mr. Stanley Parkinson, Ladies and Gentleman!"

Hector repeated both the name and the gesture. The curtains remained adamantly shut. Laddie, who had essayed an introductory crescendo the first time that Hector said Stanley's name, repeated it — this time adding a series of little trills in the high treble. The audience began to laugh.

Hector picked up his cue.

"Oh, Stanley, where are you?" Hector hallooed the question cupping a hand to his ear, and standing on his tippy-toes. He swivelled round to look askance at the audience as he did so. "Can you heee-rrrr me?" Laddie, a brilliant accompanist even when several sheets to the wind, echoed Hector's question with a thumb-numbing downward glissando after which, only a beat of silence in between, Hector, miming bewilderment, whispered, "Is anybody home?" Laddie answered with a screeching glissando upwards and the audience cheered as, slowly and very laboriously, the curtains parted.

Stanley And The Hatstand

Stanley stood alone on an almost empty stage, holding on for grim death to something that could only be described as a hatstand. The hatstand was, of course, supposed to be a lamppost. Despite the best efforts of the ancient Greek who had made such a success with the set for the play, it had resisted all attempts to turn it into a lamppost and remained stubbornly what its manufacturer had intended it to be. The hat pegs had been excised and an electric bulb inserted into its apex but still it resembled nothing so much as a hatstand. The lampshade that had been affixed to its top made it look considerably embarrassed but did not change anything. In a final, desperate attempt at verisimilitude, the ever more perplexed carpenter had hacked off the four steadying feet at its base and nailed the upright pole to a piece of board. The effect of this was that the amputated object swayed dangerously whenever anyone passed within three feet of it.

Since Stanley's only chance of staying erect was to hold on to something, the neutered hatstand was his object of choice and the two of them lurched backwards and forwards, he clasping it around the middle, looking like a child caught on a merry-go-round and afraid to get off. The lightbulb had a short and the light kept going on an off at random. The audience was enchanted.

Laddie played the introduction to Stanley's song and launched into the first line. If he expected Stanley to follow, he was sorely disappointed. Stanley stood swaying as if in a gale force wind, mesmerized by what he saw in front of him. The medication was wearing off, but, apart from that, he was finally coming to terms with what he had brought upon himself. He was terrified. The auditorium was jammed with people and they were all looking at him. He caught sight of the Vicar seated in the front row next to that dreadful Old Mr. Simms and was horrified to see him make the sign of the cross in his direction. He could hear

Laddie vamping on the piano and then an abbreviated version of the introduction was offered again as encouragement. He would have done anything to have begun, but suddenly and completely, he could not remember a single word of the bloody song. Then, suddenly inspired, he remembered every last comma in the lyrics and, to catch up, began three bars behind where Laddie had got to on the piano.

An uncertain hush descended on the audience. Stanley was not the most popular member of the congregation but to see him there twisting in the wind — the hatstand had taken on a life of its own and was going from side to side like the pendulum of a grandfather clock — was embarrassing. It was Laddie who saved the situation. Vamping once more until the oscillating soloist finally caught up with him, the two of them came together on the refrain at the end of the first verse.

In the whole canon of musical theatre there were probably no more heartfelt and thankful words than those sung in Stanley's reedy but rather sweet tenor when the piano and he came to the refrain, although, as he began it to sing it, he was less and less leaning against the lamppost than clutching it, hands wrapped around tightly, holding on. His good leg was beginning to tire and the pain in his bad leg seemed to increase with every breath he took.

It is traditional when singing the George Formby version of the song to increase the tempo during the last refrain and to repeat it twice. The song, begun at a sedate pace, finishes at a canter, whole sentences articulated in one long, almost gasping breath. Laddie and Stanley had rarely practiced together and Stanley was unaware of what Laddie began, instinctively, to do. It took him a bar or so to realize that he was in danger of falling behind again, but anything that would bring the song to an end more quickly and permit Stanley to get at the pills secreted in his pants' pocket, could not be all bad. He sped up, even managing to outdo Laddie when Laddie re-upped the tempo yet again for an encore — the audience was already applauding — in a third refrain.

Hubris, not to mention a deeply unhappy hatstand, was not to be denied. Stanley was out of breath by the last line of the song and more than slightly red in the face with the pace of it, but a little part of him was excited by what he had accomplished. Deep inside him, a showman was seeking to be born. It flashed through his brain that the best way to finish the song was with a flourish. Belting out the last note, he let go of the hatstand, extended both arms out to the audience in a gesture half of supplication and half of success, the grimace of a smile plastered across his face. His bad leg, however, had other ideas and began to give way. The last note of the song became a screech of purest panic as he began to topple. He grabbed at the hatstand as he went, of course, but that unruly object had had quite enough of being manhandled for one evening. The upright jerked loose from the base, the lampshade jumped free at the top, and the whole, Stanley clinging on for dear life, collapsed sideways onto the hard wooden flooring of the stage.

Pigalle Would Have Been Proud

It was quite some time before the cabaret could continue. To calm an audience caught between horror at what had happened to Stanley and delight at the slapstick version of the old song some thought he had given, Fanny persuaded Laddie to play a series of old-time melodies, she conducting the audience and periodically whispering over her shoulder, "Keep going, keep going! Just a couple more!" Playing the piano was what Laddie did best and gradually he worked himself out of his funk. Trills and frills were added to the tunes, and Laddie began to enjoy himself. What helped was the realization that, if nothing else, he had told Vera that he was begging off. Whatever happened next couldn't be as bad as if he had to go through with the wedding.

Laddie did not know what had happened to Vera after she replaced Stanley on the couch in the little back room — no doubt he would find out later — but for now, music was the thing. He even began to feel some sympathy for Hector having to deal with the backstage chaos. If only someone had handed him another drink, Laddie might have decided that all was, once again, right with the world.

The singsong ended when Hector appeared in front of the curtains to say that everything was fine and the cabaret began again. Everyone ooed and aahed at the little dancers as they pranced around the stage. Members of the choir performed their solos and duets, and there was even a trio from 'The Mikado.' Hector had worked hard to incorporate the various talents of the church, but some were more successful than others. A young pianist was so stricken with stage fright that her 'Fur Elise' went no further than the first two bars before she dried up and played those over and over before being led away in tears. The better of the two Ave Maria ladies had decided to sing 'Ah Sweet Mystery of

Life.' Her singing certainly mystified Laddie. Unable to determine the key she was attempting to locate, he thumped his way through three before coming across one that approximated the one she appeared to be aiming at. The woman's high notes — oh so bravely attempted — affected Old Mr. Simms hearing aids, causing one of them to whistle in competition. Hector, desperately looking for an accolade when she left the stage, fumbled badly when he said that she had the voice of a bird, although he was not sure what kind. It got him a laugh, but caused the Vicar to shake his head and mutter, "For shame."

It was during the excerpt from 'The Mikado' that Noni was decanted from her taxi at the church — and herein hangs a tale. Hector had told Roger St. John Mountjoy to go outside and wait for her. As we have seen, what Hector actually said was, "Roger, old boy, would you mind being on the lookout at the side-door for a woman arriving by taxi?" He had hardly got these words out before he realized that such a general description might be insufficient for Roger to clue in to what he was supposed to do. Hector had visions of Roger kidnapping some unsuspecting creature who might just happen to hove into view. He elucidated: "Her name is Noni Figueroa and she's in the show. She should have been here already."

These last sentences were more of an aside to himself. That he did not pay much attention to Roger as he spoke was unfortunate, for the words 'Noni Figueroa' had had a remarkable effect on him. He began to shake, he blanched and he gawped at Hector. He became more dangerously animated by the second. Hector was not to know it but, strange to tell, Roger did know Noni — oh, not in any biblical sense, but as a fan. A serious fan. Roger had been at the tail end of puberty — he was a late developer — the first time he saw Noni Figueroa perform and he had never quite recovered from it. He would have qualified as a groupie if he had known what a groupie was. He had followed the ups and downs of her career over the years and been desolated when it finally seemed to peter out. He had rather thought that she must be dead, although metaphorically he always kept a candle burning in the window for her. When Hector uttered her name, it was as if the whole firmament lit up. Since Roger was only in the play, he had not examined the latter half of the programme, and he had not realized that Noni, his Noni, was to make an appearance. Be still my heart! To be asked to bring Noni into the theatre and to actually get to speak to her, well, words failed him. And, let us be clear, this statement is to be taken literally.

Spying a man who resembled nothing so much as a cigar-store Indian standing at the door of the church, Noni determined first — Roger was able to provide a solitary nod — that she was in the right place and then demanded to be taken backstage immediately. Roger's eyes were glazed and a significant amount of saliva was dribbling down his chin, but he nodded once more and pointed the way. Noni surged past him. Following the sound of the music, she threw open the doors of the auditorium and strode forward. Roger, still mute but desperate not to lose sight of his somewhat battered grail, pointed mutely to the doors at the far end of the hall and Noni made a beeline for them. By the time she was half-way there, she was the centre of attention. The click of her heels on the hardwood floor as she stomped along was part of it, as was a slavering Roger St. John Mountjoy following behind like the man who swept up after the horses at the Queen's coronation. But it was her outfit that made every neck swivel in her direction.

Noni had dressed for the show at home and she had no intention of letting anyone see her gown before she appeared on stage. With this in mind, she had enveloped herself in a floor length, mohair cape which she had found in a secondhand store on Queen Street. The cape's origins were unknown but it appeared to have been made either for a yeti three times Noni's size, or it was not a cape at all but something that had begun life as a dwelling of some description. In it, Noni resembled nothing so much as a walking pup tent. In the dimly lit auditorium her face was hidden by the cape's hood, but if the audience could not see her properly, neither could she see them. Her ever present sunglasses caused her to walk straight into Fanny. This gave Roger an orgasmic opportunity to take hold of her hand and lead her forward. He had found true love at last.

Hector was thrilled at Noni's arrival. He would have kneecapped the soprano rather than ask her to do an encore and quickly persuaded Noni to sing not the one song they had agreed upon but two others as well. Since Noni had no intention of singing only one song anyway, she did not need much persuasion. Hector's introduction was fulsome and heartfelt. Fanny always said that when it came to old stagers like himself, Hector left reality behind, but with Noni he went more than a little overboard.

"Ladies and Gentlemen, we have a treat for you," he announced. "We have been able to bring you one of the greats of the Toronto musical stage! A woman with a tremendous talent to amuse! Someone who is always in demand!" Noni had been unemployed for years. "Someone who trod the light fantastic on the boards of Broadway!" The show had opened and closed the same night. "And someone who I have the honour to call my very dear friend!" He always made damn sure never to lend her any money, however. "Ladies and Gentleman, please put your hands together and give a hearty welcome to Miss... Noni... Figueroa!"

With the singular exception of Roger St. John Mountjoy who clapped until his palms began to hurt, the applause that followed was more polite than anything else. Half of the audience had never heard the name and the other half had forgotten it. Noni was not pleased. "Clap, you spastics!" she muttered, as she got ready to make her entrance. She had decided to perform in front of the curtains, to be nearer to, and more intimate with, the audience. A single spotlight was directed centre stage and she had demanded that the footlights be turned off. It was a wise decision. Footlights can make even the prettiest ingenue appear haggard.

It was not Noni's face that initially held the audience's attention, however. Forever committed to her signature yellow, Noni had decided on a short, canary coloured dress with a cinched waist and square, feathered shoulders. Even in the five-inch heels that caused her to totter wherever she moved, she managed to look both squat and voluminous at the same time. The audience looked on, fascinated, not quite knowing what to make of the apparition, although perhaps Old Mr. Simms overdid it when he whispered, not quite softly enough, to the Vicar, "Gawd, it's Tweetie Bird!"

Noni, however, was in her element.

"Hellooo, folks!" she bawled. "How's it going? Havin' fun? Yea! Noni's here! No kiddin' folks, I'm happy to be with y'all tonight an' I'm going to give you a medley of Eartha Kitt songs. Everybody remember Kitty? A bit before my time, but a great gal!"

The audience did not know what had hit them, but they were about to find out.

By now, they had had a chance to look more closely at Noni's face and, although the single spotlight might have helped to hide the lines on it, it had also made her eyes disappear. What was left were two slits on either side of her nose. The spotlight had done nothing to ameliorate the bloat of the Botox and it did nothing to minimize her lips, although, to be fair, Noni's use fire-engine-red lipstick was probably not her wisest decision. The spotlight had one further unfortunate effect. At the best of times, Noni's hair resembled dried straw but for the occasion she had teased it within an inch of its life. With the spotlight streaming down on her, the overall effect was of an over-the-hill hooker with a bouffant halo.

With a quick flick of her fingers in the general direction of Laddie at the piano, Noni shouted out, "Hit it, maestro!" and began to pivot and sway around at the front of the stage. Her first number completely disregarded the fact that her audience was made up of rather refined and certainly staid churchgoers. Eartha Kitt may have put a degree of innuendo into 'Let's Do It!' but Noni Figueroa left no doubt whatsoever what the 'it' was. With bosoms flying off in all directions at once, hands caressing herself from neck to crotch more lovingly than Narcissus ever did, and great pouty lips glistening in the unblinking white light, some of the people in the audience could not even bear to look. Roger, on the other hand, sat entranced on the edge of his seat and could not take his eyes off her.

"Streuth, Vicar," was Old Mr. Simms single comment. He was more voluble when Noni launched into her second number, 'My Heart Belongs To Daddy.' "If I was her daddy, I'd put her over my knee and give her a good spanking," he declared, although this time he did not turn away and might even have been seen licking his lips a little.

Noni was never to finish her third number, an even more sexed-up and certainly out of season, 'Santa Baby.' Busy undulating in her spotlight, slit eyes actually closed this time, pouting the while, a lascivious Noni was in the middle of the second verse when she suddenly found herself being unceremoniously pushed sideways across the stage, managing only with luck to stay on her feet. One of her stiletto heels snapped and she had to grab at the curtain to hold on. She hadn't the remotest idea what had happened and it took her a moment to focus. Standing at the centre of the stage, replacing her in the spotlight, there stood a woman Noni had never seen before in her life. For some reason, the woman was carrying a dog with a cone around its neck and seemed about to address the audience.

Clarence's better nature had got the better of him. He had gone outside for a smoke and found Mabel's animal shivering on the sidewalk. Clarence didn't like dogs but it got him to thinking about whether Mabel might not be shivering in the basement. True, the boilers were on and it was more likely that she would be sweating bullets, but he could not get the idea out of his head that the woman might turn into a huge permed iceberg. And what if she croaked? She looked like a frog so she might very well croak, he thought, pleased with his wit.

Wondering what he should do about her, Clarence began an elliptical conversation with himself.

"Out?"

"Maybe."

"Dangerous!"

"Run."

"Yup."

Sigh.

Holding onto Bitzie, Clarence put his ear to the door of the sub-basement. All he could hear was silence.

"You!" he shouted, "There?"

No answer was forthcoming and Clarence was beginning to wonder if there might not be a second corpse in the building that evening when Bitzie began to yelp and fuss.

"Dog," he called out, hoping the word might count as a mitigating factor for having locked Mabel up. "Safe."

Bitzie, evidently blessed with better ears than Clarence, began to demand to be reunited with its mistress. Without thinking further on the matter — it could never be said that Clarence was big on cogitation — the janitor pulled back the bolt.

"You there?" he called out, although there was nowhere else Mabel could have been.

His answer came as the door was flung open in his face flattening his nose and bruising his forehead in the process. He dropped Bitzie and cried out.

"I'll get to you later," hissed Mabel, pushing him aside and scooping up Bitzie as she went. "Don't you think that I won't, just as sure as God made little green apples!"

Thinking only to give Clarence a couple of hefty clouts with the handle of an old broom she had found with which to defend herself, Mabel sped off at a canter. Clarence didn't even try to catch up. Up the stairs she went and then down the little back corridor that led to the stage. Bitzie barked enthusiastically in her arms. Mabel could hear some woman caterwauling away about Father Christmas as she arrived in the wings. What she intended to do was tell the congregation what was what and what was not. She advanced to the curtains and flung them aside. A blinding light made it impossible to see but, gradually, she became aware of some kind of large yellow avian squawking in front of her. Thrusting the bird to one side, Mabel took a deep breath while she determined what to say. It would not be her recitation, oh no! It would not be her begging to be understood, either. It would be her telling the lot of them what she thought and what she expected them to do about it.

Unfortunately, Mabel had underestimated Noni. No one came between Noni Figueroa and her public. Noni removed the other shoe and charged. Mabel went over sideways, bouncing off the presidium arch on the far side of the stage before ricocheting back towards her assailant. Noni side stepped and aimed a kick at Mabel's ample posterior as she went by.

"Jezabel!" shouted Mabel as she flew past.

"Bitch!" responded Noni, sadly unaware of the biblical imprecations available to her.

"Hurrah for Noni!" shouted Roger from the front row. "Let's have a big hand for Noni!"

The audience was, not for the first time that evening, spellbound. Even if it had not seen Mabel teetering across the stage like a superannuated ballerina (and carrying an animal, no less), they would have loved it. Mabel had met her match. The tiny yellow turkey-bird had beaten the big bullfrog. Hallelujah! They gave Noni a standing ovation. She, in her turn, received it with a curtsey so low that she seemed to be settling down to lay what would presumably be an enormous egg, and threw kisses to the cheering audience. Roger caught several of them.

Mabel's reappearance tottering back out from the wings cut the cheering short. The audience held its collective breath. Noni, sensing her presence, turned back to face her, hands on her hips. Mabel wasn't interested in Noni, however. She marched to the front of the stage and surveyed the audience once more.

"I have…" she began sententiously.

What Mabel had, however, was to remain a mystery. As she began, a voice, female and clearly nervous, was heard from the back of the auditorium where the Ladies of the Church were huddled together for protection.

"Go home, Mabel," it said.

"And don't come back!" Another, stronger, voice joined the first.

Then the clapping started, not the fevered clapping of adulation but the slow rhythmic clapping of derision. It was as though the mob was turning on Madame Defarge. Noni, nonplussed by the whole bizarre situation — a kind of audience participation she had never witnessed before — began to cackle. Her laughter and the little dance, rather like an Indian war dance, she sketched behind Mabel's back, broke the tension and derision was replaced by wild whoopings of joy and thunderous applause. Mabel could have stood there for all eternity but she would never have gotten further with her speech. She stormed off, her coned pooch still in her arms, leaving Noni to bask in both the applause and a series of wolf whistles that Roger and Old Mr. Simms competitively embarked on to attract her attention.

And Bitzie had barked throughout.

A quasi-theological note: While all this was going on, the Vicar sat silently bemoaning his fate. He was disappointed in his congregation and it would be he who would have to pick up the pieces of Mabel when the dust settled. The dratted woman deserved something, he agreed, but surely not this. On the other hand, he had to admit that if he never saw her again, he would be a happier man. Mabel might be the second woman the Fall Follies had managed to rid him of. He sighed, and, man of the cloth that he was, cheered himself with the thought, "The Lord works in mysterious ways, Gilbert," Then he sighed and settled down to see what could possibly happen next.

The final act was, of course, to be Hector. He was two steps from making his entrance when Vera wandered onto the stage looking rather like a pregnant version of Banquo's ghost. She was disheveled and she had been crying but she did not seem to care.

"I'm going on," she announced grimly. "And he's not going to stop me." Hector was pretty sure who the "he" was — he could hear Laddie playing incidental music in the distance — but Hector was not about to stop her either. He confirmed what she was going to recite and disappeared through the curtains to introduce her.

"And now," he announced, "I have the great pleasure of introducing you to the someone who put our wonderful programme together and with whom Stanley spends most of his days." Many in the audience, Laddie included, assumed that Faun was about to appear. "She will tell us the tale of a braw wee Scot." Hector always rehearsed his introductions and what he had to say next came out of his mouth before he could stop it. "She is very fond of a certain wee Scot herself as some of you may be aware." He said this banteringly before he caught sight of Laddie shaking his head vigorously. "So," Hector continued, desperately trying to swallow words he had already uttered, "I offer you the delightful and talented Miss Vera..." And he forgot her name.

The curtains opened on a solitary Vera. The small bucket for emergency use was tucked in the crook of her elbow, oddly out of place but assumed by most people to be a prop for her performance. It shimmered in the spotlight. Like most of the other performers that evening, Vera hadn't the slightest inkling of how bright the stage becomes when the auditorium lights have been turned off and reflexively she lifted a hand to shield her eyes. She stood very still, then, lowering the hand to her belly, she cupped it around the fetus inside, took a deep breath and, eyes closed, began.

"Sir Patrick Spens," she announced the title of the poem. "The King sits in Dunfermline town, Drinking the blood-red wine..."

Many in the audience had learned the poem in their first year of high school but they had never heard it read half so well. Vera fell in with the cadence of the iambic pentameter for which it is famous, but she brought to the story an emotion that many a teacher never managed to achieve. Her voice was never shrill. It was never too loud, but every last word could be heard at the back of the auditorium and, long before it was over, the tension a great storyteller can bring to a piece held the audience in thrall.

When she was finished at last, applause rolled through the auditorium. Most of the audience did not know who Vera was, but her dishevelled appearance, not to mention the delicate condition that she did nothing to hide, played on their sympathies even beyond the power of her performance. Vera, however, was unaware. She made a move to turn and leave the stage, but as the applause continued and increased, she seemed to change her mind. She turned again to face the audience. She held up an arm, in a gesture of asking for silence, and when it did not come immediately, seemed quite willing to wait. Hector, standing in the wings, frowned. There was no encore planned; he himself was waiting to go on. Only when the applause died did Vera lower her hand and begin again.

"I am a pregnant woman," she began sonorously. "I am with child." That much was obvious. Her voice was solemn, however, and she spoke with a dignity and with a cadence that matched her earlier rendition. Such was the truth of the emotion in her voice that a complete hush fell upon the auditorium even with so few words spoken. Vera surveyed the people in front of her until, at last, her gaze came to rest on Laddie, still seated at the piano. "I gave myself to a man," she continued, slowly moving the hand that had been cupping her belly higher so that it caressed and pressed against her breast. "And I have been betrayed!"

This was not a piece that anyone in the audience knew, but they were enthralled.

"Jumping Jesus!" Hector, still standing in the wings, said the words aloud.

"I was used." Vera spat out the words volcanically, a cross between Ophelia and Mother Courage. "I was abused. And I have been cast aside!"

Vera took hold of the bucket tucked beneath her arm, and flung it in the direction of her late intended. The audience flinched. The bucket bounced once on the stage and jumped the footlights. Laddie shrieked and lifted his feet to avoid being hit before it came to rest against the pedals of the piano. It hit him anyway.

"But I will survive!" Vera pounded her chest with a fist and struck a pose. "I will go forth!"

Unfortunately, the audience was not to learn Vera's destination. Once more a rolling, tidal wave of nausea struck her and she fled precipitously from the stage. The waves of applause that washed over the empty stage were cataclysmic. Those few in the know breathed sighs of relief that she had gone, but the majority, who thought they had been watching an Oscar-worthy performance even if only in a supporting category, stamped their feet and bellowed their bravas and called for an encore.

Minutes passed before the applause ceased and the low buzz of wonderment subsided. Fanny would have prevailed on Laddie to provide incidental music but she did not have to heart to ask him. He was shaking like a feather in a hurricane and, to confuse similes, gulping air like a landed mackerel. She would have fed him liquor if she had had any and, desperate to do something since Hector was on next and would need his accompanist, she whispered urgently into Laddie's ear.

"Now Laddie, calm down. She's gone. She won't be back." Fanny prayed fervently that this might be so, although not as hard as Laddie himself. "And she didn't mention your name. She didn't, did she?" Fanny punched him lightly on the arm, wanting the thought to take hold. She nodded sagely. "No one knows." This might almost have been true, although there were a fair number of people who would make it their business to find out before they went home that evening.

Laddie looked at her balefully, "Why me?" he whined.

Fanny felt an urgent desire to box his ears.

"Why indeed!" she replied, shaking her head. "You're not exactly love's young dream."

Laddie stared blearily at her and seemed to find reassurance in her words. The two of them began to nod at each other as though some great wisdom was being shared. Then Fanny had had enough. Laddie had gotten himself in this situation and he could get himself out. She had Hector to think about. She stood, and, towering over him, commanded, "Now for heaven's sake, buck up, and play the damn piano.

Hector's Turn

Vera would be a hard act to follow, but Hector, always the professional, was going to give it his best shot. The show was running late, but no one had left the auditorium and he said to himself, relishing the moment, "Tonight, it's my turn." And as the thought took hold, he repeated it, "Finally," he said, squaring his shoulders and pushing his chest out, "it's my turn." The showman in him knew what he had to do and the performer in him knew that he was up to the task. He had decided with Laddie weeks ago that he would do a medley of songs by Ivor Novello and Noel Coward. A mixture of romance and sophistication. He had tales to tell about both men and it would not be a hard sell with a crowd brought up on such songs.

The curtain opened on a smiling and tuxedoed Hector, a straw hat set at a jaunty angle, a cane held lightly in both hands in front of him. He maintained the pose for a long beat before tipping the hat to the audience and strolling to the front of the stage to begin his patter. He was to sing five songs in all and he began with Novello's 'We'll Gather Lilacs' which most everyone knew. Hector did not have a loud voice and these days it was not particularly strong, but he knew how to breathe and he knew how to put over a song. He painted a picture with the words and before it was over the audience had joined in and was singing with him. This both pleased and annoyed Hector. He liked that he could bring an audience along with him, but he was also enough of a performer — a thin slice of well-cured ham really, as even he would wryly admit after a couple of Harvey's — that he didn't like it when they didn't pay every last bit of attention to him. An impish smile at the end of the song acknowledged their participation but he hoped the raised eyebrow that went along with it would give them pause before joining in again.

Changing the tempo, the next song was 'And Her Mother Came Too,' a story-song to be acted out with expressions of exasperation, frustration, and choler. The counterpoint between Hector's precise and woeful words and Laddie's musical reaction to them had the audience in stitches. When the song was over, Hector drank in the applause but, as he always did, he listened to the effect that the performance had inside of him. He was not sure how he felt this time. There should have been a wonderful warm feeling of internal mirth, but for some reason it seemed to be cut across with something else and he wasn't sure what it was. Wondering how he might come to understand it better, Hector signalled to Laddie that he wanted to change the order of his programme and go straight into the other comic song on the programme, Noel Coward's 'Mad Dogs and Englishmen.'

It was one of Hector's party pieces. He could have performed it in his sleep but that was never Hector's way and he invested every syllable with Coward's clipped diction and his own inventive bits of business. The audience adored it, but, again, as he listened to himself, part of him able to assess what he was doing, he remained uncertain. A feeling of unquiet remained. When the song was over, he stood still, resting against his cane, looking down at his shiny patent leather shoes. He decided to do something he had never done before in any of the many shows he had put together over the years.

"Ladies and Gentlemen, I wonder if you would indulge me a little?" he said, the warmth of his voice drawing them to him, "I wonder if you would permit me to bring my good lady wife onto the stage with me?" Several wolf whistles and much laughter greeted the question and, beckoning to Fanny, he called out, "Come on up, Fan." Laddie reprised 'We'll Gather Lilacs' while Hector arranged a chair just off centre in the spotlight. When Fanny appeared, he led her to the chair and bowed to her as she sat.

None of this was rehearsed and Fanny, who was never entirely comfortable on a stage, smiled cautiously at her husband. She was aware that he was feeling his way but she did not know his direction and she felt quite unable to assist him. She squeezed his hand to offer the only support she could. Hector squeezed back and turned to the audience to explain what he was going to sing next.

"Ladies and gentlemen," he said, "Ivor Novello wrote a beautiful song that never became quite as famous as perhaps it should have been.

I'm going to sing it for you tonight," Hector paused, "but, if you will permit me, I am going to sing it to my wife as well. Laddie, my friend, if you don't mind, could we have 'I Can Give You The Starlight'?"

Hector sang the ballad tenderly, never quite looking directly at the audience, but never paying so much attention to Fanny that they would feel left out. Fanny did not know where to look. She was moved and also suddenly frightened. She did not doubt for a moment that Hector was singing to her but in all their years together he had always insisted in keeping the personal separate from the professional, sometimes even being almost hurtful in the process. Fanny wondered, with a lurch, whether he was ill, but she put the thought aside because surely she would have known. She had seen the doctor's report and all Hector had to do was be careful. She wanted to cry but he would tease her about it afterwards, and she thought ruefully that he wouldn't much like her mewling on while he was singing anyway. Hector would want all eyes on him.

As for Hector, he hardly knew what he was about. The feeling of melancholy had passed but the one which replaced it was of a bittersweet twilight that escaped further definition. He felt a great tenderness inside him. A tenderness for Fanny but also a tenderness for the life he had led and for the theatre he loved. Not calculating what he was about to do, he went slowly down on one knee and kissed Fanny's hand as the melody finished.

The last song of the evening was Noel Coward's 'I'll See You Again.' Hector sang it through and then the audience joined in. And when it was over, they sang it again. This time Hector took Fanny into his arms and they waltzed around the stage. Everyone urged them on. When the curtain finally closed, Fanny and Hector embraced, both of them a little uncertain about what had just happened until finally Hector was able to snap out of it.

He had to get down to the serious business of curtain calls.

Exeunt All

Hector had seen too many shows marred by people who didn't know what they were doing when it came to taking a bow. A performance, he always said, was not finished until the applause was over and people began to put on their overcoats. He intended both the cast of the play and the performers in the cabaret to take curtain calls and the Sergeant Major in him had drilled how they were to come on, what they were to do when they got there, and how they were to move to the side to allow the next person to appear. The play came first. Each actor walked to the very front of the stage, bowed deeply or curtsied, and moved to a different side of the stage. Clarence, grinning broadly, hitching his pants high as he approached the footlights, received 'bravos' and whistles along with his applause. Roger St. John Mountjoy stumbled a bit but seemed to have a little more bounce in his step than usual. Next came the dancers and singers from the cabaret. Vera, alas, did not appear, although had anyone been listening carefully, she might have been heard retching backstage.

Noni's appearance was a production in itself. She shimmied forward, perforce barefoot, laughingly shaking her bosoms but refusing to curtsey, preferring to bow and let the front row peep down her décolletage. No one quite knew what to make of her but there was much to be said for the person who had whacked Mabel Green. The applause went through the roof. At length, she moved alongside Roger who beamed down at her like the village idiot. Old Mr. Simms peered up at them and shouted out, "It's the monster and Igor. Oh my Lord, save us all!" At last, Hector appeared. He waved his straw hat and bowed right and left, wandering about the stage and breaking every rule he had laid down for his cast. He kissed Noni and all the females and shook hands with the men. Then, remembering, he called out, "And don't shoot the pianist, folks. Take a bow, Laddie!" Laddie swayed and beamed and bowed next to the piano.

Mabel and Bitzie were nowhere to be seen.

The applause continued until the Vicar came out from the wings to congratulate everyone and to thank them on behalf of the church.
"I think you will agree," he said, "that we have had an evening like none other."
A voice was heard from the front row. "You've got that right, Vicar."
"Yes, Mr. Simms," replied the Vicar, "I have indeed. A wonderful play followed by members of our choir and our Sunday School, in addition to guests and even a professional artiste." He stressed the French pronunciation of the word and a fine spray of saliva descended on the footlights. "All have outdone themselves. I want to thank everyone — but most of all," and here the Vicar stopped and waited until he had the attention he required, "most of all, of course, I want to thank Stanley and Hector. This was their brainchild and their idea and how grateful we are!" The Vicar sailed slowly over to shake hands with Hector and whispered congratulations in his ear. Then, frowning, he asked loudly, "But where is Stanley? We have to see Stanley!"

Stanley Parkinson, meanwhile, had been off in the wings. He lay half seated, half sprawled, on a chair put there for his comfort by Faun so that he could listen to the rest of the cabaret. He had wanted to go home, and then he hadn't. The evening had been his idea in the first place and he would have been less than human if he did not want to share in the glory of it, but his leg was still throbbing like the dickens and he was weary. Hector had urged him to stay, to see it through to the end — very probably his end — but the main reason he was still there was that it hurt too much to even contemplate having to reverse his steps through the auditorium, go up a flight of stairs, climb into the car and be driven back home. He would have been quite happy if they had just let him die where he was. Faun wasn't sure how she was going to get him home either. Every time she touched him, he whimpered. Nevertheless, Faun wanted her Stanley to have his taste of glory. Too often, it seemed to her, Stanley was the man in the shadows. He did the work and someone else got the accolades. There was Hector bowing and scraping, stage centre, lapping up the adulation and where was her Stanley? Cowering in pain in the wings was where he was. It was the same at the bank. He should have been a Senior Vice President by now — if he had been willing to put himself forward, to push a little, to let people know that it was he who did the work and kept the place running. Faun sighed, acknowledging to herself that she and her husband were rather alike. Too hesitant and not aggressive enough. Too polite for modern life. Her father, after he had met Stanley a few times, had said he was a nice guy but not a man for the trenches. For a long time, she hadn't understood what he meant but, gradually, she came to see the sense of it. Stanley was not the heroic type. A good man, yes. Efficient, certainly. Competent, always. But a man, she had come to realize, compromised by his own lack of pushiness. He should have been striding out boldly onto the stage right now, she thought, waving to the audience, grinning just like Hector, although that would have been physically impossible at the moment of course. She had to admit that.

In another time and in another place, Stanley might have agreed with his wife, although he was not exactly a man prone to accurate self-analysis. At the moment, however, he was incapable of analysis of any kind whatsoever, having two completely irreconcilable desires. The first was to stride out onto the stage and take his bow; the second to disappear from the place and never set eyes on it or anything to do with it again.

The pain of childbirth, he was sure, was nothing compared to what he was feeling. Faun used to go on about that at length, but what did she know? Why hadn't they given him an epidural? Stanley wasn't exactly sure what an epidural was but he remembered that Faun had begged for one and had behaved very badly until she got it. He could remember her yelling as they wheeled her away down the corridor that she could not take it any more in a most embarrassing manner. Stanley, of course, had no intention of behaving like that but if somebody didn't do something soon, he wouldn't be responsible for what happened next. He grabbed hold of the sleeve of Faun's dress, twisting it tight as he pulled her towards him.

"Faun," he hissed at his spouse, waving his other hand in the general direction of the stage, "will this never finish?"

"It will be over soon, Stanley," Faun, still barely able to speak, croaked her words back at him with a little smile. "They're nearly done. The Vicar can't be much longer and then you and Hector will take your bows. I think they have a bouquet for you!" She made it sound as though it was to be a treat; a child given a lollipop.

The thought went through Stanley's head that his wife was an imbecile. Taking a bow was about the last thing of which he was likely to be capable. To bow you had to be perpendicular to the stage and, indubitably, to accomplish such a stance would be to put more reliance on what was left of his leg and what remained of his ability to cope with the torment he was suffering than he could manage.

He shuddered.

"I don't need a bouquet. I want to go home."

The wheedling tone in Stanley's voice was new and Faun might have taken it more seriously had not the audience cottoned on to the Vicar's query about his whereabouts and demanded to see him. It was probably Old Mr. Simms who started it, but the words, "We want Stanley," began to be heard throughout the hall. The chant began in the front rows but soon spread towards the back of the auditorium to include persons who had only the remotest knowledge of who Stanley was and dozens more who couldn't have cared less. A chant is a chant. Fanny began clapping to accompany it and Laddie got into the spirit of the thing by vamping in time on the piano.

"Can you hear that, Stanley?" said Faun, a little in awe at the commotion going on just outside her line of vision. "They are calling your name. Oh my, Stanley! They want to see you!"

Stanley was many things, but deaf was not one of them. At first all he heard was noise, and noise, at that, which exacerbated the throbbing that now ran down in a pulsating line from his groin to his big toe and all the way back up again. From where he was, he could see the Vicar on the stage beaming beatifically at him and beckoning him to come forward. His first thought was to somehow lunge forward and pummel the man to pieces, but as the noise swelled and the chant grew — the floor of the stage even beginning to vibrate with the simple statement it put forward — something of its message began to lodge itself in Stanley's cranium. We have seen that Stanley Parkinson had never been a man to put himself forward, but this did not mean that he had no pride in himself, had no self-respect, no wish to enjoy the appreciation of his peers when such a thing was appropriate. 'Leaning On The Lamppost' was evidence of that and perhaps it was the very volume of the chant which in some way went to mitigate the wretchedness of his physical condition and make him change his mind. Perhaps it was the very challenge of moving himself into a position from which he might, just for a moment, acknowledge the applause — not bask in it, of course, but at least doff his hat at the justice of it. And so, for the second time that evening, there began a process in Stanley's head that would lead him to step forward into the arms of his fellow man's approbation.

Well, metaphorically anyway.

"Help me up, Faun," Stanley said the words in a whisper, a look of supplication on his face that would have softened the heart of a Medusa.

"Oh, Stanley love, are you sure? Be brave. You can do it." Faun stroked his damp brow and kissed a fevered cheek, "You'll be all right, Stanley. Just one step at a time. Say a little prayer."

Stanley was of the opinion that the Pope in Rome hadn't a prayer big enough to dull the agony in his leg but the chant continued and its message had percolated into his brain. They wanted to see him. They were, in fact, demanding it and, appearances sometimes to the contrary, Stanley was a human being after all. At the end of the day, it was he who had conceived of having a social event and, however turbulent the journey, he had been there every step of the way. And just now, steps were what counted. Almost before he thought about it, Stanley stood. He leaned on his one good leg and stumbled forward. He grabbed hold of his crutch and began to lurch towards the limelight. Sometimes teetering on the spot, holding onto Faun for grim death and with a bovine kind of lowing each time he moved, the two of them began to inch towards the light of the stage. Hector and the Vicar could see them and both urged them forward: Hector with a wide grin and nods of the head, the timing of which he seemed to have coordinated with the clapping of the audience; the Vicar with great windmill gestures of his arms that would have been a danger to life and limb had Hector not ducked to get out of the way.

And so, at last, Stanley emerged from the wings. The crowd roared and the room rocked.

"Well done, thou good and faithful servant," declaimed the Vicar dramatically as he hove towards Stanley across the stage. Hector followed behind still nodding his head. "A triumph!" he said, grinning from ear to ear. "We did it, Stan, old man, we did it!" he added, his eyes glistening. "By George, we did it!"

The two men embraced. Hector was on the verge of tears and Stanley, carried away by the moment, gave him a big wet kiss on the neck.

"We did indeed, Hector, my friend!" replied Stanley, choking up. He was breathing in the overpowering scent of Hector's Old Spice and he tried to laugh. Out of the corner of his eye, he saw two little girls coming towards them carrying bouquets. Where the little girls came from he had no idea. A random thought jumped unbidden into his head that the church had no access to little girls; perhaps Hector had had to hire them for the evening. A second banker's thought was that the cost of the flowers would come out of the profit column on the final balance sheet. His third thought revolved around the fact that he hadn't the vaguest idea how he had got onto the stage but that amputation would be the only thing that — just possibly — might be what would get him off it.

The flowers were wrapped in cellophane and about as tall as the girls themselves. Hector managed an expression of 'what me' surprise when presented with his bouquet and then he moved away towards the centre of the stage, again bowing to the audience, waving the flowers above his head and revelling in the moment. The second little girl moved towards Stanley hesitantly and, just as she had been coached to do, curtsied, holding the giant flower arrangement out in front of her. Faun stepped back not wanting to tread on her husband's moment of glory and stood quietly smiling, saying to herself that they would be home soon. Everything would be all right after all.

In a perfect world and also, most probably, in a work of fiction, this would be the end of our story. Hector and Stanley would stand together at the front of the stage, acknowledging the applause, smiling and bowing while the curtains slowly closed and the footlights dimmed. Stanley's pain would somehow dissipate so that he would be able to attend the cast party, Fanny would flirt outrageously with him, while Hector, getting his second wind, would plan another convivial event for somewhere around Advent with, possibly, a reading of Dickens's 'A Christmas Carol' performed in the sanctuary and carol singing around a creche, the appropriate biblical characters in attendance. Faun might be prevailed upon to play a post-menopausal Virgin Mary and since it was a non-speaking part Hector would not have to worry about another attack of hoarseness.

This is not what happened.

It was true that neither Mabel nor Bitzie had appeared during the presentation of the cast and that no one had set eyes on them after they fled the stage at the end of Noni's performance. They had not left the church, however. Mabel, made of very stern stuff indeed, had merely retired to the vestry to consider her next move. Unable to think of one that would satisfactorily embrace the whole congregation, not forgetting the Vicar, Clarence and the apparition in yellow whose name she still did not know, she sat there engorged by wrath and overcome with righteous indignation. She remained there until the show was over. Bitzie was made of even sterner stuff. Having been picked up, flung about, deposited outside in the cold, shouted at and unceremoniously dumped hither and yon, the animal was, by this time, full of the finest Prussian pugnaciousness. Not helping matters was the dratted cone that, while it had served its purpose of not letting the dog bite itself, had also had the unsatisfactory effect of not letting it bite anyone else. Oh, it could nip, but it could not get a grip. It was the animal's continuously shaking its head frantically back and forth in an attempt to rid itself of the cone that eventually caused Mabel to lose her temper and eject Bitzie from the room.

Once on the other side of the door, Bitzie could hear the chanting far below in the auditorium. For reasons beyond the scope of human understanding, the chanting infuriated the animal even more and it took off at a brisk trot towards the sound. Skidding into a wall and tumbling down a flight of stairs did not help maintain the dignity that Bitzie always strove to present but it did have the salutary effect of loosening the cone and by the time the dog reached the back of the stage it had left the cone behind. One might have thought that an animal with such a militaristic background might have stopped at this point to decide tactically what to do next. Bitzie, however, had a weakness and it was one that caused the creature to throw caution aside and to engage the enemy without so much a pausing to consider its options. Bitzie, you see, hated cellophane. And there, right in front of it, was

Stanley receiving a giant bouquet of flowers wrapped in the stuff. Where such an irrational hatred came from even Mabel did not know, but it was something so ingrained that one can only presume that Bitzie had learned it at its mother's teat. The crackling of the cellophane drove the little animal berserk. The dog could hear the stuff now as the little girl handed the flowers over to the man. Bitzie recognized the man and knew he was an enemy, but it was the bouquet that drove the little dog insane, and, primed for battle, the animal flung itself across the room to attack it.

If Bitzie abominated cellophane, the little girl — a wise child, indeed — abominated little dogs. Shrieking loudly, she thrust the bouquet at Stanley and fled. The wrapping of the bouquet sizzled against Stanley's face and, momentarily, he was unable to see. More to the point, however, the flowers, thrust against his chest and into his face, caused him to lose what little balance he had achieved when Faun let go of his arm and moved away to allow him to bask alone in the limelight. Stanley began to teeter. He also became aware that in addition to all his other troubles, a small snarling dog had begun to savage his ankles. It was unwise, however, for Stanley to attempt to shake the animal away, especially when he did so with his injured leg, an action that introduced him to a degree of pain previously unimagined.

The howl uttered by Stanley Parkinson had an instantaneous effect on the audience. The chant ceased most ungrammatically in mid-sentence and the applause ended mid clap. Only Bitzie was impervious. Its mind inflamed by the crackling of the bouquet to which Stanley was clinging like some kind of floral lifejacket, the animal began to leap up in an attempt to demolish the loathsome package. Stanley, vaguely aware that he was about to loose his balance, in the throes of an agony that felt as though his leg was being operated on with a hacksaw bereft of anaesthetic, began to beat the dog with the bouquet. Being hit over the head with cellophane was not what Bitzie had contemplated as an outcome of the engagement, but nothing if not willing to soldier on to the bitter end, the little obersturmbannführer sank its teeth into the crinkling transparent viscose and refused to let go. Stanley, mid-swat, lifted the bouquet high above his head. Bitzie came with it. Stanley brought the bouquet back down and whimpering silently at every last thing that had befallen him that evening, cast it away as, unable to remain upright a moment longer, he fell forward onto the stage in front of him for the second time that evening. Bitzie fell underneath the bouquet and the bouquet, alas, fell beneath Stanley.

And so the Fall Follies came to an end. The audience stood, stunned and immobile, while an unconscious Stanley was carried off into the wings and Clarence ladled the corpse of the little schnauzer onto a shovel for disposal at a place and time to be determined at a later date. It was left to Hector to close the curtains, dim the lights, and stand alone at the centre of the stage wondering what the reviews would say. He stood for a while until he heard Fanny call his name, telling him that they wanted to lock the building and that it was time to go. "Well," he thought walking jauntily off into the wings, "that was something! A night they will never forget! Stanley, old bean, that's what we gave them. Something they will never forget!"

And with that, Hector left the stage. The vestigial aroma of his cologne lingers still.

Whither They Went Afterwards

Mabel Green was unable to retrieve her position as commandant of the Ladies of the Church and, in time, she moved herself to sit, in solitary splendour, in a pew at the back of the church. It became her chief goal in life to get rid of the Vicar.

Bitzie's burial place remains known only to Clarence and he isn't telling.

The Vicar fought Mabel Green for as long as he was able but eventually decided to settle for a quieter life. He applied to become a chaplain with the Canada forces in Afghanistan. He failed the physical.

Lilith Payne finished her Ph.D thesis on deviant behaviour and is now an Assistant Professor at York University. In her spare time she travels and recently visited the Galapagos Islands. She was unaccompanied.

Old Mr. Simms, worn out at the end of the Fall Follies, took himself off to the Emergency Department at Sunnybrook. After a great deal of prodding and poking — all of which he made comments upon — it was recommended that a pacemaker be implanted. He will live forever.

Clarence was not rehired. Unable to find alternative employment, he attempted to hold up a convenience store with a toy gun. He currently resides in the Kingston Pen.

Roger St. John Mountjoy married Noni Figueroa, eighteen years his senior, and knew ecstasy for the first time in his life. He expired in the Latin Quarter of Paris on their honeymoon. A debonair coroner, commenting on the unusual circumstances, was heard to say, "Vive L'Amour!"

Noni Figueroa lives on in Roger's house in North Toronto. She entertains frequently and can be persuaded to perform at the drop of a hat. Do not drop your hat anywhere in the vicinity of Mrs. St. John Mountjoy.

Vera Tilsley gave birth to a ten pound baby boy. It was not an easy birth. The baby cries whenever he hears a piano. Vera left the bank to become an advocate for Planned Parenthood. She recently toured India and West Africa handing out condoms.

Laddie is alive, if not quite sober, and still in demand as an accompanist. He does not see his son and owes a wash of money in child support. He manages to stay one step ahead of Vera's solicitors.

Hector Hammond suffered a serious coronary before the autumn was out. He lived on quietly for two years during which time he, Fanny, Stanley and Faun often dined together and went to the theatre. The Fall Follies was the last time Hector performed on stage. Stanley gave the eulogy at his funeral.

Fanny returned to Jamaica after Hector's death. She bought a cottage from which, across the bay, she can see a house once owned by Noel Coward. Stanley and Faun visit her each February.

Faun became interested in amateur theatricals and has appeared in several productions across the city. Her first priority, however, is to make sure that Stanley has a hot meal when he comes home from work. She is a good soul.

And Stanley?

Well, he, um, he wrote the book, of course.

Feci quod potui, faciant meliora potentes.

I have done what I could, let those who can do better.

Printed in the United States
By Bookmasters